OPENING GAMBIT

THE ENEMY SERIES
BOOK TWO

JOHN PARK

SNOWY RANGE PRESS

Opening Gambit
Book Two of The Enemy Series
Copyright 2024 by John Park

ISBN: 979-8-9866376-2-4
All rights reserved
Printed in the United States of America

No part of this book may be used or reproduced in any manner whatsoever without the author's written permission except in the case of brief quotations embodied in critical articles and reviews.

This book is a work of fiction. Names, characters, places, and incidents are either a product of the author's imagination or are used fictitiously. Any resemblance to actual events, or persons or locales, living or dead, is purely coincidental.

Published by
Snowy Range Press
Laramie, Wyoming

Cover design by SweetnSpicyDesigns.com

*To my wife, Jane,
without whom it would have taken me much longer
to complete this book.*

CHAPTER 1

The sun was out, and the weather was getting chilly for early August. Sahar wished she could jog outside instead of being stuck in this windowless van.

"General Hermann is gone, and we have a runner," Agent Sahar Hatem said while looking at her monitor in the command van.

Their agents had had the suspect under surveillance for a week without gaining any significant new intelligence, and General Hermann never showed up. The tennis ball-sized drone had been hovering over the suspect's house for two days. Thanks to the alien Thrultak battery technology, their improved drone could fly silently for over three days on a single charge, and the HD camera had thermal as well as night vision capability. Agent Hatem watched her screen while Agent Mark Russell waited in his SUV, monitoring the drone footage of a small house in Green Acres, near Woodlawn Cemetery in Detroit, Michigan.

"I've got him," Agent Russell said from the black Suburban at the other end of the block. "Let's take him down."

"Yeah, go ahead, Mark. We need to question him."

Agent Hatem used the control pad and the drone's autonomous surveillance function to follow the suspect. She watched the suspect walk down Bloomfield Street toward Woodlawn Cemetery. Mark's SUV slowed to a stop to help take the suspect down. A separate crew was going to intercept the suspect before he reached the cemetery. Two other SUVs were also converging on Agent Russell's position.

Sahar zoomed out the camera and got a better overhead view. *This is better than a helicopter*, she thought. That's when she noticed an unmarked vehicle driving toward Agent Russell's SUV at a high rate of speed.

"Heads up, Mark, you have a white Chevy van headed your way."

The van sped down Shrewsbury Road.

"Heads up, Mark! We have a problem," Sahar said.

Before she could say anything more, the van plowed into Agent Russell's black Suburban. Three masked individuals jumped out and opened fire on the two approaching SUVs, which blocked the road in front of Mark's. The FBI agents didn't stand a chance as rifle fire riddled the first SUV, killing the two agents. The second one swerved while another masked gunman opened fire at it with an M4. Agent Hatem saw the driver of the second SUV slump in his seat. Agent Andrew Garcia managed to get out of the passenger side of the still moving car and fired seven rounds with his Glock. The suspects returned fire immediately, and Andrew went down.

All the gunmen were wearing black balaclavas underneath their Halloween ice-hockey masks and tactical plate carriers. Two of the shooters helped the suspect run back to their van. Sahar saw Agent Williams stagger out of Agent Russell's damaged SUV from the passenger side and draw his pistol. He looked unsteady from the collision. Before he could fire his Glock, one of the gunmen shot Williams several times with what looked like a 1911. The masked figure walked back toward the van while shooting out Agent Russell's tires. Before getting in the van, the gunman holstered his pistol and unslung a strange-looking, rifle like device, pointing it at the surveillance drone. A few moments later Sahar lost the signal, which should have been impossible.

Agent Hatem looked at her blank monitor and got on the radio. "We have agents down. Head toward Agent Russell's position and get a medic there now! I'll call an ambulance."

She then turned to the van driver. "Agent Kendall, start rolling toward Agent Russell now!"

***

The war between humans and aliens had begun because of a series of mistaken assumptions. The fighting had become deadly, with human governments on the verge of collapse. But the war ended as quickly as it began when direct communications was established and both sides negotiated in good faith. Lieutenant Julieta Alba Cruz Lopez, or Julie as her friends called her, was a former police officer. Like so many others she joined the Army at the beginning of the conflict when human civilization was in danger and fought with distinction with the 2nd squadron of the 102nd Calvary Regiment. Later, she was assigned to Dr. Khan's team, now officially called the First Contact Group (FCG), which helped establish communications with the aliens. Her transition from the stressful life on the front to a desk job was made easier because of her boyfriend Danny.

Since the signing of the peace treaty in New York at the United Nations, Lieutenant Lopez and the FCG had been kept busy with translations and smoothing over cultural differences. Today the group gathered in a large conference room to get to know each other better. There were many humans who remained hostile to the aliens, although most people were glad the fighting was over. The aliens were vegetarians who loved eating fresh fruits and vegetables from Earth. Their biochemistry was compatible with humans, and they were well suited to the Earth's environment. The catering staff always supplied their gatherings with a nice assortment of fruits, vegetables, and sandwiches.

"Hi, Odortor," Julie said.

"Hello, Julie, my friend. This is the Master of Arms, Makro. I told him about our discussions, and he liked the idea of fighting together against the Qhasloi."

The Thrultak sent different individuals to these group meetings to practice their English. However, the majority of their population remained in stasis because their ships were unable to house and support a larger number of them. Julie helped supervise and organize these meetings and ensured that different groups of humans were able to meet with their new allies. The meetings helped build informal ties to the Thrultak. Today Borlinn, the arts councilor, wanted the contact team to meet with Makro, Xeegi, and Orclite. Julie was nervous because this was her first meeting with Makro, the Master of Arms. Since the discovery of the Qhasloi spaceship, ongoing high-level negotiations took place at the UN with all the world's leaders with the aid of the Thrultak translators and the FCG. The enemy ship was just beyond the heliopause, and light took twelve hours to reach the observers on Earth, although the only leader the contact group they had met was Borlinn.

"Pleased to meet you, Makro," Julie replied.

"Nice to meet you." Makro turned slightly red with joy. The Thrultak were direct, and Makro was no different. "I was wondering if you could introduce me to one of your military leaders. Odortor and Hancear have told me about some of your ideas, and I would like to explore them further with your military leader without further delay."

"We have the president in charge and many military leaders but I can ask General Ross if she would meet with you." Julie found this directness refreshing.

"Yes, please ask as soon as possible. I want to start conversations about creating a joint independent defense force. How we respond to the Qhasloi will depend on which Qhasloi slaves we face."

Julie looked at her smartphone, which had a Thrultak translation app designed by Noah Green on it. It was not as good as the dedicated translation units, but it was more convenient.

"I don't understand," she said. "What do you mean depending on which Qhasloi slaves?"

"We have never met any of the real Qhasloi but we have fought at least two different enslaved races. They fought differently. Their level of aggressiveness and tactical sophistication were not the same. The slave races fight in their own way; there is no uniform military doctrine."

Julie was surprised. "How can we tell what we're facing?"

"We'll know soon enough when they send their first video demand for surrender; then we'll get a look at who we're facing," said Makro as he retracted his limbs and rested comfortably on the floor.

Julie found the idea of fighting enslaved aliens repugnant.

"Can you excuse me for a moment? I'll make the call now."

She walked away from the group and dialed General Ross's personal number. "Hi, General. Can I ask you a question?"

"How are you, Julie? Sure, go ahead."

"I know it's irregular but Makro, the Master of Arms, would like to meet with you. I think he has an idea he wants to talk to you about. I think he wants to cut through the red tape. And I think we misunderstood the Qhasloi threat. We may be facing several different kinds of enslaved aliens."

"Well, you are in luck. I'm in New York attending a meeting with a small delegation of all the theater commanders, their NATO and Asian counterparts. With the destruction of most of the world's nuclear weapons, we have a mess to deal with on the planet. The Russians and Chinese may think this is a time to fulfill their territorial ambitions in Eastern Europe and Taiwan, and everyone is scrambling to rebuild their nuclear arsenals. We created a special task force just to deal with North Korea and Iran. And Africa is a mess; the African Union is the only real multilateral organization still functioning. Most of Sub-Saharan Africa is tearing itself apart, and it's been difficult reinforcing our units there. On top of all that, we still don't really have a plan for the Qhasloi."

"Sounds like a mess. I'm glad that's above my pay grade. What time will you be free?"

"We'll break for lunch in two hours, and I don't need to attend the small group meetings afterward. The others can take over," replied the General.

"Thank you. I'll let Makro know."

Julie walked back to join Makro who was having an intense conversation in French with Claude.

Claude smiled at Julie and reached out to kiss her on each cheek.

"*Bonjour,* I was just telling my friend here that he must visit my country when he has time. I have to go and chat with my friend Borlinn. She wants me to meet someone."

Julie waved goodbye and turned toward Makro. "Well, we got lucky. General Ross will be able to meet you in two hours."

"Thank you, I hope we'll have a chance to talk together soon." Makro's eyestalks waved along with two of his arms as he turned to leave.

***

"What happened?" Agent Russell was just regaining consciousness at Sinai Grace Hospital.

"You got hit by a van. They were waiting for us. It was another ambush," said Agent Hatem, pushing back her shoulder-length black hair.

Agent Russell sat up in the bed, winced, and felt the bandage on his head. "What about the other agents?"

Agent Hatem grimaced. "Agent Collings was killed. Agent Reddy was hit several times with one round to the head, which fortunately was just a glancing hit. He's recuperating from surgery. The doctor said he is going to fully recover. Agent Doyle was hit in the arm and his plate carrier. Agent Garcia just came out of surgery; he got hit in the leg. Both of them will be fine. I asked headquarters to analyze our surveillance video. The techs said they'll also ask Hancear to look at the recording and give us his analysis. It might take a while but I've been going over the video myself. The attack looked coordinated, and the gunmen were well trained. Something bothers me. I can't put my finger on it."

"Shit, we almost had Hermann and 'General' Williams."

Agent Hatem frowned. "This is the third time we came up empty. We've never been ambushed before. This can't be a coincidence. There has to be a leak. Or they're really good at gathering intelligence on us."

Agent Russell tried to get out of bed. "We've got to find out if there's a leak before anyone else gets killed. From now on we keep everything inside our group, and everyone else gets nothing."

Agent Hatem stepped in closer and used her hand to gently keep the older agent in bed. "I know you don't like hospitals and this is not a particularly pleasant one, but you have to stay here overnight for observation. Besides, you still need to get an

MRI to make sure you don't have a brain injury. I'll work on the video with the techs and keep you informed. Just try to rest for now. I know you liked my mom's Knafeh. She sent me a batch a couple of days ago, and I brought you some."

Agent Russell reluctantly laid back and took the small plastic container. "Thanks, I love the spun pastry and the way she flavors the syrup."

Agent Russell had developed a taste for Lebanese food while on assignment to help investigate terrorist cells in the Middle East. He found he like Lebanese cuisine the most out of all the ones he'd sampled so he immediately took one and savored the taste.

"Enjoy, I'll be back later," Agent Hatem said as she walked out of the room. "By the way, I asked the local PD to post a guard outside."

In between chews Agent Russell said, "Thank you, and I'll see you later."

***

Hancear got the video feed from Agent Hatem's drone before it died and, in a few seconds, analyzed the video. "Helzul, I have some disturbing news."

"Well, what is it?" Helzul asked as he stopped his work on improving the ship hull material.

"The video was sent by our friends in the FBI. They were attacked, and one of the enemy shot down the drone with a directed energy pulse," said Hancear, the Thrultak AI.

"Yes, and why is that interesting?" asked Helzul.

"Humans do not have the capability to make such a weapon. It is Thrultak technology," said the AI in definitive tone.

"Are you sure? I'm going to have to have a talk with Metlob. Don't send the results yet. We'll find a way to work with these FBI to find out what's going on."

***

"We have to have a real discussion on how to deal with the Qhasloi ship. I know at their current speed it will take three years to reach the Earth's moon but we need to prepare," Makro said, waving his two arms as his body turned blue with excitement, then white.

His people had already voted on helping the humans as much as possible; eighty-seven percent of the voters were for helping the humans against the Qhasloi. Everyone eligible voted through their personal computer pad, and Hancear tallied the results immediately. Over the centuries the Thrultak used the intelligent computers and their personal pads to conduct voting on important matters as situations arose, and elected leaders were able to make decisions if voting hampered quick decision-making. Certain votes were binding for a minimum length of time before another vote on the same matter could be undertaken, although the leaders had the discretion to stop implementing the voters' decisions if there was a material change in circumstances.

General Ross looked at her translator and then at the small screen's color interpreter.

"General, white means that Makro is displaying anger," added Julie.

"I agree with you, Makro. We must start planning our defense as soon as possible. I know the United Nations along with the United States and all our allies have recognized the Thrultak as a sovereign nation with all the concomitant rights and duties. But unfortunately, not all humans have welcomed your presence, and many still harbor ill will toward your people."

"I understand the anger and sadness. I want to suggest that we create a joint defense force against the Qhasloi," Makro said, turning purple. "This will help us become closer allies."

General Ross stopped to take notes on a notepad.

"I personally agree with the idea but I have to take this to our president, and she has to get approval from Congress. For it to be an international force you have to present it to the United Nations as well. We can start by asking our ANZAC, NATO, Japanese, Korean, Indian, Israeli, and ASEAN allies. I also want all the information you have on the multiple slave races of the Qhasloi. We have to know what we are dealing with."

"I'll have Hancear transmit everything we have to the Cyberinfrastructure Center. By the way, Hancear would like to rebuild the radio telescope at the Arecibo Observatory so that we can aim our communications to a fixed ground receiver from the deployed satellites. This will make communications easier if we have to move the Homeship."

General Ross said, "I'll make sure the president understands the urgency of this request."

"Thank you. Please excuse me; I have other duties here before I go back to the carrier here in New York. Tell your president we took her advice and we're going to hire several law firms, public relations firms, and financial institutions to manage our economic and social integration with humans. I think one idea we might use is to give our allies preferred trading partner status. We will not trade with those who are not friendly toward us; we'll charge them extra tariffs. Take care I'll speak to you soon. We've taken on projects with other government entities and private companies to pay for the agreed reparations for damages caused to your planet offset by the damage you caused to our Homeship."

"Good luck. That sounds like a lot of work." General Ross stood and watched the large alien trot out of the meeting room on six legs.

"Well, what do you think, Lieutenant Lopez?"

"I think we should work with them, and we need a plan if what they say about the Qhasloi are true."

"Do you trust them?"

"Yes. They are generally peaceful and, although they have a lot of technology, they are not very good at fighting. They depend on their technology and are passive. I don't know if it's because they are herbivores and didn't evolve from hunting societies, but they do tend to be reactive and defensive."

General Ross thought for a moment. "I've been briefed but the Thrultak don't seem to have much on the Qhasloi."

"Yes, I've studied some of the new information, and they were completely overwhelmed by the Qhasloi's tactics. They faced two different races, the Ktols and the Mirlaks. I've seen what data Hancear had on them, and it's not much. They have little data on the other slave races and even less on the actual Qhasloi," said Lieutenant Lopez.

General Ross stood and picked up her notes. "The good news is that the Thrultak seem to like a democratic way of doing things and appear to be receptive to us and our allies. The totalitarian regimes remind them of how the Qhasloi do things. This will make it easier for me to push our allies to join the Earth Defense Force."

Lieutenant Lopez stood and waited for the General to finish gathering her things. "Good luck, General."

She snapped off a smart salute. The general returned it, smiled, and left with her waiting staff officer.

***

Agent Russell felt all his aches and bruises as he climbed into the wheelchair. All the tests had come back negative, and he was going to get discharged after two days in the hospital. After reading the name tag on the orderly's scrubs. Agent Russell said, "Hi, Jason, I'm Mark. Before I leave can you take me to see a couple of my agents? They were brought in with me, and I think they are still in ICU."

"Sure, I'll take you to their rooms," said the orderly, smiling at the older agent.

Agent Russell felt old, having to be pushed around in a wheelchair, but was glad when the tall African American nurse guided him through a maze of corridors and elevators. Once in the correct wing, Jason got directions from the nurses' station and wheeled Agent Russell into the room.

Before leaving he said, "Hey Mark, I think your other buddy is just next door. I'll be at the nurses' station when you're done."

Before Agent Russell could say anything, Jason left whistling a familiar tune.

"Agent Garcia, how are you doing?"

"Hey boss, I'm fine. They are letting me out of ICU later today. This is nothing. A round hit the edge of the plate, and a couple of fragments hit my leg. The bullet fragments had lost most of their energy and barely penetrated the skin. I'll be back on duty in no time. How are you?"

"I feel like I got hit by a truck," replied the older agent.

"Because you were. Did we find those bastards?" asked Agent Garcia.

"Not yet. Agent Hatem is on it, and we're getting our

surveillance video analyzed."

"Hello, boss," came a voice from behind Agent Russell.

"How's the arm, Agent Doyle?" asked Russell.

"It was a clean through and through, didn't hit the bone or anything," Agent Doyle replied, standing there with his left arm in a sling.

He was a six-foot three former Penn State linebacker who looked goofy dragging an IV stand with his right arm and wearing a hospital gown that barely covered his large frame.

"I can't wait to get my hands on those fucking guys. Any luck finding who set us up?"

"Not yet, but we'll get them," replied Agent Russell.

Garcia sat up straighter on the bed. "They knew we were coming and Hermann, our target, wasn't there."

"Yeah, they must have known, and those guys that jumped us were trained," added Doyle.

***

"Put everything that we're not taking inside the van. Make sure there's plenty of gas. I want to make sure the fire is hot enough to melt everything," Ambrose said while he packed his rifle in a hard case.

He towered over the rest of his crew at six foot five. He placed the case in his government issued car. The mission had been successful: They had relocated General Hermann and General Williams before the FBI caught up to them.

"We should have made sure those alien lovers were all dead," Jeremiah said as he took off his dark base layer and exposed his tattooed covered body. After he dumped his clothing, he brushed off his sweat-soaked blonde crewcut.

"We didn't have time, but if we run into them again, we'll make time," Dinah said as she took off her mask and freed her long brown hair while she put her gear away in the rental car. She came around and hugged everyone.

"I'll see you guys soon. Got to run and catch my plane."

"Wait a second." Ambrose handed out a new burner phone to each member. "Give me your old burners."

After collecting them, Ambrose put them into a large Pyrex baking tray and poured concentrated hydrofluoric acid over them before placing the tray on the floor of the stolen van.

After getting her new phone, Dinah got into her rental car and drove away from the abandoned garage in the Deanwood section of Washington, D.C.

Ambrose waited for Hiram and Jeremiah to get into Gideon's truck before he ignited the signal flare and tossed it into the gasoline-soaked van. Through the van's growing flames, he watched Gideon's Ram TRX truck drive off. Ambrose got into his dark blue charger and hoped they would soon do something more significant for Christian Patriots everywhere. The liberals and aliens were taking over the country, and he didn't want to just hide in the shadows.

CHAPTER 2

"How are they making all this money?" asked President Lana Gallo, sitting at her desk looking at the report on Thrultak activity.

Emmet, her Chief of Staff, said, "They really took your advice and created a large international corporation. They are calling it Thrultak Interplanetary Partners or TIPs. The first thing they started was contracting with large cities around the globe to haul their recycling away for a reasonable fee. They're unbelievably efficient, and they sell their remanufactured raw materials back to private industry. They have also reached out to our Department of Energy and can recycle radioactive waste. What little they can't recycle they haul and launch into the sun. Their economic team has priced all their services competitively. They also use local private and municipal garbage haulers and small businesses so there isn't a negative impact on the labor market. They accept US Dollars, British Pounds, Euros, Japanese Yen, Korean Won, and Singapore Dollars. They have set aside some of the funds to help rebuild the damaged global infrastructure, and they are funding victim aid programs as well."

"This is almost too good to be true. I know people are still angry about the war but this will go a long way to make things better. What are they asking for, and how did they come up with this economic model?" President Gallo asked as she adjusted her reading glasses.

Once the short but deadly war was over, the Thrultak moved quickly to establish relations with every nation on Earth, and they helped repair as much of the damage as possible.

"You're going to love this. The Thrultak hired a team of experts to design their five-year economic plan. They specifically are using the Korean Chaebols and Japanese Zaibatsu as models for their conglomerate. They have already shared some of their patented technology."

"I know. I had one of their batteries installed in my smartphone. They have a partnership with several battery manufacturers. Now I don't have to charge my phone for days. I know everyone is trying to tear these batteries apart to reverse engineer them. I hope they don't run into any of the negatives of that kind of financial and vertically integrated business conglomerates, like the Empire of Japan experienced," said the president.

Emmet stood and thought for a moment. "I don't think they will. Their corporation will have the ability to become involved in every type of business. They'll be able to produce all manner of goods and services. Although they are willing to use the free market corporate model to interact with the world market, internally, they live and interact without money in a democratic and cooperative way. They use Hancear and their personal comm units to vote on everything at frequent intervals."

The president sat back and relaxed for a moment. "What else are they asking for?"

"As part of the payment for the damage to their Homeship, they want market access and intellectual property protection. The Chinese, Russians, and North Koreans are having a fit over these demands. But if they want access to the Thrultak technology, they'll comply. The Thrultak are very good at enforcing their rights with Hancear and shutting down and destroying computer systems that violate the agreements. They're helping us enforce our trade agreements against the Chinese and Russians. Interestingly, they also are creating a huge demand for real organic produce, which is giving the giant ag industry fits. As vegetarians they don't want anything with corn syrup or bad seed oils. They apparently get bad stomach aches."

President Gallo added, "I've heard from the EPA. They said that the Thrultak will be willing to take out greenhouse gasses from the atmosphere and plastics out of the ocean for a fee."

Emmet took a sip of coffee and nodded. "Right now they are doing this to pay for the damage they caused. But soon we'll owe them money."

This was a rare private moment between them, and the president felt relaxed talking to her trusted aide. "Interesting. I just got word from General Ross. She talked to their military leader, Makro. He wants to start an international Earth Defense Force independent from all national governments. He thinks this force should be free to make their own decisions and start preparations to deal with the Qhasloi threat."

Emmet raised his eyebrows. "Will the Thrultak control this force?"

"No, they understand that humans on the whole don't trust them yet. The force will be independent and make their own decisions, no single country will control it."

"But they have the spaceships," said Emmet.

"They are promising to create a unified leadership, and everyone will have a chance to be part of it. Makro also asked if the FCG could continue to work with them as teachers and advisors as they start the selection process for this defense force. They're willing to share their technology with all members of the defense force."

"What kind of tests are we talking about?" asked Emmet, a little skeptical and wary.

"From what I could gather, they want the FCG's help finding suitable Earth Defense Force personnel quickly so they can come up with a strategy."

"Are you going to keep Dr. Khan in charge?"

"Yes, for now, and I'll allow him to expand his group to get the expertise he needs."

"Sounds good," Emmet said.

"Is there anything else?" asked the president.

"Yes." Emmet seemed reluctant to continue, holding a folder in his hands, and stood there.

"Is that for me?" she asked, reaching out for it.

"Yes, we have a serious problem. I think we have a security leak. The director of the FBI, Wyatt, sent me these files. Their investigations into Bishop Jones, General Hermann, and the white supremacists have failed, and their surveillance operations were compromised."

"What did the Attorney General have to say?" Lana asked.

"The FBI suspects that white supremacists and their sympathizers have infiltrated the highest levels of government and present a huge security risk," Emmet replied. "Attorney General Ben agrees with Wyatt: They want to keep things as low profile as possible, and they are going to give more latitude to Special-Agent-in-Charge Mark Russell. They trust both him and Special Agent Sahar Hatem."

"That's interesting. Makro said they were concerned about the potential leak of technology. They want to be involved in the investigation; we have to find out where the security leak is coming from."

The president looked out the window and wished she could go outside and just play with her chocolate lab, Buster.

"Why the interest?" Emmet asked, curious.

"The short version is that Agent Hatem asked the FBI techs to examine a surveillance video, and the FBI sent it up to the Thrultak. Now they want to be part of the investigation."

"I'll tell Wyatt but he's not going to like it, nor is Agent Russell." Emmet picked up a notepad and jotted some notes. "One last thing. Both the Democratic and Republican leadership want you to appoint more members from their own party."

Emmet was worried about Lana losing support from both political parties because she was an Independent prior to the arrival of the Thrultak.

"I've tried to be even-handed. But it's hard to figure out who is in it for themselves and who to trust," the president said, trying to rub away her growing headache.

"I don't envy your position. But you do have to think about the midterm elections next year, and you need to start thinking about your own reelection campaign," Emmet reminded. He wanted her to get ready to raise funds for the campaign.

"When I ran as an Independent, I just wanted to get a few things done. I didn't want to run for another office. I just wanted to serve my district. I don't like either party. I agree with the Dems on some issues and the Republicans on others. But I wonder if I can stay Independent or if I should rely on one of the parties."

Emmet said, "I know, but I'm going to make sure that we build our own grassroots organization and begin the process of getting you reelected. I think it was a mistake to appoint Michael, a Republican, as your vice president. I think when you run you need to find a moderate, maybe even a Democrat or another Independent. We have to get rid of Michael. I think he has been in touch with the most extreme Republicans with ties to right-wing extremists, and some of them have links to Bishop Jones."

"Okay, keep on top of it. Now I need to go over more of these reports before the NSC meeting. Make sure Wyatt and Ben find the security leak and shut down those right-wing terrorists. I also want a report on how the Thrultak carriers are doing in their new locations."

It had been her idea to have the Thrultak carriers in the United States move away from population centers and land in remote national parks till a more permanent solution could be found while their Homeship orbited the sun like a new moon.

CHAPTER 3

Julie was allowed to reoccupy her apartment located in Alphabet City. It was a large one-bedroom with a huge, professional eat-in kitchen. The apartment was owned by a wealthy professional chef who retired to a country house in upstate New York and rented it to Julie. She stood over the forty-eight-inch Wolf Dual fuel range and watched the herb butter sauce simmer and reduce. She had half of a whole wild-caught salmon cooking with herbs and lemon in a sous vide cooker. The salad was finished, and the Korean rice cake dessert, which she bought in Korea Town, was ready to be served on the tray. While she worried over the sauce, she ate another morsel of the delicious rice cake and rearranged the others to fill in the vacant spot.

She was cooking a real meal for the first time since the whole comet war had begun. Danny had finished the full-length OCS and the Advanced Infantry School and was about to graduate from Ranger School. She hadn't spoken with him since he started the last phase of school. She missed him and looked forward to seeing him. This was his welcome home dinner party, which she had planned for days. She invited Agnes and Connor to join them in the celebration.

***

Danny sat back on the couch and savored another Korean rice cake. "Dinner was so good. I've been craving this for so long. We didn't have enough to eat while we were at Ranger School. Florida was even worse."

Agnes, who had her left arm around Connor and a glass of wine in the other, took a sip. "The salmon was so moist and flaky. It's good to get some time off."

Connor looked at Agnes and smiled. "I feel like we are finally catching up with all the work. I'm not sure but I think Dr. Khan is even busier these days. I think they are going to ask him to take on more responsibilities."

Danny finished another rice cake. He had put on some muscle and had lost all his body fat. "That sounds like more work for you guys."

Julie sat next to Danny and took a sip of her Pinot Grigio. "I like this job; it's relaxing and not much stress. I just meet with new Thrultak, talk with them, and help them deal with humans. I like helping humans adjust to working with the Thrultak. In fact, I've helped Dr. Padget's son, Trevor, and Dr. Kim's daughter, Dalia, meet with Borlinn and a few of the other Thrultak. It would have been nicer if they could have met Thrultak children as well. But because they have been in space, they do not have children among the crew yet."

Danny perked up, "What did the kids think of the Thrultak?"

"They thought the aliens were cool, and we arranged for their school to meet with them," Julie replied.

"Most people aren't afraid of the Thrultak," Agnes added.

"True, but it seems like the people on the fringe of society can't accept the aliens," agreed Danny.

Julie smiled and took another sip of wine. "I like my job because it helps people get to know the Thrultak. The FCG has been essential in creating a good working environment. I've even had time to ride my bike and cook."

Danny didn't want to be a party pooper but let out a sigh. "We still have the Qhasloi out there. The Thrultak are afraid of them, which means we should be worried as well."

Julie rested her head on her right shoulder as she looked at Danny. "You're right but we're ground pounders. If there is any fighting, it's going to be up to the Air Force and the Space Force."

"Unless the Qhasloi make a ground assault," Danny added, taking another sip of his wine.

"I don't know what's going on but Dr. Khan and Colonel Gardner have been meeting together every day for over a week.

I have a feeling they've been tasked with something new and important. I've had to help expand Capstones' capability," said Connor.

Danny asked, "What's Capstone?"

"The Supercomputer at the University of Maryland."

Agnes laughed. "Capstone? When did we start calling it that?" She stifled a yawn. "We should get going." She gave in to the yawn, took a last sip, and nudged Connor with her elbow.

Connor nodded. "I'm tired, and you look like you're about to fall asleep, Agnes. Let's go back to the Best Western."

"I've got to get up early and put together a first contact briefing for a human and a Thrultak," Julie mentioned.

Dr. Montfaucon and Dr. Padget would be helping her. Dr. Claude Montfaucon was also a neurologist, while Dr. Anthony Padget was a trained psychologist. Her team worked with Baxso, the Thrultak's chief medical officer, to prepare a short introductory briefing for a human and Thrultak separately before they had their first contact. With their expertise plus outside consultants, they developed a basic protocol for first contact, which stressed the importance of accepting each other's cultural norms and being open to an exchange of ideas for the betterment of both humans and Thrultak.

After Agnes and Connor left, Julie let Danny rest on the couch. She rinsed and loaded the dishwasher and then hand-washed the wine glasses. Tears formed as this simple act reminded her of helping her mom in the kitchen when she was in middle school. She smiled at the fond memories, and her smile widened when she thought about Danny in the small living room. Her mom would have liked him. She finished in the kitchen and grabbed her wine glass and walked out. She found Danny passed out on the couch, exhausted from the training he had just finished. She got a throw blanket, covered him, gave him a kiss on the cheek, and turned off the lights before going to bed herself.

CHAPTER 4

"Absolutely not! Come on, Wyatt, I can't have a tech and an alien on this team." Special-Agent-in-Charge Russell said from his hospital bed.

Wyatt frowned as he looked at the files marked Top Secret that he had on his desk. "Look, Mark, I just got out of a meeting with the president and the AG. This is not a request. It's an order from the top, and I'm sorry you lost three agents."

"I can't babysit two untrained techies, and I don't want more field agents I don't personally trust. Whoever is behind the security leaks must be very high up."

"I know, and I did my best to vet the new agent. His name is Lucas Hill. He's extremely qualified, and I trust him. I'm also going to give your team security clearance, second only to me and the Deputy Director."

"I don't like it, Wyatt."

"Mark, these two are already on their way to your new field headquarters at the Seventh Regiment Armory in New York City. You'll work in the building next to the FCG, and that'll give you priority access with the Thrultak."

"Is that wise? I'll need to be able to travel out of state on short notice. Getting out of New York City will be very difficult."

Agent Russell was trying to give as many excuses as he could think of to stay away from New York and avoid babysitting two tech nerds.

"No problem. I've authorized a dedicated helicopter for your team on the newly created helipad at the armory, and you'll have access to a private jet out of Teterboro Airport in New Jersey. Mark, I need you to do this, and I need you to find the white supremacists and those traitors. I'm asking you as a friend, not as the Director of the FBI. The president and the AG are authorizing you to add any personnel and equipment to your team as you see fit. This has the highest priority. You may ask for support from all federal and state counterterrorism agencies, access to any support you need from Quantico, and additional help from any of the field offices in the country. But on a day-to-day basis you will operate independently."

Agent Russell was silent for a moment. Wyatt had been his supervisor when he first joined the FBI, and he now trusted him with his life. "I'll do it. I don't have to like it but I'll find those bastards."

"Thanks, and get well soon. How is Agent Hatem working out?"

Agent Russell didn't hesitate. "She is one of the best I've worked with."

***

Gretchen Braun was one of the assistant directors to Wyatt Thomson. She had lost her husband, a Naval officer, on a guided missile frigate in the opening days of the attack by the Thrultak. She just couldn't believe that the president and the unelected government had capitulated and agreed to surrender to the alien menace. Gretchen was sure the aliens were planning a wider takeover; she just couldn't prove it yet. The Bishop was right. The weak liberal sinners were willing to sacrifice Americans and the world to the aliens for personal gain. She had already given information about Agent Russell's investigation to Bishop Jones and Secretary Kelly.

After the recent deaths she was finding it more difficult to get access to Agent Russell's activities. She had to be more careful around Director Thomson, lest he become suspicious of her. He was already more cautious and kept some files only for himself.

***

Lucas and Metzul were both waiting in a large conference room. They didn't look at each other and just kept to themselves. Metzul was sitting on his haunches and looking at his computer pad, recalling his conversation with Helzul and Klopzar. They wanted him to find out how their technology had gotten into the hands of human enemies who opposed the peace between the Thrultak and humans.

Metzul was young and feared the humans' propensity for violence. The humans were so strange. He tried not to glance at the man in the room with him but he couldn't help himself. So Metzul turned to his computer pad and studied English idioms and recorded human expressions. But he kept one of his four eyestalks on Lucas, who had his own laptop open. The biped was probably bored and playing video games since he kept looking at his watch and checking his phone repeatedly.

Metzul didn't realize Lucas Hill was a shy nerd, not good in social situations with humans or any living creatures. Like him, the human just didn't know what to do when faced with a new situation.

Lieutenant Lopez from the FCG had given them a short briefing. Metzul noticed that Lucas had tried not to gawk at the female's face and figure as she had told them to act normal and just relax. She stressed the importance of communication and acceptance. With time they could work together as a productive team. After the presentation was over, she left them to wait for their supervisor. Metzul was glad the human just sat there watching his laptop and didn't attempt to communicate. Metzul called up the drone surveillance video again, trying to see if he could find any clues to the gunmen's identities. He swore and noted that the video was being accessed by someone else in the room. He turned another eye on the human but quickly glanced away when the human turned to look at him. After a few seconds Metzul turned one eyestalk slowly to the human who had returned to watching the screen.

Metzul was thankful when the door opened and a young woman walked in and introduced herself.

"I'm Special Agent Sahar Hatem. Welcome to the team."

Metzul turned green with blue and yellow spots because he felt apprehensive and shy. He tried his best to stand at attention with appendages sticking straight out and all four eyestalks pointing straight up.

Agent Hatem turned to the alien. "Hello, you must be Metzul. Nice to meet you." She extended her right fist.

The alien used one of its arms and touched the fist. "Yes, I'm here to help you as much as I can and report my findings to Helzul and my leaders."

The human walked closer and extended his hand. "I'm Agent Hill. People call me Lucas. I'm a tech specialist."

Agent Hatem shook his hand and smiled. "Both of you can call me Sahar. I assume you two have met?"

The alien turned to the human and turned a little red with embarrassment. "Actually, no."

Agent Hatem looked at them both. "What have you been doing all this time?"

Neither responded.

"Never mind. We'll be based here at the Armory, and most of your work will be here. You'll meet Special-Agent-in-Charge Russell after you get settled. Agent Garcia and Agent Doyle will join us after they have recovered. Any questions?"

"Where will we stay?" asked Metzul.

"Both of you will be quartered at the Best Western Plus Stadium Inn, which is very close by. We have extra security there, and we're all going to stay there while in New York. Most of the FCG and the Thrultak delegation is staying there for now as well."

"Am I going into the field?" asked Lucas.

"We have a small team. You might have to come with us when we travel. You do have weapons training, don't you?" Agent Hatem asked.

Lucas stammered blushing slightly. "Ummm. Yes, I passed my pistol qualifications."

She smiled. "Don't worry, you're not here as a breacher. But I would like to see you at the range."

"Metzul, are you qualified with any of your weapons?"

The alien shrank a little and turned green with fear. "I've never touched a weapon. Do I need a weapon?"

She smiled and in a soft, gentle voice said. "No, you do not need one. I'll take you to your workspace. There's a secure high-speed link to Quantico and, Metzul, you'll also have a secure link to Hancear there as well. I'll come get you guys for lunch."

The alien tech only carried a small case and a small satchel around the upper part of his body, while Lucas had two rolling bags and a backpack. Agent Hatem took them to a large, locked office. It was in the middle of a hallway with other offices but theirs did not have a room number or any other identifying markers.

"We'll have this door replaced with a more secure one, and we've already swept it for any kind of surveillance. I cannot stress this enough: You cannot talk to anyone about your work here, not even the director of the FBI or the AG. Do you understand?"

The look on Agent Hatem's face scared Metzul, causing him to struggle with the translator.

Before he could form a reply, Lucas said, "Yes, I was told by the Director about the need for top-level security."

The serious frown on Sahar's face was replaced by a warm smile. "Good, I'll get you boys for lunch around 11:30." She handed Agent Hill a set of keys, turned, and left.

The alien turned all four of his eyestalks toward Lucas, and his mouth emitted soft squeaks and clicks.

After a slight delay his translator said in a soft voice. "She is a little scary."

Agent Hill said, "Yes, I wouldn't mess with her."

***

President Gallo looked at her notes as she spoke into her phone. "Hello, General. I don't have much time to talk but I have to ask you a big favor."

"Yes, Madame President, I'll do what I can," said General Ross.

"I'm asking you to step down as the Chairman of the Joint Chiefs of Staff."

General Sharon Ross almost slammed the phone down. "What?"

"You've been doing a great job, Sharon, but I have a new important mission for you."

The General breathed deeply, relaxing a little. "What is it?"

"Makro and Klopzar want to start a joint human and Thrultak defense force to prepare for the approaching Qhasloi. I want you to be part of it. You can pick anyone you want to be on your staff, and you'll get priority support from both the US government and the Thrultak."

The General's anger dissipated. "Thanks for your vote of confidence. I would like to keep working with the FCG since they've become comfortable working with the Thrultak. We can add more personnel and experts as needed."

"I agree the people on the FCG can be trusted. I've asked Dr. Khan to work closely with the Thrultak to develop a selection process for this new combined Earth Defense Force. I want to have it started before the end of October."

"Great. I like Dr. Khan. Are we going to continue to use the facility at the University of Maryland?"

President Gallo looked at her watch. She had another private meeting with the vice president in half an hour, then a cabinet meeting. "Yes, temporarily, until we can rebuild some of our bases and launch more communications satellites."

"How's the investigation into the Bishop and his followers going?" asked the General as she remembered the attack at the University of Maryland and how a small group had almost prevented the first contact.

"Sharon, we're facing a growing security leak. We still haven't found Bishop Jones, and we've had a hard time locating his followers. They're planning something but we don't know what. Look, they have supporters at the top levels of government. That's why I need you on this. I'll get a more detailed briefing to you as soon as possible. I also want your recommendations for a new chairman."

"Okay, I'll send the recommendations right away. Will there still be Senate confirmation hearings?" asked the General.

"Yes. Talk to you later," said the president after she was reminded of her next appointment by her Chief of Staff.

***

Dr. Kareef Khan sat at his desk looking over the set of recommendations from his team. All the original members of the FCG were multitalented, and each contributed to the list of items that should be included in the test for the Earth Defense Force candidates. Some of the ideas were taken from various aptitude tests and psychological tests available in the commercial market and the military. Kareef was glad that he could count on Anthony, Patricia, Jan, and Claude to put together this test for him.

While he was looking at his printouts, someone knocked at his door.

"Come in."

Klopzar and a small six-legged droid walked into his office. Helzul spoke first.

"It's good to see you again. Hancear will join us through the droid."

He was still not settled into his new, large office at the Armory, but it had a large, clear space for several Thrultak to sit on the floor comfortably for face-to-face meetings. Dr. Khan stood, came out from behind his desk, and guided Klopzar, followed by the droid, to a cleared space with one comfy chair near a fifty-inch LCD display on the wall.

"Come in. I printed out the list of qualifications we've been working on."

After a short discussion on the progress of human and Thrultak integration, Hancear produced a soft chime.

"I've prepared a presentation and ranked the qualities in order of importance by both human and Thrultak."

He gave a brief explanation of how it had come up with the list of qualifications after studying human and Thrultak databases. Kareef looked at the long list of qualities and found them interesting.

"How soon will you be able to use our data and yours to compile a sample test?"

"I have already made fifty sample tests for you to consider. You will need to construct new physical tests for the human members of the defense force."

Dr. Khan was still getting use to how fast the Thrultak did things when they built consensus. They operated very efficiently and without red tape.

"How many teams are we trying to build?"

Klopzar moved his arms around and regarded his human counterpart with two of his eyestalks while his two other eyes studied the LCD screen on the wall.

"I think for the moment we should start with five teams and move up to ten teams after the initial phase. Each team should consist of ten humans and one Thrultak to operate our technology. We also need to have at least two hundred replacements in case of injury or illness. After that we will build larger units for ground and space operations."

Dr. Khan took some notes on his legal pad. "I'll have FCG look at the sample tests, and we'll begin sorting through the potential pool of applicants as soon as possible."

Klopzar said, "We've already chosen our candidates, and Hancear has begun making changes to a few of our larger flyers to accommodate human passengers. We are also sharing some of our medical and scientific technology with your scientists."

"Thank you. I will bring this up with our president, and I know you'll be sharing this with the United Nations this afternoon," Dr. Khan said.

Klopzar turned different shades of blue with light blue spots indicative of his happiness and excitement and extended his legs to leave.

"I think some of the training and selection will take place in Western Europe, India, South Korea, and Japan. We've not selected Russia and China as training sites because they have not agreed to some of the basic principles of freedom of information and protection of our intellectual property rights. We'll move ahead with our planning as is."

The director of the FCG stood.

"Thank you for visiting, and I'll get this started as soon as I can."

CHAPTER 5

President Gallo sat at her desk and finally signed the executive order allowing the United States to join the Earth Defense Force along with NATO, ASEAN, South Korea, Japan, Australia, and New Zealand. No country was excluded, and any country could provide personnel, even the Russians and Chinese. While the North Koreans and Iranians pretended there were no aliens on Earth, all other nations would be included as part of a general United Nations agreement. The creation of the Earth Defense Force was still not going to magically fix the socioeconomic political issues the independent countries continued to face.

***

Dr. Khan's FCG, with the help of many experts across the country, modified Hancear's suggested questions and pieced together a grueling multiple-choice test. Before they finalized the test, they met as a group and agreed on the qualities they would test for in the candidates for the new Earth Defense Force. The group came up with a list of seventeen qualities. They wanted all the candidates to demonstrate each of these in some way during the entire selection and training process.

Colonel Gardner read the list: "Compassion, Creativity (knowing when to break the rules), Intelligence, Leadership, Motivation, Manual Dexterity, Physical Condition, Mental and Physical Perseverance, Patience, Zero and Advanced G Capability, Spatial Orientation, Decisiveness (quick thinking during emergencies), Adaptability, Confidence, Self-Discipline, Mathematical Ability, and Teamwork."

The group all nodded their heads. Claude Montfaucon, who

had degrees in mathematics and physics as well as linguistics, looked at the group and touched his perfectly groomed, grey-streaked beard.

"I sure as hell don't want to take this test," he said in a thick French accent and looked toward Dr. Padget and Dr. Kim.

The two educators had initially been chosen for their linguistic and teaching ability. They helped teach English to the aliens and designed a curriculum that others could follow. However, because of their expertise in different areas of psychology, Dr. Khan increased their involvement in the FCG, and they became part of his core group. Dr. Patricia Kim was an expert on group learning, group dynamics, and their impact on learning impairment, while Dr. Anthony Padget was an expert on how stress impacted learning, which prevented sound decision-making. Both insisted that during the test all the candidates should be put under different kinds of stress.

Dr. Kim asked, "Are we making this too difficult?"

Dr. Padget took a sip of his black coffee. "Maybe, but this has to be hard. We need to weed out as many unqualified people as possible."

Jan Kowalczyk, ever the skeptic, was given the task of looking at potential problems and any possible underestimated dangers. "No, it has to be difficult."

"I agree we only have a limited number of spots, and we are not taking that many alternates," said Dr. Khan.

Dr. Montfaucon nodded in agreement. "I just want to remind you that the test is only the beginning of the selection process. Only those candidates that pass the test will be allowed to continue to an exhaustive interview by a panel of humans and Thrultak."

Dr. Kim still frowned. "I hope we're doing the right thing."

She glanced at her watch and said, "Anthony, we have to get going or we're going to be late for your son's birthday party."

Dr. Khan smiled at his friends. "That's enough for today."

Dr. Padget turned to everyone and asked, "Why don't you all join us for the barbecue?"

***

The chicken and lamb kebabs were delicious, and the entire

scientific team was sitting around and sharing some beers while Trevor, Dr. Padget's son who had turned twelve years of age, and Dalia, Dr. Kim's daughter, watched an old black and white pirate movie, arguing with the other children at the party on the realism of the movie. While all the other adults ignored them, Jan Kowalczky's ears perked up when the children began discussing how the pirates captured the British warships and merchant ships so easily with so few people.

Jan turned to Trevor and asked, "How did these pirates capture those ships?"

Trevor had a sustained interest in pirates and spent his entire free time learning as much as he could about them. His enthusiasm had infected Dalia as well. They often played together since their parents worked together.

"During the age of sail they would use small boats to sneak up on the enemy ships and overpower the crew. Or they would get close without a flag and, once they were very close, run up the Jolly Roger and make the merchant ship surrender," replied Trevor. "They got to keep all the booty."

Dalia, not to be outdone, added, "Then there were privateers who captured and destroyed ships for their country and captured enemy shipping."

"Interesting," Jan said, stroking his scruffy beard.

Trevor began speaking more quickly and louder when he realized that Dr. Kowalczyk was really interested. "There are modern pirates."

Jan's eyebrows rose and said, "Really?"

"Piracy has never disappeared," replied Trevor.

Anthony noticed his son and Dalia talking nonstop to Jan.

"Are they bothering you, Jan?"

"No, not at all. I'm getting a good lesson on pirates," Jan replied.

Sitting on the floor with his Eli Fish sour beer, Jan turned to the children and said, "Please continue."

Trevor was happy to share his knowledge and proudly told all he knew.

"In 1998 the Cheung Son, a cargo ship traveling from Shanghai to Malaysia's Port Klang, was hijacked. The ship and cargo were never found again. There's a great book called *Pirates: A New History, from Vikings to Somali Raiders* by Peter Lehr."

Dalia, not to be outdone said, "People make the mistake of thinking pirates act like people in the movies. They're actually dangerous and deadly."

Patricia raised her voice, "It's cake time, everyone. Trevor, come blow out the candles."

Patricia and Anthony were spending a lot of time together, especially since Trevor moved from his grandpa's Colorado ranch to New York. Patricia was happy they had a chance to have this celebration after a tumultuous year.

Claude walked over to Jan and asked, "What was so interesting, my friend?"

Jan took another sip of his sour beer. "Well, the Qhasloi ship is more advanced than the Thrultak ship, and it's a warship, unlike the converted civilian Thrultak ship. We could learn a great deal from the Qhasloi ship. So why not capture it like pirates?"

Claude smiled. "If you can get close enough. I don't know much about space but I'm pretty sure you can't hide any energy signatures, no matter how much stealth material you use to build the ship itself."

Jan scratched his beard as he saw Colonel Gardner and waved him over. "Hey Oliver, can you have stealth in space?"

Claude added, "What Jan is asking is, can you fly any kind of craft without it being detected?"

Oliver didn't have to think at all. "No, you simply can't hide energy signatures in space; it will be like having a bonfire in a small, dark room. Why do you ask?"

Jan took another sip of his beer. "The kids were telling me a big problem with modern pirates is that they're able to capture huge merchant ships with only a handful of people in small boats. I thought it would be wonderful if we could capture the Qhasloi ship. After all, it has a hyperdrive, and it's a warship. Even the Thrultak don't have a hyperdrive."

"As far as I know, the only way modern pirates have been successful is when they can sneak up on the merchantman. And in the cold of space, any large energy signature would be detected easily."

"But if they could get close, could a small group take control of the ship?" asked Claude.

"I'll have to check with a Naval officer, but I assume that both modern and old merchant ships don't have enough fighting men to stop a pirate boarding party. However, a warship will have armed sailors or marines to repel boarders. I'll give Commander Martin White a call. He was involved in getting you here, Claude."

"*Mon Dieu,* do not mention my trip here again. The food was terrible, and we almost died. Let's have cake and forget about the sea."

Jan put his beer down and picked up the cake Julie had baked for Anthony and promised to get more information from Hancear about the Qhasloi ship.

***

Julie stood in line with her laptop with thousands of people trying to enter Madison Square Garden. Once inside, she saw that the venue would be filled to capacity. The Garden floor was filled with chairs. Danny had gone to see his parents and told Julie he would meet her at the Garden. But because of the large crowd she couldn't find him. Each person was required to bring a laptop capable of wireless connectivity, a black pen, a legal pad, two number two pencils, and a ruler. Julie got a seat in the bleachers close to the exit and the bathroom.

I've never taken a test like this before, she told herself. *What a cluster fuck. People are jammed into this arena. There must be more than twenty-three thousand people here.*

A disembodied voice came over the public address system. As soon as the voice started speaking, she recognized it as Hancear. He had taken on a slightly Irish lilt to his English.

"Ladies and gentlemen, this is a grueling twenty-hour multiple-choice examination. It is designed to test you in many ways and will only be given once today all around the world. Millions of people are taking this test. Many are already serving in the military or working for the government. However, it is also being given to any individual who wishes to take it. The physical conditions in the building will be manipulated as you take your test. Do not be alarmed. You may hear noises or feel a change in temperature. However, your priority is to finish the test. Here are the rules: First, you cannot leave the complex. Second, there are no rules. Third, physical violence will not be tolerated. Please take your seats."

Julie heard a voice mutter, "What the fuck." She grimaced and thought, *This is a disaster*. Then she heard a female voice call out to her.

"Lieutenant Lopez! Julie!"

She looked to find the voice in the crowd was Captain Egorova.

"Hello, Captain. I haven't seen you in a while."

"Tati, please," she said as she hugged Julie and kissed her on both cheeks two times. "May I sit next to you? I've been busy talking with aliens. I know our government and the aliens haven't reached any comprehensive bilateral agreements, but I was asked to participate. There are many who want to leave behind our old ways. However, some refuse to change and don't want to give up any power even if it ruins the motherland."

"Sure, these seats are not taken."

Julie took another look around for Danny. Then she heard him scream her name.

"Julie! Where are you?"

He was standing on top of a seat across the arena twenty or more rows down. She felt her face turn red and just looked down at her feet, trying not to feel embarrassed.

"Isn't that your man?" asked Tati.

"Yes, that's Danny."

Tati stood up and started waving.

"Wait, what are you doing?" Julie reached up and held the Russian Captain's wrist, feeling embarrassed at the attention they were getting from the people around them.

"Hold me steady," Tati said, then stood up on her chair. In a surprisingly loud Russian accented voice, she yelled, "Hey, Danny boy!"

Tati was not shy at all. She turned to their neighbors and asked them to help her, and in a few seconds a whole group started chanting, "Danny! Danny! Danny!"

He spotted them, started running up the aisle, and reached them as the announcer started talking.

"Please take your seats. We will begin the test in fifteen minutes."

***

Julie sat and opened the file after logging into the secure server set up by Hancear and the Capstone team down in Maryland. The human Supercomputer was now far superior to all other supercomputers on Earth, thanks to its Thrultak modified servers. The small ten-thousand-square-foot space, which included space for offices and meeting spaces, had at least quadrupled the capacity of the largest data centers such as The Citadel, which had more than seven million square feet of space. Now Capstone was used to showcase joint human and Thrultak achievements.

Julie glanced at the Table of Contents and sighed at the test; it was over ten-thousand questions. After reading four questions Julie said, "There is no way I can finish this in twenty hours."

"Yes, I agree," said Tati while she looked around the testing center. "We should work together."

Danny looked at them both. "Yeah, the rules didn't prohibit it."

"Let's find two more. Five is a good number. What did you study in school?" Tati ignored Julie's objections.

"History, and I have a culinary arts degree," Julie answered.

"I studied English literature," Danny added.

"Good, I am an electrical engineer. We'll need a biological science person and a math person. Let's ask the people around us."

They started talking to their immediate neighbors and found Asher Tang, a Singaporean Naval Special Operations First Warrant Officer. Asher was a certified paramedic with advanced combat medical training. As a bonus he had a math degree from Nanyang Technical University. Tati found Captain David Ohayon of the IDF. He seemed lost but Tati was not shy and convinced him to join the group. He was a fighter pilot who flew helicopters for fun with an aerospace degree from Iowa

State University. The group decided to go out to the concession area and found a space near a wall outlet just in case they needed to recharge. They sat in a circle, introduced themselves, and began to work on different questions. Others formed groups of their own, and the entire arena became abuzz with conversations.

After three hours of working on the test, an announcement came over the public address system: "Meals and snacks are available for pickup at all the concession stands. You can pick them up at your leisure."

Since their group was already near a concession, Danny and Asher took turns getting the group drinks and snacks from a nearby stand.

Julie nearly dropped the cup of coffee Danny had given her when the MSG concert sound system started playing loud bone-shaking explosions. Loud music was interspersed by recorded gunfire and explosions. She quickly cleaned up the mess. Although not as loud as the real thing, Julie could feel the bass in her body. It became difficult to concentrate, and some of the participants were clearly having PTSD responses from their recent combat experiences. Julie and her group worked together well and finished five hours early. The five of them hit the submit button at the same time. Because Hancear was administering the test, they received a reply in less than ten seconds.

Julie stretched her arms overhead and read the message: "You have passed and may leave. You will be contacted in three days to set up an interview. If you have not been called for an interview, you have not been selected. Thank you, Julie."

Julie smiled, remembering her interactions with Hancear and how it loved playing with animals while in its robot extension.

Tati turned to Julie and asked, "Did you get a message?"

Julian Danny replied at the same time. "Yes."

"I passed," added Tati.

"That was quick. I passed," David said.

Asher put in, "Me, too. Thanks, guys. I hope we can work together in the future. Good luck."

Julie said bye to everyone as Tati gave each person a kiss on each cheek and got Julie's number.

***

The very next day Tati invited Julie for coffee at a local pastry shop. She had spent a great night out on the town with Danny, but he had to return to his parents and get his gear before shipping out for training with a K-9 unit specializing in combat patrolling.

Julie sat there and remembered the nights they had spent together in her apartment. Meanwhile, her Americano and Tati's espresso arrived with a doughnut made from croissant dough. They sat together in comfortable silence and sipped their coffee while nibbling on the confection.

Julie asked, "I thought your government didn't want to participate in any propaganda activities the Western countries have set up?"

"Officially, the government is angry that the Thrultak had become so close to NATO and all the American allies. However, in private, many recognize the Thrultak are advanced and can do what they want. Many moderates understand the appeal the open societies have for the Thrultak. Many young Russians want to change for good; they want to reform Russian society but those who are in charge are afraid of change. The conservative Russian Orthodox Nationalists are too entrenched and will not give up their privileged positions without a fight. I hope the arrival of the aliens will change things. I'm a simple soldier, and I was told to try and get into the Earth Defense Force and make sure that Russian interests are not overlooked."

"It's too bad, really. We should try and get along," Julie said.

Tati took a sip of her espresso, and her Russian accent thickened. "I know. We need to work together against these Qhasloi and help each other rebuild a better planet. I don't know anything about these Qhasloi. But they defeated the Thrultak, and that means trouble."

Julie's hand trembled slightly. "Yes, the Qhasloi must be dangerous, and I can't imagine what they could do to us."

CHAPTER 6

Onboard the Qhasloi ship, the Clutch Leader of the Ghakeols, Gurjin, waited for reports from his crew. Two, his second in command, was on sensor duty.

"Our hyperfield has fully dissipated. Our sensors are operational again, and we have detected the Thrultak ship's energy signature," he said.

From a human viewpoint, the Ghakeols were the size of an average child at four feet tall. The facial structure of the reptilian Ghakeols also made them look like they had permanent grins. Their shiny smooth skin had a plastic-like appearance with large green eyes and red pupils. Their skin sported a variety of bright colors, adding to their toy like appearance.

Two continued, "Clutch Leader, I have detected a planet that is inhabitable. We don't have any visuals yet of the enemy. They may be hiding behind a moon or the primary star. We can launch a probe now."

Gurjin scanned his own data pad. "Wait till we pass the asteroid belt, then launch both the reconnaissance drone and the navigation buoy so that our drones will have a zero point on their X, Y, and Z axis, creating a reference for their internal guidance and navigational systems."

Two bowed his head. "Yes, Clutch Leader."

"Make it so, and good work, Two. Seven, calculate a course for the planet, secure the hyperdrive and the quantum generator, and make sure the ship and crew are ready for normal space."

Gurjin hated what the Qhasloi had done to his people and to his family. But unlike other slave races, he did not enjoy killing or enslaving other sentient beings. Yet what choice did he have?

The four-foot-tall reptilian helm operator clicked his tongue and began the process of retracting the hyperdrive field generator. The generator consisted of two pylons, fore and aft, that deployed a translucent cocoon membrane around the ship. When energized, the cocoon took the ship out of normal space. He looked over his control panel and sent a message to engineering to confirm that the quantum field generator that powered their hyperspace drive was offline. He prepared warship number 23158 for normal space travel. They had remained stationary in space for many weeks, recovering from jump sickness, and were also blind because it took time for the hyperfield generator to collapse its field before they could move in normal space. Otherwise, their ship would be torn apart at the quantum level.

Gurjin looked at the upper arms of the science officer and saw the thirty-eight tattooed in bright red on his yellowish skin as well as eighteen smaller digits. The masters did not allow most slaves to have names, only twenty-digit alpha numeric designations. He was allowed to have a name as part of a reward for being promoted to the commander of this warship, but even he had a slave race number on his arm.

"Science Officer Thirty-Eight, begin scanning the planet and prepare a detailed scan of this system. We will need the navigational data for our attack drones."

"Yes, Clutch Leader Gurjin."

The Qhasloi ship began the slow process of retracting its hyperspace field generator membranes into its hull, and the warship transformed itself into a sleek spaceship roughly seven hundred meters long and fifty meters wide. The ship had a crew of one hundred with an additional five hundred warriors in stasis. The warriors had a complement of one thousand drones for subduing alien races, and the ship had the ability to remanufacture drones if they had enough raw materials.

***

Bishop Jones lay naked in his king-sized bed and watched Maggie and Lilith dress after they had both spent the night pleasuring him. The first time he took them both to his bed, Lilith cried all day afterwards. Now she was happy to please him. The failed attack on the Supercomputer had been a disaster that forced him into hiding. His true followers and allies made sure no one could find them. In fact, his sermons were reaching more receptive minds. People were living in fear of alien domination and an uncertain future. "Maggie, get my blue Armani suit ready for the meeting."

The Bishop's entourage traveled by motorcade from his fortress in Idaho to the suburbs of Denver. He visited and preached at different churches affiliated with the New Patriotic Sword of Christ Church. His new aide, Amos Boseman, took care of his security. Amos was an ex-Green Beret and had worked for the CIA. But as a dedicated Christian, he had become an important part of the church. With Amos's help, they had collected more than five million dollars in donations from patriotic supporters in the past few months.

This upcoming secret meeting would help him gain even more power; it had been set up by Shane Kelly, the Treasury Secretary who had provided valuable intelligence and was great at recruiting dissatisfied people in the government. Today he would meet with US Vice President Michael Landreneau. The Bishop had grown to hate President Gallo and found a likeminded ally in the vice president. The weak woman had given in to the aliens without putting up a serious fight. A man would have done a better job of leading this great Christian country, he believed. Now they were allies against some new alien threat, the Qhasloi. None of these demons should be trusted. He opened his laptop and scanned the new sermon he had written for broadcast by the underground network of Christian internet radio stations and AM radio stations. The file would also be copied to thousands of flash drives and distributed through the underground network of the New Patriotic Sword of Christ Church. Since the failed attack on the communications array and the signing of the New York Peace Accords, the number of followers had grown. Jones sat back and listened to the sermon once again over his ear buds.

"Brothers and sisters, you cannot drink from the cup of the Lord and the cup of demons. You cannot partake of the table of the Lord and the table of demons. If you believe in the Lord, you cannot pretend to keep his commandments. You cannot mix with alien idol worshipers, sit next to them, and take their evil offerings. You cannot give up your freedoms to follow their evil desires to kill other beings after they have killed so many of the chosen people. The Lord's table lies before you. Do not deny our Lord, the one and true God. Even before the arrival of the demons from space, true believers were persecuted by liberals. Too many true believers were tested by money, pleasures of the flesh, and the evils of the internet. Remember, brothers and sisters, do not conform to this world but be transformed by the renewal of your mind, that by testing you may discern what is the will of God, what is good and acceptable and perfect. Our Lord has shown us the way to salvation and everlasting life. If you affirm his words and commandments, he will save you. Brothers and sisters, when faced with enemies on all sides, put on the whole armor of God that you may be able to stand against the schemes of the devil. Become the warriors of Christ. Do not succumb to the devil and his ways. Amen."

Bishop Jones smiled, pleased with the sermon, and pushed the laptop away. "Maggie! This is ready for distribution."

"Yes, master," Maggie said as she laid out the Bishop's white shirt, a red tie, and his suit at the foot of the bed. Afterwards, when she set the laptop on a small desk, the Bishop walked up behind her to fondle her from behind.

***

Vice President Michael Landreneau sat in the fast-moving motorcade. He spent a lot of time handpicking his Secret Service detail. He knew them all by name and could count on these men to say nothing. He tapped the armrest in the limo nervously and turned to Henry James Perez, his aide.

"I don't like the way the president seemed to just listen to a bunch of soft, weak, liberal Democrats, who are such libtards. She's not acting like an Independent or an American. She concluded the peace treaty and signed all sorts of agreements without consulting me. She even let the god damned United Nations lead the way in negotiating multilateral agreements, and the shell-shocked Senate just rubber-stamped whatever she put in front of them."

Perez clutched his hands and felt his anger grow at the mention of the "libtards."

"You know, sir, she's going to use this national crisis to help Democrats take away people's Second Amendment Rights, expand healthcare to every poor, unproductive member of society, and give every homeless person money to live. I think she'd like to implement a Universal Basic Income as well. She may even propose the building of massive low-income housing projects when the damaged areas are rebuilt. She's also letting the aliens put in their alien clean energy technology into our national energy grid. Who knows if it's safe for humans?"

Michael nodded his head at the rant. "We can't let that happen. We have to protect our sovereignty and our industries and energy infrastructure."

Perez thought about how his grandparents escaped from Cuba, built a small business, and didn't get any handouts. "It's typical for the liberals to use a national crisis to advance their crazy globalist agenda and give handouts to welfare moms."

"I know, Henry, I know."

Michael was worried about the negative impact all this was having on the business community and the stock market. The lazy poor would always exist, and he had to help those who had made something of themselves in the business world. Things had to change before the president could give away all their freedoms and make Americans slaves to this alien menace. If this Bishop Jones could help him secure a large popular base, he could run against President Gallo, an Independent without a political party behind her. All he had to do was secure the backing of the GOP and this Bishop Jones. Then the rest would be easy.

***

Bishop Jones walked out the front door alone and watched three armored Suburbans drive up the road in a cloud of dust. He stayed under the awning of the large ten-bedroom house to avoid any chance of being photographed by a surveillance satellite. As the SUVs came to a stop, four agents jumped out, two from each SUV. One of the agents from the trailing SUV deployed a cell signal jammer while the other swept the area for electronic surveillance signals. They didn't have to worry about GPS tracking because they had deactivated it the night before. When those two gave the all clear, the lead agent signaled, then the vice president was quickly escorted into the house by Perez. Once inside, the Bishop and the vice president disappeared into a private study where the Bishop shook Michael's hand and guided him to a leather chair. They faced each other in a well-appointed private study. A large desk was on one side of the room and a bar on the other side.

Bishop Jones didn't waste time. He knew the vice president was busy, and Amos had stressed the importance of brevity since the man was traveling to Utah for another round of fundraising and recruiting.

"Thank you for coming, Mr. Vice President."

"Call me Michael. Shane has told me a lot about you and what you are trying to do. He also told me that you're being persecuted by the FBI. I think the president blames you for the violence at the Supercomputer Center in Maryland."

"All I did was encourage a group of concerned citizens to protest. I'm not sure how a small group of violent men was able to create such a mess. But I guess the FBI and the president needed a scapegoat so they blamed me. We cannot have a government that oppresses religious freedom. The government cannot take away our rights," said Jones in his most sincere tone.

Michael listened to the Bishop, then leaned forward. "I agree. I think the president is overreaching, and she's not looking out for the best interest of the country. With your support I'll be able declare my candidacy and run against her."

Bishop Jones smiled, pleased that the vice president shared his views. "We can't have her ruin the country for another two years. The aliens will control everything. Now I fear we're going to become their slaves," added Jones, playing on the fears of many Americans.

"But what else can we do?" asked Michael who wanted the Bishop to offer suggestions.

"She could disappear," said Bishop Jedediah Obadiah Jones in a low voice. "With a little help from you we could make sure she does not completely ruin the country."

Michael felt beads of sweat form on his forehead and felt sweat run down his back. Was he really going to do this?

"Say no more. I agree. She cannot be allowed to destroy the economy and fund all these liberal policies with our hard-earned money."

The Bishop grasped his hands. "Amen, Brother. Let us pray for the salvation of this great nation and the true believers."

Michael felt some discomfort. He was never really religious but the Bishop was absolutely right. If he was going to save the country, President Gallo had to be stopped. Since the alien attack, all the people he ran into at the country club and at the Yale Club in D.C. told him how this administration was destabilizing the financial markets. There were even rumors that the capital gains tax would be increased and the federal estate tax exemption amount will be decreased to only two million dollars. Something had to be done.

"Amen. I'll get my aide, Henry, to help you and be your contact person. He'll be able to get more people to help you. But I cannot know anything. I need plausible deniability."

Bishop Jones grinned. "I already have a team that Shane helped put together. What we need is more access to information and authorization from your office. Once you're sworn in, I'll need a presidential pardon and my Church assets freed."

"Done."

Michael stood, feeling a slight unease but knowing that he had taken an important step for true patriots and his people.

Bishop Jones stood and smiled as he thought, *God is great, and the demons and those who consort with demons will tremble before the Lord.*

Michael strode to the waiting SUV with Henry jogging to catch up to him. Perez was loyal but out of shape and out of breath.

"Well, sir, how did it go?"

Michael waited till Henry opened the door for him to get in the armored SUV. "Good. What are you willing to do to take back our country?"

Henry didn't even pause for one second. "Anything, Michael, you know that."

"I want you to start communicating with the Bishop and Secretary Kelly regularly, but you have to make sure it can't be traced back to me. Give them anything they need. You'll be contacted by someone working for us soon. We need to call upon all our trusted friends to help rebuild this country. I can't know any of the details but the president has to go sooner than later. I want you to make sure everyone on my security detail is loyal to me. Do you understand what I'm asking of you?"

"Yes, sir. I will make sure that everyone is a true patriot," said Henry, eager to be rid of all the liberals ruining the country.

***

Secretary Shane Kelly was in another boring meeting with other cabinet members when he got a simple untraceable text from the Bishop: "We will cleanse the country and rebuild it with God's help. The meeting was a success. Begin Operation Hidden Redemption. We will not be replaced!"

Shane smiled and forwarded the Bishop's message to Agent Ambrose, adding, "Forward all future messages to Bishop Jones and Henry Perez."

He included their numbers and finished with these words: "It's now the time to kill."

Shane had used his contacts and recruited Secret Service agent Ambrose Hall from a list of suspected right-wing extremists compiled by the FBI for President Gallo. He introduced the agent to the Bishop and became part of the trusted brotherhood. Once recruited, Shane helped Ambrose delete the FBI's list and recruited more patriots.

Shane received an answer right away.

"Yes, it's time to tear down."

***

Ambrose smiled at Shane's message and stretched his six-foot three frame. He and his team had been lying low since they extracted Gideon from that FBI team led by that nosey Agent Russell. Gideon had been a little careless when he relocated General Hermann and allowed himself to be tracked to one of their safehouses. But now they were going to do something that would change the country. He almost couldn't believe that they were going through with the mission. *I will be the sword of the Lord and bring down the evil liberal regime*, he declared to himself.

He then sent a group text: "Operation Hidden Redemption is a go. We'll meet in three days."

Ambrose didn't have to wait long and got replies from Gideon, Hiram, Jeremiah, and Dinah. *I'm going to be the sword of justice, restore the country with a righteous God-fearing leader, and get rid of these unelected liberals.*

CHAPTER 7

Metzul and Lucas both looked at the video from the shootout between Agent Russell's team and the unknown light blue Chevy G series van with blacked out windows. It hadn't taken long for the two to figure out how to work together but the alien was still uncomfortable with humans. Metzul reviewed the data from the van that was recovered a day after the shootout; no forensic evidence was found. It had been stolen from a used car lot near Detroit a few days before. Metzul was tired but he looked over the same video once again, now going frame by frame in super slow motion, with three of his eyes on the screen while the fourth kept an eye on the human.

At the same time he investigated who might have had unauthorized access to Thrultak technology. He submitted his queries to Hancear and waited for a response. How did rogue humans get the weapon to shoot down a Thrultak modified human surveillance drone? He had a list of ninety-six names that had direct access to the technology; many worked with the FCG.

The human threw a small yellow toy animal across the room, yelling, "Come on Pika!"

From Julie's briefing, his workmate Lucas was displaying both frustration and anger.

"What is the matter, my human friend?" asked Metzul, turning all his four eyestalks to gaze at the human.

Lucas was startled and jumped a little as the alien turned blue with yellow spots. Lucas pointed the built-in camera on the human translator, then looked at the translator, which said that the colors indicated excitement and confusion.

"I'm frustrated by this video. The resolution is amazing. But I've looked at it over and over again at different speeds and zoomed in, and the only clue is a small segment of a possible tattoo on the right wrist of one of the gunmen."

"Here let me take a look at the tattoo," said the alien, moving uncomfortably close to Lucas and still keeping three eyes focused on the screen and one on Lucas. It took a moment for Metzul to see the small image of a partial tattoo.

He huffed and asked, "Lucas, can you zoom in and switch to the thermal setting available on the drone footage? Tattoos can influence thermographic examination; we might be able to get a clearer picture of the design."

Lucas was amazed he hadn't realized that this drone camara could do that. He adjusted the camera settings.

"Here we go."

Some of the clothing obscured the tattoo, but with the enhanced thermals they saw the man had most of his body covered in them. The chest plate and Nomex balaclava obscured some of his neck and face, but the arms and leg tattoos became visible.

"We should look at the other suspects and see if they have these body drawings." Metzul felt pleased and turned a light blue.

"That was great. We should work together more often," said Lucas.

"I thought we are working together?" he replied.

"I mean we should ask each other for help. You know, trust each other."

"Yes."

The alien considered the human for a few moments. The alien hadn't made any progress in finding out how Thrultak technology got into the hands of violent human rebels. He couldn't accomplish his mission by himself so maybe this human should be trusted.

"Do you know why I'm here?"

Lucas turned to face Metzul and made sure his translator faced him. "No, I was just told to report here and provide tech support. I don't even know what exactly Special-Agent-in

Charge Russell is investigating. I definitely don't know what you're doing here."

Metzul's eyestalks lowered and looked around. He also checked his translator.

"I also do not know what Agent Russell is doing. You know this video you are examining came from a drone that was developed using a combination of human and Thrultak technology."

"Yes, I know, but I'm still learning about its capabilities. Those guys at Area 51 and Langley are working with Helzul and Hancear to build surveillance and communications equipment through the Thrultak Interplanetary Partner Group and using their proprietary technology."

Metzul paused and decided to take a risk; after all most of the humans were friendly.

"Hancear thinks that the drone was shot down using our technology, and I'm here to find out how these criminals were able to get their tentacles on one."

"We should definitely help one another, and we need to figure out what Agent Russell is trying to do."

"Yes." The alien fumbled with his translator. "We need to be part of the party cabal."

Luas stifled a laugh and frowned, "I'm not sure I understand. You mean become part of the team?"

"Yes, I was trying to use one of your idioms. I preprogrammed it into my translator to make communicating easier. We must work in harmony as a large, friendly gathering of likeminded individuals who work for the greater good of the pod."

"You mean like a team?" asked Lucas.

"Yes. I need help with the list of names I have compiled who may have been the source of the leak. Many of the names are on the FCG."

"We have a few things we need to do before we can move forward. First, we need to know what's going on. Second, we need access to the FCG. Third, I'm hungry so let's go get something to eat before we talk to Agent Hatem."

Lucas saw Metzul turn light blue with lots of yellow spots

from happiness and saw the four eyestalks stand straight up and wave lightly side to side. "Are you hungry?"

"Oh, yes. But can you do the talking? I'm afraid of Agent Hatem scolding me. When I met her she had just come back from the hospital and seemed very angry."

Lucas swallowed; she was very attractive but he remembered her getting out of the van with her jacket off. She had on her tactical vest and was carrying a shotgun in one hand and an AR 15 in 300 blackout with a suppressor in the other. She carried all the gear without breaking a sweat and had barked at him the first time he introduced himself to the group after he got assigned here.

"We'll go together and talk to her after we eat."

***

Agnes Nelson received another email from Agent Ambrose Hall. She verified the email address and that he was an actual agent working for the Special Branch of the Secret Service. His requests seemed reasonable as was his requirement for secrecy. She gave him access to their work and one of the anti-drone rifles the FCG, in conjunction with the scientists in Area 51, had created with Thrultak technology. This time Agent Hall wanted access to anything she had on the Creation of the Earth Defense Force and to other weapons that they were developing. After reading the email she began to have some doubts about the legitimacy of the request. She quickly erased the message with a shredding program.

"What's wrong?" asked Connor from the breakfast table across from her at the Best Western.

"Nothing," Agnes replied.

"You can't fool me; I see that worried wrinkle on your forehead."

"It's just work. I have to get some information for the government, and I'm not allowed to talk about it."

"Okay."

Connor knew that much of their work was secret. They often didn't share their work with each other so he didn't bother her anymore about it. But he was worried about Agnes. This was the first time she seemed stressed since they started working together.

***

Dr. Khan was reading through the requirements for the Earth Defense Force personnel. Out of more than two hundred million hopefuls worldwide who took the written test, only 1,902,230 individuals passed the test. Some didn't pass because they didn't work in groups; only one person had passed the test working alone, someone named Mark Giambalvo. That name seemed familiar, but he couldn't remember him. Dr. Khan noted that Hancear informed the people who passed as soon as the grading was finished. The candidates were required to have an interview prior to actual selection for the Earth Defense Force.

Dr. Khan sat drinking the instant chai tea he had just made. He winced. Not like homemade but better than coffee. He didn't have to wait long in the small conference room for Dr. Montfaucon and Dr. Kowalczyk.

"Good morning, Claude, Jan, please make yourselves comfortable. There's coffee over there and water."

Claude sat down, then grabbed a water bottle while Jan walked over to pour himself some coffee.

"I have a favor to ask you both. The test results are in, and we will proceed with the next phase of the selection process."

Claude took a sip of water. "That was quick."

"What did you expect?" Dr. Khan asked. "Hancear finished grading all the tests the same day. We've been waiting to help set up interviews."

Dr. Montfaucon replied, "I helped Dr. Kim and Dr. Padget design part of the interview. I insisted that the interview should be conducted by three people and the candidate must have the support of all three. The next interview will be conducted by the Thrultak themselves with Hancear."

Dr. Kowalczyk listened and stated, "I think you have something else in mind, Kareef."

Kareef Khan took another sip of his chai tea.

"Yes. General Ross has already asked various groups to conduct studies on how to combat the approaching Qhasloi warship. One of the possible requirements for the new Earth Defense Force is humans may have to take a hibernation or stasis drug and be subject to neuromuscular stimulation. The sample drugs and the electronic stimulation device have been sent to Stanford, Yale, and the University of Pennsylvania. I was wondering if you had connections to other research labs we can ask for help. Chaoxiang Feng from the People's Republic of China was also given samples, as were many other countries."

Dr. Montfaucon scratched his head. "I know someone at the Max Planck Institute in Germany. She can help get the right people testing the drug and the medical devices."

Dr. Kowalczyk asked, "Why do the Thrultak think we may need this?"

"One of the options Hancear had come up with is deep space combat with a combined crew of humans and Thrultak. The AI suggests a deep space intercept with several smaller ships supported by three carriers could destroy the coming warship."

The Frenchman was puzzled. "Why three carriers? The Thrultak ships seem powerful enough."

Dr. Kowalczyk interrupted, "Claude, their ships were not designed as warships; they are commercial ships or passenger vessels."

"You're right, Jan. Hancear told us the Thrultak have very high levels of technology but their Homeship is a hastily built colony ship, and the carriers were modified from deep space exploration vessels," said Dr. Khan. "One Thrultak carrier is no match for a Qhasloi warship."

***

Julie was finishing up her portion of a report on the integration of human and Thrultak work crews. All she had left was interviewing the latest two she had worked with for the FBI. She texted Lucas and Metzul: "I have a few questions. I'm stopping by for a few minutes." She grabbed her notepad and walked to their office.

"How are you guys doing?" she asked.

"I'm okay," said Lucas as he took a drink out of his Star Wars Darth Vader mug.

Metzul fumbled with his translator, which said: "Everything is forthcoming thorny smelly flowers."

All four of the alien's eyes were turned to Julie, and she could tell by his reddish hue the young alien was happy with the translator.

Julie didn't have the heart to correct him and smiled.

"Good," she said, then thought to herself, *I have to talk with Hancear and make sure the AI takes a look at Metzul's translation software before he really puts his feet in his mouth.* "I just want your feedback on the FCG's briefing on human and Thrultak collaboration. Just send me an email on our secure server."

Just then Agent Sahar Hatem and Agent Mark Russell walked into the room.

"Lieutenant Lopez, it's great to see you," said Agent Russell.

"I've been meaning to come see you, Mark. I heard you were injured."

The older agent just shrugged his shoulders. "I'll be fine."

Julie nodded to Agent Hatem. "I guess I'll be going. It looks like you guys have something to discuss."

"Wait. I think it might be good for you to hear this since you've been involved since the beginning and we may need your help," said Agent Russell.

Agent Hatem frowned a little, then nodded her agreement. She turned and locked the door, then took out an electronic RF detector and camera finder and started to sweep the room.

Lucas stood from his desk and said, "Umm, Agent Hatem, I've already scanned the room."

Agent Russell waited for the female agent to finish and give the all clear. "I'm including Lieutenant Lopez here because we'll work with her as our main contact with the FCG, and I want to brief Agent Hill and Metzul on what we're up against. Lieutenant Lopez, do you remember General Hermann and General Chester Williams?"

Julie frowned and her body tensed on hearing Hermann's name. "Yes, I thought you guys had him under surveillance?"

"We did. But someone helped them go into hiding. We were following a lead when they ambushed us. The thing is, very few people knew about our operation," said Agent Russell.

"There've been other security breaches," added Agent Hatem

with a deep frown on her face.

"I'm not sure how I can help with any of that," said Julie.

Those names reminded her of all the good people she'd lost, and she had a difficult time keeping her own anger in check.

"Agent Hill and Metzul had a few ideas about how to track down the security leak. Helzul and Hancear sent an email suggesting that the guys who ambushed us used a new experimental anti-drone weapon designed by a joint human-Thrultak partnership from Area 51."

Julie remembered all the people she knew who died defending the Supercomputer. "I can't believe this. Is Bishop Jones behind this?"

"Yes, we think so, and he's getting help from very powerful people inside the government," Agent Hatem said vehemently.

Agent Russell put his hand on the younger agent's shoulder, "We've lost agents. But we may have gotten a break. Agent Hill and Metzul found some clues on the criminals that just attacked us. Using a new thermal feature from the advanced drone, they were able to recreate the tattoos of two of the attackers. We're in the process of identifying them, and that's where we need your help, Julie."

"Sure, I'll do anything I can," said Julie, eager to see the Bishop behind bars or better yet dead.

"Metzul and Hancear were able to trace the security breach to the FCG. I want you to introduce Agent Hill and Metzul to everyone. They'll go undercover as tech support, scan everyone's computer, and trace their computer activity."

"Sure, come up to our offices before lunch. I'll get you guys started," said Julie.

"That's it for now, but everything you find will go through me. No one else can have access to our findings," said Agent Russell as he pinned everyone with a deadly look.

Metzul eagerly tapped on his translator. The little speaker blurted out: "I'll beware of unguarded talk or ships will start to leak."

All the humans looked at the earnest alien and smiled but didn't correct him.

As Agent Russell, Agent Hatem, and Lieutenant Lopez

walked out, Russell whispered to Julie. "Did he mean loose lips sink ships?"

Julie stifled a laugh. "I think so. There might be some translation issues, I'll tell Noah. Maybe Hancear and he can figure it out."

***

Julie went straight to the lady's locker room and changed for her daily workout. She looked at her workout schedule for today, a 5k run on the indoor track, and it was shoulders day for weights. Afterward, if she had time, she would at least use the heavy bag for a few rounds. *I should really go visit Master Mau more often,* she thought.

She was almost finished with her third two-minute round when her workout timer was interrupted by a priority text: "Congratulations again, Lieutenant Lopez. Since you have passed the written portion of the Earth Defense Force selection process, you are now required to have two interviews as part of the selection process."

Julie smiled but then noticed the time and place for the interview and told herself, *Shit, I have an hour to get ready. At least I don't have to go anywhere.*

The Armory had become the headquarters for alien-human interaction in the United States. It was a beautiful building; one section was a medieval style brick building with terra cotta parapets, the other was Art Deco. It also had an indoor running track and other athletic facilities. Julie knew of two other major sites where the Thrultak kept a permanent presence. One was in Geneva, Switzerland, at the old League of Nations Museum and the other was located in Kyoto, Japan, at the Biwa Otsu-Kan Hotel. Julie jumped in the shower, then blew out her shoulder-length hair as fast as she could. Finally, with her hair in a neat bun, she slipped into her green Service Uniform. She decided to wear the regulation skirt for the interview and took out her cover.

As she finished dressing, she got a text from Danny: "Miss you. I passed the test. Did you? I'm sure you did; I have an interview today. After that I'm going to be in Arizona about two months for training."

Julie sent a heart emoji and typed: "Miss you, XOXO, and I'm headed to the interview now. When we have some time, we'll take a trip to upstate New York or maybe we can meet in Vegas for a short vacation."

"Sounds like a plan. GTG."

Before heading into the interview, she texted Agent Hill and Metzul and told them to join a FCG meeting after lunch. Julie forwarded the text to Dr. Montfaucon who was running this meeting.

The Earth Defense Force interview felt a little weird because Julie knew two of the three interviewers: Dr. Patricia Kim and Dr. Padget. However, she didn't know Dr. Silverman who was a practicing psychologist in New York. The interview was more relaxed than a job interview, and Julie felt calm throughout the meeting.

Dr. Silverman threw her a curve ball as the interview ended. "So, Lieutenant Lopez. Do you enjoy killing? Do you feel bad? How do you deal with the stress?"

Julie didn't know how to answer that and looked at Dr. Padget and Dr. Kim for some help. Both sat back and looked uncomfortable. Julie took a deep breath.

"No, I don't enjoy killing. It's necessary sometimes, and I try to talk to my friends who were there with me to process what we went through."

Dr. Silverman was relentless. "So are you getting professional help with your PTSD?"

"I meditate," Julie said as she thought about her sessions with Master Mau, who she had started seeing again for advanced training when she had time. "I also talk to my counselor regularly, Dr. Ayana Goswami. She helped me get through my first deadly force incident."

After that answer Dr. Kim spoke up. "Dr. Silverman, I think that is enough. Clearly, Lieutenant Lopez is doing her best to address any lasting psychological scars."

When the interview was over and Dr. Silverman left, Julie went to give both Anthony and Patricia a hug and told them about Agent Hill and Metzul, the new tech personnel that would be around to evaluate their computers and ongoing security needs. After chatting for a few more minutes, Julie left feeling like she had failed the interview. *Oh well, I guess I don't get to go into space.*

***

It has been a grueling three weeks, Danny thought. Only eight more left. He was on his knees examining the gear in front of him, ready for the in-quarters inspection. He finished laying out the kit when he got notification that he had passed the Earth Defense Force interview. He sent a quick text to Julie: "Love you. I haven't scheduled mine yet." He put the phone away before he could see Julie's reply. He had to get her out of his mind and focus on the upcoming inspection. He looked at the mandatory list of gear and recounted the leashes he had in his dog handling bag. He had the required five different leashes and a choke collar. After his work as a police officer, this seemed like a better career path than being assigned to a Ranger battalion. He didn't want to go back to the civilian world; he could do more good in the army.

His choice was made easier when Captain John McGlinchy had called and asked him to come back to the police force. During the conversation Danny realized he wanted to stay in the army. The Captain told him he could have his old job back anytime. It seemed strange to Danny that since the peace accords people returned to "normal" very quickly, including all the societal problems. Overseas, small, low intensity conflicts broke out in Africa and the Middle East, and the Americans, Russians, Chinese, Iranians, and the North Koreans found it difficult to intervene militarily without their former naval and air assets but continued to conduct covet operations against one another. The United States was on a crash ship-building program in partnership with their closest allies. Shipyards were laying the keels to new vessels that would incorporate some of the new technology, although it seemed like a waste of resources when the enemy was out in space. It seemed strange to Danny that people were still focused on terrestrial problems when the Qhasloi were out there. For him, it was easier to ignore these regional conflicts and focus on the approaching enemy. But these regular problems persisted. Danny heard from some of his friends that the Navy had taken some private yachts through eminent domain and armed them for anti-pirate and drug interdiction.

After this training Danny wanted to be stationed with Julie and have a chance to stay together. Every time he thought about her, he had to pinch himself and question if he was good enough for her. His mom liked Julie a lot but his dad wanted him to marry a Korean girl. Luckily, his mom promised him that she would have a talk with his dad.

***

President Gallo took off her reading glasses and rubbed her eyes. She had just reviewed the briefing for the new legislation for fully funding the Rebuilding Stronger initiative and was waiting for the Senate to pass it. The infighting between the Republicans and Democrats was even worse than before the aliens showed up. There was a knock on her private office. Emmett Haskell walked in with more files for her to look at.

"I want to remind you that you have a call with General Ross in five minutes."

"Great. Thanks, Emmett. Any news about the security leak? And find out about what progress Dr. Khan has had with the Earth Defense Force Screening."

Emmett took some notes on his phone. "Neither Director Thomson of the FBI nor Attorney General Geller had any news about the security leak. But I've been told that Vice President Landreneau has been floating the idea that you should not run for reelection as an Independent. He thinks you owe it to the American people to either join the GOP or the Dems. I have it on good authority that he has suggested that he'll accept the nomination of the GOP to run against you. As far as I know, Dr. Khan and the Thrultak have already begun the selection process."

The Chief of Staff looked at the text on his phone. "General Ross is on the phone."

President Gallo picked up the phone and threw her reading glasses on the table. "Good morning. How are you?"

"I'm well. I'm ready to move and work on the Earth Defense Force full time. I've already been briefed by Dr. Khan, Klopzar,

Makro, and Hancear.”

“Great. Have you had the chance to look at the files on your replacement? Do you have any recommendations?” Gallo asked while she sat back and closed her eyes.

“Yes, I think General Miguel Angel Bienvenida from the Marine Corps will be great. He has a lot of experience with the Special Operations command and is also a trained engineer.”

“Yes, I have his file, and that’s a great choice, thanks. His name came up several times from my other advisors. Is there anything else you need?”

“Well, I would like to have different groups study how we should handle the Qhasloi. I really want options. I have asked the war colleges to come up with solutions. I would like your permission to ask civilian think tanks for other solutions. The Thrultak are advanced but they aren’t good at war planning.”

“Sounds reasonable I’m having the Secretary of State and Homeland Security working on how the United States will participate in the Earth Defense Force. I’m trying to convince everyone that we should cut back on some of the conventional military spending and put more money into the new EDF. We’re also looking at the United Nations Peace Keeping Force, the French Foreign Legion, and the Spanish Foreign Legion as possible models.”

“To be effective, the Earth Defense Force-EDF must be allowed to operate independently. I want the Army Futures Command to work closely with me and help create new strategic doctrines and building programs. They need to help us modernize and develop new ideas not only about using the Legion but how we’ll update our own conventional forces and NATO. Can you also have other general officers from the other branches work more closely with the Futures Command?”

“Yes, I agree. I’ll make the changes to the Futures Command as soon as I get off the phone and make it a priority for the Joint Chiefs. I’m working with our allies and private industry in rebuilding our own forces. We may have a problem with the Russians, Syrians, Iranians, Chinese, and North Koreans. I have to go soon; I have another call. By the way, how is the selection process going?”

"It's going well. I have to admit the Thrultak don't like to waste time. The written tests and interviews are already completed. Once Hancear has the data, candidates will be chosen and the physical tests will commence. It's going to be a very difficult test. Hancear came up with it after examining every major Special Forces testing requirements."

"I have to go. Send me a copy of the physical test, and thanks, Sharon. I'm counting on you to make the EDF a success."

"I'll do my best, and you're welcome, Madam President. I'll send it now by phone."

Sharon found a file on her phone and forwarded it to the president.

Moments after she hung up her desk phone, President Gallo received a small file called EDF test requirements. She opened it and gave a short whistle, "Well, this won't be easy."

5k run in under twenty minutes

100-meter swim with clothes

200 lbs. dummy drag for twenty-five meters

200 lbs. dummy carry for twenty-five meters

Fifty push-ups

Fifty sit-ups

Ten pull-ups

Agility test run

Physical combat with a larger opponent for two minutes

A coordination test in zero gravity

Puzzle solving while undergoing heavy acceleration

CHAPTER 8

President Gallo ate her breakfast in the White House kitchen with her protective detail nearby. Chef Jadyn Rodgers and the main kitchen staff prepared for an afternoon luncheon for U.S. House of Representatives leaders to help pave the way for a New Reconstruction Bill. She was working hard with the leadership on both sides of the aisle to cut out as much of the pork barrel spending as possible.

"How is the shrimp and grits, Madam President?" Chef Jadyn asked. "It's my grandmother's secret recipe from South Carolina. She got it from her ancestors who worked on the rice plantations."

"Come on, what is the real secret?" she asked with a smile.

"Well, you're my best customer. You have to cook grits low and slow with just a pinch of salt, pepper, and sugar. The shrimp is sauteed with my own Cajun blend," he replied with pride in his family's recipe and heritage.

"Thank you. I wish I had time to slow down and try to make this myself. Sometimes I don't feel like I can even sit down to enjoy a good cup of coffee. I looked at the menu for the month, and everything looks good. But tomorrow I would like a good cheesesteak sandwich and beer for dinner."

"I'll see what I can do. Do you want a regular steak sandwich or a Philly cheesesteak sandwich?"

As Chief of Staff Haskell entered the kitchen, President Gallo stood, eating the last shrimp and wiping her mouth with a napkin.

"Thank you, Chef, and Philly cheesesteak with provolone, onions, and peppers."

"Considered it done. And what kind of beer?" replied the Chef, picking up the half-eaten plate of food.

He shook his head and wished the president would just sit and have a relaxed breakfast. At least she ate something this morning. She would often just drink a cup coffee and grab something off the pastry tray.

"You pick one out for me, Chef."

She turned to Haskell as she walked back to the Oval Office.

"What's on the agenda today?"

He replied, "Before the House Leadership Luncheon, the Republican minority leader and the Democratic majority leader want to meet with you. I think they are going to ask you to align yourself to a party before the midterm elections and endorse their own batch of candidates."

"Okay, anything else?" asked President Gallo.

"You'll leave for your upcoming tour of the New Reconstruction sites in Colorado, Wyoming, Utah, Arizona, Texas, and California in a week. But you need to have a phone call with each of the governors before that. After California I scheduled a few days off in upstate New York before your visit to New York City and northern New Jersey."

"I can't take too many days off."

Her Chief of Staff frowned. "Look, Madame President. Lana, you have to rest and recharge. There's so much to do, and you can't wear yourself out. You need to be fully rested to rebuild the country and get ready for another alien encounter."

***

Ambrose sat in a rocking chair on the porch, his HK 416 with an aim point and a PEQ 15 laser target pointer leaned against the wall next to him covered by a towel. He had told his team to rendezvous at the farm by noon. He felt nervous and excited at the same time; this was going to be the moment when patriots took back the country. He rocked the chair back, gazed heavenward, and repeated part of Nehemiah's prayer out loud.

"O Lord God of heaven, the great and terrible God, that keepeth covenant and mercy for them, that love him and observe his commandments: Let thine ear now be attentive, and thine eyes open, that thou mayest hear the prayer of thy servant."

His squad had dispersed since the last run-in with the FBI. He thanked God that Agent Jeremiah had worn his disguise to prevent identification by surveillance drones. But now, with Operation Hidden Redemption getting the green light, his crew just needed to keep their heads down and stay at this upstate New York farmhouse in New Paltz until the mission. The farm belonged to a church in New York City that used it as a weekend Bible study retreat. All the members of his squad worked for the federal government and were given orders to join a special investigative multiagency task force. The orders came from the Office of the Vice President through one of Directors of the FBI, Gretchen Braun, and Homeland Security. The orders filtered down to the different agencies where his squad members normally worked. His multiagency task force was created to investigate organized crime, counterfeiting, and the continuing supply chain issues plaguing the world even after the New York Peace Accords. Now his squad would coordinate with Assistant Director Braun exclusively and would not contact anyone else until the operation was completed. Their true mission was to assassinate the illegitimate president who was an unelected usurper.

He heard the rumble of the exhaust before he saw a green Ram 1500 TRX appear at the edge of the private driveway; the custom bed cap was wrapped with a bald eagle carrying an American flag. Ambrose reached for his HK 416 even as he recognized Gideon's massive truck. He and Jeremiah Sullivan were army veterans, and both worked in the Secret Service. As Ambrose watched the truck roll toward the farmhouse along the long driveway, he received a text message from ATF agent Hiram Martin: "I've landed but I need a ride to the farm."

Ambrose texted him back: "Okay, sending Gideon."

He sent another text quickly to Dinah Smith, a DEA agent: "Where are you?"

She texted back immediately: "Ran into traffic on the thruway. Be there in half an hour at most."

"Good, keep me posted," Ambrose replied, then put his phone in the back pocket of his Wrangler jeans and walked off the porch. He waved at Gideon to drive up to him.

When Gideon rolled his window down, Ambrose said, "Hiram's stuck at the airport in Newburg. Go pick him up."

Gideon frowned. "Yes, brother." He began programing his GPS.

"You want company?" asked Jeremiah.

Gideon finished programming the GPS. "Naw, I got this. Take the gear out of the bed."

Ambrose and Jeremiah opened the truck bed and took out five large pelican cases.

"Is this all the gear we need?" asked Jeremiah.

Ambrose looked at the pelican cases and began opening the long rifle cases. "No, we still need a few more things, but we are going to liberate them from some local private sources. I'll text you a list of groceries, and you guys can hit the supermarket on the way back."

Gideon stuck his head out of the window and asked, "Sure, text me. You done?"

Ambrose slapped the side of the truck. "You're good to go."

As the trucked drove away, Ambrose opened the two rifle cases and smiled.

"I'll handload the .408 Chey Tac rounds myself. For the M200, we need to buy some match grade ammo for the SCAR 20s."

Ambrose picked up the Cheytac M200 intervention and looked through the Leupold Mark 8 CQBSS, smiled, and put it back in the case. He opened another case and picked up the SCAR with the Nightforce ATACR scope with a MIL-XT reticle. He was glad that both had Mil Dot Christmas tree style reticles. The two snipers could spot for each other without the need for a spotting scope. They could also shoot at the same target to ensure a hit; one would aim high while the other aimed low to bracket the target.

"Check the other boxes, and let's see what we else we need to get for the mission."

Jeremiah nodded and began opening the three other large Pelican Cases.

"These have all the night vision equipment, comms, and other electronic gear."

Ambrose opened the fourth case.

"This has one of those new drones that the boys down in Area 51 developed with the aliens."

Jeremiah opened the last case. It was filled with new camo uniforms that were invisible to night vision, and there was one bulky suite that was even invisible to thermal imaging devices as well as night vision.

"Where do you want this stuff?"

Ambrose closed the rifle cases.

"Store these in the dining room. It's on your left as you enter. I'll be right with you."

The church retreat was a large, ten-bedroom farmhouse with a huge kitchen and dining hall. They would have the facility to themselves until the mission was over. He didn't like reporting to so many people; it was not good operational security. But the Bishop, Director Braun, and the vice president's aide, Henry, were trusted believers. He reread the text message before hitting send: "All set to start. This will be the last group text. I'll text you individually if I need anything. I need to know the president's schedule as soon as possible."

Bishop Jones smiled and typed back: "God is on our side. The diversion will be planned out as soon as we have a date."

Director Braun nodded at the phone.

"Good. I'll send info as soon as possible," she sent back.

Henry replied: "Good luck and let me know if you need anything."

***

Thirty-Eight was standing at the sensor array and couldn't hide his excitement as he started emitting a trilling noise, almost like a cat purring but louder. "Clutch Leader, we have sensor confirmation of the Thrultak. The criminal's information was buried in the old database of known fugitives. A fairly large ship is near the planet where we detected signs of technology but no sign of their colony ship."

"Don't get over excited, Thirty-Eight. We have time to stalk the prey," Gurjin said, realizing he'd have plenty of time to study the old database before he encountered these unknown aliens. "Eighteen, prepare to start transmitting the Qhasloi demands once we are past the last planetoid of this system."

Eighteen looked nervous and didn't obey his commands right away. Eighty-Five, a big ancient security officer. turned toward Eighteen and grabbed the youngling's shoulder.

"Didn't you hear the Captain?"

The youngling cringed with fear.

"That's fine, Security Officer Eighty-Five. Eighteen is new," Gurjin said.

He hated the Qhasloi for forcing these younglings away from the nest before maturity. This one didn't look like he had molted more than ten times. Normally, younglings stayed close to their mothers for at least fifteen moltings before going anywhere alone. A long time ago he'd dared to suggest that younglings stay with the nest till they had a chance to molt at least twenty times before entering into Qhasloi service. He was ignored and treated to days of electric shocks. The Qhasloi never listened to the slave races.

Eighty-Five looked around, nodded, and patted the youngling on the shoulder. Every Ghakeols knew what it was like to be taken at such a young age.

Eighteen replied, while moving his hands as fast as he could, "Yes, Captain, and I'll do better next time."

Eighteen couldn't hide his fear and nervousness because he was trilling involuntarily fast in between his words.

***

The Bishop lay in bed getting massaged by both Maggie and Lilith. He was naked, and they were just wearing t-shirts. He smiled to himself; General Hermann was a drunken fool, but he would be useful to the movement one more time. Bishop Jones would use these men again in Operation Hidden Redemption. He knew that a small group would not be enough to take on the protective detail. When the operation kicked off, he would have General Hermann and General Williams ready to conduct diversionary operations with seventy hardcore militiamen and a few of his regular followers. *With the Lord's help, Operation Hidden Redemption will succeed*, he thought. *I will rebuild this country and the world.* He turned over to his back and reached up to feel Maggie's breasts and allowed Lilith to rub him all over.

Bishop Jones began thinking about the next sermon. He remembered God's message in Zechariah 13. He turned on the digital recorder while Maggie lay next to him as Lilith worked on his legs.

Jones spoke into the recorder: "Brothers and sisters, I want you to remember God has graciously provided a fountain for sinners to be cleansed so that they may become His holy people. Never doubt that God is watching, and he is angry. We've broken his covenant and sinned with alien unbelievers. We've defiled this sacred land. We've turned away from him and sold our souls for shiny alien technology and their empty promises. But God's fountain is here and is open to all believers who turn to him and cleanse their souls."

Maggie kissed his neck, and Lilith kissed the inside of his left thigh. Bishop Jones stopped recording and smiled at his faithful girls as they pulled their shirts off.

I'll finish this later, he told himself.

In his lust-filled vision he didn't notice Maggie's obvious discomfort and anger.

***

Julie walked as fast as she could toward the outdoor café. She was running late and found Tati already sitting in the outdoor seating area of the fancy coffee shop. The Russian Captain was dressed in jeans and a pink blouse. Julie glanced at her dad's old Omega Seamaster and smiled. He would often look at his watch and tell her they were running late for church or an appointment. Julie waved as soon as Tati saw her coming.

"Good morning, Julie," Tati said as she kissed Julie on both cheeks.

Julie was wearing a black dress shirt and grey slacks.

"So what is so important that you couldn't wait to tell me?"

"Did you get a chance to look at your emails?"

"No, why?" asked Julie, a little worried.

"Look at them now." Tati smiled and waved for a waiter to come.

Julie opened her phone and found several unread emails. She

found one from 1Hancear.com. She opened it and looked at Tati. The waiter was there before she could speak but some of the names on the list struck her immediately: Danny Lee, Sandra Cunningham, Tatyana Egorova, Jurgen Moller von Heytzenstein, David Ohayon, Fetu Tupuola, Damian Hill, Asher Tang, Mark Giambalvo, and Oliver Gardner.

"May I take your order?" asked a tall waiter.

Julie looked up at the man and smiled at him, "An Americano with cream and sugar and a Madeline."

Tati sat closer to Julie. "Well, did you get the email?"

"Yes, I got it. We're going to be in the same unit, and I know some of the other people as well."

"I'm glad we'll work together." Tati grinned and took a sip of her cappuccino. "I hope they have a plan."

***

Gretchen smiled as she sent the group email to Bishop Jones, Secretary Shane, and Henry Perez, the vice president's aide. She had been friends with the vice president prior to the war. After the Peace Accords were signed, she turned to him for advice. He had brought her into the fold; she had doubts but she had to do something, didn't she? Operation Hidden Redemption would use several diversionary operations to mask the real attack that would be conducted by Ambrose's group. This would be the last time they would communicate as a group until the operation commenced. She would maintain communications with Ambrose and provide him with support. She had managed to get the president's schedule from Haskell. She prepared a secure text message for the group and sent the schedule. She also made sure that her hacker was aware of the situation but not the details of the proposed mission. The president or "Ace" as she was fondly called by her security detail, a recycling of her call sign as one of a handful of Apache pilots who had shot down a MIG-25, would be going to her family cottage near the Shawangunks after her tour of the West Coast. Gallo was scheduled to arrive at the cottage on October 25 and would stay till November 1.

***

Hermann looked at his unshaven face in the bathroom mirror.

He could see the naked blonde woman on his bed still sleeping since he had paid for her to stay overnight. He was hungover but felt renewed energy after being with a woman. Bishop Jones had finally sent him a message. It was time to fight against the government again. He was ordered to prepare for an operation against the Picatinny Arsenal as other patriots prepared attacks against Thrultak controlled sites. He would have at least one hundred veterans for this mission. He broke the phone and planned to burn and dump it later. He smiled and walked toward the naked blonde. On the way he took another swig of Stolichnaya Vodka before he grabbed the blond woman's hair and began to kiss her.

***

"General" Chester Williams was tired. He wanted to stop running and get revenge against those alien lovers. He was hidden in a safe house in Florida. The Bishop had helped him avoid arrest after the defeat at the University of Maryland. Now he found himself staring at a new message on his secure phone: "Operation Hidden Redemption is a go." He didn't know the details but he knew the mission was vital to the movement. He was going to receive weapons from South America and help patriots attack the illegitimate president. He knew several smugglers were going to bring in plastic explosives, Russian MANPADS, detonators, and fuses from Columbia. He would help get these weapons into the right hands all across the country. Patriots would stage simultaneous attacks on the federal government as his group attacked the presidential motorcade just outside of New Paltz.

He knelt and prayed for the soul of his son who had committed suicide after returning from the Middle East. His son served with distinction as an army sniper. But the VA failed him; they didn't treat his son's PTSD. He prayed for his wife who passed soon after their son's death after a long battle with stomach cancer. Her illness had not been fully covered by medical insurance. He sold the farm to pay for her treatments; now he was alone and broke. He prayed for their souls, and he prayed for strength to take down the crooked system.

CHAPTER 9

"Brothers and sisters," came a voice from the internet radio. "The Lord told us in 1 Timothy: 'Understanding this, that the law is not laid down for the just but for the lawless and disobedient, for the ungodly and sinners, for the unholy and profane, for those who strike their fathers and mothers, for murderers, the sexually immoral, men who practice homosexuality, enslavers, liars, perjurers, and whatever else is contrary to sound doctrine.' We must include aliens who do not follow the Word of the Lord. We must include those who would benefit from these ungodly beings exploiting us. Prepare for the day when we will rise up and strike down the unbelievers destroying our land."

"That's enough," Agent Hatem said to Agent Hill and Metzul. "This is interesting, but can you trace where it came from?"

"Not yet," replied Metzul. "The web broadcast is being routed through many servers, and we're having difficulty locating the source. We'll find them when they make a mistake. Then they will receive the many deserts they qualified for."

"So what else do you have for me?" Agent Hatem asked.

She didn't want to correct the alien who was turning magenta with green spots. She looked at her translator, which indicated the alien was anxious.

Both techs looked excited.

Metzul said, "Go ahead, my human companion."

"Right. We used Thrultak technology and reconstructed the tattoos of the gunman firing the anti-drone weapon. He was only wearing a thin, long-sleeved tactical shirt, and we used the thermal imaging capability of the drone to reconstruct the tattoos along his arm.”

Metzul kept two eyes on each of the humans and looked for any signs of approval. He found the human's inability to change colors difficult.

“Yes, the drone's visual sensors were able to detect thermal anomalies all along his arm.”

Agent Hatem didn't want to belittle their accomplishment. She waited for the techies to finish their explanation, then smiled at the eager faces and eyestalks waving at her.

“Do we have a useful image to work with?”

“Yes,” Agent Hill replied.

A few seconds later Metzul's translator chimed in. “Yes, we have four possible variants of the image. These should be close approximations.”

Agent Hill was holding a few of the hi-res printouts.

“Here are the most interesting ones. This is definitely a Ranger tab and jump wings.”

He handed Agent Hatem the first printout, then said, “Now this one is pretty unique. It's a rat holding a knife and a severed head.”

“Email me the files, and I'll get this out to our field agents around different bases across the country. We'll make sure to pay special attention to all the tattoo parlors near Fort Benning.”

The need for secrecy prevented her from telling any of the other field offices what they were doing and why.

Agent Hill handed her the other printout while Metzul emailed the files to her phone.

Agent Hill added, “I think we could ask tattoo artists in some of the largest conventions and see if they recognize the style.”

“Great idea. Any progress on how they may have gotten the anti-drone weapon?” Agent Hatem asked.

Metzul replied, “I'm going to examine three more laptops and phones from the FCG today. Afterwards, I'll compile the data and will have an analysis soon. But I have to weigh each variable to draw any meaningful conclusion. Don't worry, we'll find the breach. These bad doers cannot play hide and investigate with us forever.”

Agent Hatem smiled and told herself, *I think he means hide and seek.*

"Good work."

Agent Hatem hoped they found out what was going on before it was too late. These extremists were up to something but what? She really should tell someone about Metzul's translator. But she didn't have the heart to saying anything to those puppy dog eyes looking at her. He seemed so eager.

***

"Looks like the repair of the Arecibo radio telescope is complete," Klopzar said, turning red with approval while stroking his pet ferret who he kept in a pouch in his satchel.

Helzul extended his two green fronds from his back and faced the tropical sun to maximize his symbiote's photosynthesis. The Thrultak were capable of a chemical process called kleptoplasty, in which they retained the chloroplasts from the algae and green vegetables they ate. Some of the algae lived in the fronds resupplying the Thrultak with chloroplasts, which also gave them a very robust immune system and evolutionally lessened the need to compete for food resources. These factors, in turn, enabled the development of a cooperative society.

"Yes, the dish has been repaired and will be stronger than ever. We'll begin testing the communications gear later today. Is there any news from Metzul?"

"No, not yet. But Hancear is keeping track of his progress. I wish I could join you, my friend, and bask in the sun for a while."

"You should come to this island. The sun is nice, and the lush vegetation is beautiful. How are the plans for the Earth Defense Force progressing?"

"Hancear has been talking with Dr. Kowalczyk and Dr. Montfaucon about the possibility of capturing the Qhasloi. So we have divided the candidates into three groups. The first group will be the largest, out of which we will create the core of First EDF Combined Arms Brigade. They'll become the main joint planetary surface fighting force. The second group will train in teams with Thrultak pilots, prepare to intercept the enemy ship in space, and engage them in direct battle with drones. The FCG will assist us in developing some new weapons for space combat. The third and smallest group of fifty humans and five Thrultak will be trained to capture the enemy ship if the opportunity presents itself."

Helzul moved a little to make sure his green fronds were getting the optimal exposure to the sun.

"I know Jan and Claude. They are very intelligent and have been helpful. I don't know of any way to approach a spacecraft without getting detected. Have they found a way?"

"No, every permutation that Hancear has simulated has failed because they can't get close to the ship in any of our current vessels without detection. The third group may never be needed. There is no way to hide any kind of propulsion system's energy signature."

"Perhaps we can run a contest open to all humans and Thrultak. We can offer a prize if someone can come up with a way to reach a spacecraft without getting detected. We can offer Earth currency and some access to our technology, though our people would be happy just for the opportunity to help."

"I'll talk it over with the Council members, my friend. This proposal may not bear fruit, and we should plan on integrating the third group into the first brigade."

***

Hancear didn't know why it had never considered the option of capturing the Qhasloi warship in the first place. *I must do a diagnostic and set aside time to ponder why I hadn't considered this*, he thought. Hancear was asked to monitor the conversations between Klopzar, Makro, and Sharon Ross, the new human commander for the EDF. Hancear refocused a larger portion of its available memory and consciousness to the video conference call.

"I just don't know how they would get close to the enemy ship but if they could reach it, just like Dr. Kowalczyk and Dr. Montfaucon suggested, a small group could capture the Qhasloi ship," Makro said while turning light blue with darker blue dots.

On General Ross's screen were English subtitles: "Light blue is indicative of happiness, and the darker blue spots indicate interest."

The General was pleased with Noah Green's work. He had

continued to improve the human version of a portable translator but had also written a program that used cameras to decode the meaning of the various Thrultak colors. This allowed humans to get a better sense of what the aliens were saying because the translator did not convey emotions or nuanced meanings that were associated with their metachrosis. At the same time General Ross knew that Hancear had devised a system of looking at human body language and physiology to help the Thrultak understand human vocal communication better.

"Where did they get this idea?"

"Jan said he got the idea from some children watching pirate movies."

"Yes, I've analyzed all the available pirate movies. I've also conducted research on all historical incidents of piracy and privateer activity. I am studying and monitoring all the current International Maritime Bureau documents and studies on recent criminal activity," Hancear said.

"What conclusions have you drawn?" General Ross asked.

"I'll send a detailed report to all of you, but these are the key elements for a successful pirate or privateer action that would apply to our case. First, we have to find and identify their target. Second, we have to trick the target to get close without fighting. We should not have to show our colors until the last moment or not at all if possible. Third, when real pirates board, most merchants would not fight because these merchants do not have sufficient crew for a fight. In our case the Qhasloi are in a warship with a substantial crew and warriors."

General Ross sat back in her chair. "Are these all examples from the age of sail?"

Hancear answered quickly, "No, and I've noted that warships were often captured during your age of sail but piracy continues to this day. Warships are not regular victims of pirates but even warships were captured during modern times as an aftermath of fierce fighting. For example, the German U-boat 505 during your Second World War was captured on June 4, 1944, by United States Navy Task Group 22.3. Historically, only one United States Ship was captured after fierce fighting. The USS Pueblo, a Navy intelligence ship, was attacked and captured by

North Korean forces on January 23, 1968."

"I don't see how we're going to get close to the enemy ship. Even if they do get onboard, they'll have a substantial number of warriors," Makro said, turning white.

Sharon read the subtitles: "The subject is very angry."

Klopzar was also white and spoke louder than usual. "Yes, we can't get close to the enemy ship to even try any kind of subterfuge. Anyway, General Ross, you and Makro will serve as the first two commanders of the EDF and will have access to Hancear. I wish you both good luck before I leave this conversation for another meeting with the United Nations Council."

General Ross smiled and said, "Thank you, Klopzar. Makro, can you stay on for a few minutes? I have a couple of questions."

After Klopzar left the video conference, Makro said, "I was thinking we should prepare a small group from our candidates to attempt a boarding action. Perhaps if our main attack group can cripple the Qhasloi, we can board and capture it."

"I was thinking the same thing. We're going to work well together."

General Ross noticed that Makro had turned light blue, indicating happiness. She opened Hancear's report and noticed that the details on the enemy ship were slightly vague.

"Hancear, can you clarify your data on the Qhasloi ship? The numbers don't make any sense."

"Long range sensors indicate that it's a standard light attack craft with four drone launchers, two close range projectile launchers, and two energy beam weapons. There will be around eighty to one hundred and thirty crew members and three hundred to six hundred warriors."

"That's what I mean. Why is there such a range in crew numbers?"

Hancear sounded surprised, "Oh, that's because we don't know which species we are dealing with yet. The Qhasloi slave races are physically different from one another, and some are much larger than others and have to adapt themselves to the Qhasloi designed ships. By the way, I agree with you both: We need to have three different groups in the EDF."

Makro leaned closer to his screen. "What do you mean?"

Hancear replied, "Besides the spaceborne force and the boarding party, we need an integrated ground force in case the Qhasloi break through and conduct a landing with massed drones. I have studied the candidates and have already marked those suitable for the three groups."

General Ross added, "Yes, I think that would be wise. Can you forward the names of the candidates in the various branches?"

Hancear said in a softer than usual voice, "I have included suggestions for uniforms, rank structures, and distinctive names."

"That's wonderful work, Hancear. I wasn't even thinking about that," replied Makro.

General Ross felt nervous but knew she had been outmaneuvered by the AI. She realized a need for new distinctive names for the EDF, but letting the AI name them might be a mistake.

"Ok, tell me."

As soon as she said the words a large file appeared in her inbox.

"The EDF should be called a Legion, and the three groups will be called the Space Legion, the Planetary Legion, and the Privateers," Hancear said after a brief pause. "I suggest using a combined British and American rank structure with modified badges and insignias."

General Ross opened the new file and saw a whole array of work uniforms, combat uniforms, service uniforms, and dress uniforms. The service and dress uniforms were navy blue with red and silver accents. The dress uniforms had a matching cape with red, silver, or gold lining depending on the branch.

"Wow, you gave this a lot of thought, didn't you?"

She didn't complain because this issue was not worth fighting over.

"Yes, I did give it my full attention for six minutes. The dress uniforms are based on the Italian Carabinieri uniforms. I designed all the insignias and uniforms for the ground and space forces."

The names of the ranks were familiar to General Ross. The noncommissioned officers had diagonal straight bars descending from right to left. They looked similar to the IDF and South Korean military NCO's insignias. The officer ranks looked a little like the British military, but instead of stars the EDF had silver planets, instead of a crown it had a sunburst, and instead of the British crossed baton and saber, the EDF had crossed missiles.

"I think Klopzar forgot to tell you the news. It's not official yet, but you and Makro will both be given the rank of Lieutenant General of the EDF," added Hancear.

"Thank you, Hancear," Klopzar said. "I was going to tell you once it was approved by the newly formed UN Special Council on Interplanetary Affairs."

The new body was created so no single member could veto the efforts of the other members, unlike the Security Council. The Special Council could act with a simple majority or a two-thirds majority depending on the question at hand.

"That's okay. I thought that something like this would happen. I guess I'll have to order some new uniforms. What will the Thrultak wear?" General Ross asked while she copied the materials and forwarded them to the White House.

"They will wear a simple sash and harnesses, but their spacesuits and combat armor will match the new human uniforms," answered Hancear.

***

Danny stood in the middle of a small room, his hair cut super short. The room was more like a closet. He turned around once to make eye contact with everyone.

"I know we all got the list of names and some of us know one another already but let's go around the room and introduce ourselves. Name, career experience, military rank if applicable, and a fun fact about yourself. I'll start. My name is Danny Lee, I used to be a cop before the Thrultak arrived. Now I'm a second lieutenant in the U.S. Army. I love animals and have a degree in modern English literature from Princeton."

Danny pointed at Sandra because he wanted to start with

someone he knew. She had cut her long light brown hair to shoulder length and was wearing grey sweats.

Sandra stood and smiled at Danny and Julie, then did a cute wave at Mark.

"I'm Sergeant Cunningham, U.S. Army. I went to the police academy before all this, and I have a degree in accounting. I love to sail and surf at the Jersey Shore."

Danny nodded and added, "She's modest, but she's a great shot with the Carl Gustaf."

He then looked at Tati to start.

"My name is Tatyana Egrova. I'm what you call a Captain in the GRU of the Russian Army. I have an electrical engineering degree from Saint Petersburg University. I like to read and go for long walks."

Before Danny could add anything, Julie almost laughed out loud; it was like a dating profile.

"Hi, I'm First Lieutenant Lopez, and I also used to be a police officer. I have a degree in European History and love to cook."

Danny pointed to Mark.

As he stood, he waved to Julie and Sandra. He was unrecognizable. He had lost almost a hundred pounds and looked like a gymnast. Since joining the army, he exercised as often as he could and changed to a high protein gluten-free diet.

"Hello. My name is Mark Giambalvo. I'm a corporal in the U.S. Army, but I was in the Coast Guard before. I have a degree in computer science from Rutgers University, and prior to all this I worked as a consultant maintaining large servers. I like to build radio-controlled planes, cars, and boats for fun."

Danny said, "Thanks, Mark. As you may have noticed, some of us served together in combat prior to the peace treaty. I want to make sure everyone knows that all are welcome into this crew. We need to work together."

Jurgen was a huge, older man with a thick German accent. He stood six foot five and hadn't smiled once since he was put into the group.

"My name is Jurgen Moller von Heytzenstein. I'm an Oberstabsfeldwebel Kommando Spezialkräfte and trained as a combat medic. I like to listen to opera music and go underwater diving for fun.”

Danny asked quickly before the next person could start, “Can you explain what the Kommando is?”

Jurgen frowned, “Yes, it is also called the KSK. We are like your Rangers or SEALS, and we can fight as soldiers or conduct anti-terrorism missions.”

David was medium height with close cropped, curly black hair and didn’t wait for Danny. He stood at attention and said, “My name is David Ohayon. I’m a retired Captain in the IDF, I flew F35’s, and now I’m an aerospace engineer. I was also trained as an infantryman in the IDF. I fly helicopters and build my own drones as a hobby.”

Danny nodded to the next man, who had visible tattoos all over his arms and neck.

“My name is Fetu Tupuola. I’m a sergeant in the 1st New Zealand Special Air Service Regiment. I joined the military straight out of high school. I’m an Olympic shooter and jungle survival instructor. I like surfing, open ocean sailing, and canoeing.”

“My name is Damian Hughes. I was a Lieutenant Commander in the U.S. Coast Guard and have experience in the MSRT and search and rescue. I left the service a couple of years ago to work on my Ph.D. on the History of Naval Warfare at the University of Miami.”

“Thank you, commander,” said Danny as he pointed to the last human.

Asher was very tan in contrast to the very pale, red-headed lieutenant commander.

“So far I think you are the most senior officer in the group.”

He gave Damian Hughes a salute, then continued.

“My name is Asher Tang. I’m part of the Singaporean Naval Special Operations group. I’m a warrant officer and joined the Navy after completing my degree in Biomechanical Engineering at the Nanyang Technological University. I’m a foodie, and I like to go scuba diving, as both a job and for fun.”

Damian raised his hand. “If I may, I think as part of this new EDF we should forget our previous ranks and just use our first names until we are told differently.”

Everyone nodded.

"Last but not least is Odortor, the Thrultak member of our crew," Danny said.

Odortor stood on his hind legs and turned green with a few light blue dots. The colors indicated that he was feeling shy. A soothing male voice came from the translators: "My name is Odortor; I was a farmer before the escape on the Homeship. I'm now a trained soldier and computer systems technician. I can operate all the different Thrultak vehicles both in atmosphere and in space. For fun I like to grow my own food in a hydroponics garden."

Just as Odortor finished, Hancear's voice came over the new wireless intercom in their squad room. If Danny wasn't mistaken, Hancear had developed an Irish brogue since he'd initially spoken to the alien AI.

The voice said, "Every crew will fail or succeed as a single unit. If a single individual fails, the crew will be disqualified. You will receive the last member of your crew this morning. Get settled and rest for now. Your last teammate has arrived and is available at the sidewalk-level entrance at 103 East 66th Street, just east of Park Avenue. Please go there to greet your teammate and let her out of the cage."

Danny said, "Let's go."

As they walked out, Julie waited to be the last and kissed Danny and hugged him.

"I'm glad you're here. But let's keep it on the down-low. What is this about a cage?"

Danny hugged her back and smiled, "Down-low? I think everyone knows about us already."

They hurried out to the hall and caught up to the rest of the group who were all gathered around a large crate. Inside the crate was a black and tan dog. A tall, older woman with white hair stood protectively next to the crate.

"Hi, I'm Mary. I'm here to drop off Coco. She's a Belgian Malinois. I was told to hand her over to a Mr. Daniel Lee."

Danny moved closer and noticed the dog was alert and looking at all of them from inside the cage with a guarded expression.

"Yes, I'm Danny."

"Good, I was told that you have some experience handling dogs," Mary said as she handed him a binder. "My husband and I usually train Belgian Malinois for the police and as private protection dogs. But we got a few great Belgian Malinois puppies, and Coco had the best temperament to become a protective working dog. She has a stable temperament and is very confident. She is watchful and naturally protective but also very friendly. She's still a puppy, only a year old, and she will grow more."

Mary bent down, opened the kennel, and had Coco come out and sit. "I have some extra food and toys for her."

Mary turned to Coco and said, "This is your new pack, your family now. Be a good girl."

Mary stood and gave Danny the leash.

"Here you go. You must continue to reinforce her training and give her daily exercise."

Sandy knelt down, gave Coco a hug, and petted her. "She's so cute."

The entire group moved back to their small squad room. Mark and Jurgen carried Coco's kennel and bag of gear.

***

After their group settled into the cramped quarters, they eased into a training routine with Hancear's and FCG's help. They often did everything as a group including their PT.

Julie broke into a slow jog with Danny and Coco on the Armory track. Coco was very happy to run in the morning off leash.

"Where are all the other teams?" Julie asked.

"I don't know." Danny looked around the empty complex.

"I don't understand this training," Julie said. "All we do is train in close quarters combat, learn to fly the Thrultak craft in case Odortor goes down, and pilot squadrons of drones."

"Yeah, I'm getting sick of all the medical classes, learning about the signs of space adaptation syndrome, and trying to patch people up in Zero-G," Danny added as he looked at his watch and remembered how difficult it was to even begin the process of intubation and starting an IV with a pump in micro gravity.

"At least Coco doesn't seem to mind the Zero-G, and she's learned to orient and propel herself in the simulator. But I hate that we have to do it so often."

Julie rubbed the bruise on her shoulder from the last time they had Zero-G fire suppression training on board a Thrultak craft. Julie learned that there were only a few ways to fight a fire in Zero-G. First, starve the fire of oxygen and turn off all the equipment to prevent its spread. Or depressurize the ship. Julie had hurt her shoulder when she unbuckled from her seat to get the Thrultak fire containment acoustic device and hit the bulkhead hard. The sound emitter was designed to contain a Zero-G fire from erratically spreading in an uncontrolled manner.

Danny said, "Do you know what I hate the most?"

He didn't wait for Julie to speak up. "I hate it when we're practicing close quarters battle drills in Zero-G, and they just turn the gravity back on. The last time, when we breached the hatch, Damian and Fetu both fell on top of me because they were above me in Zero-G. The breacher drone lost its orientation as well and looked like a dead bug."

"This is just silly. I reached out to a couple of Rangers I know who have been assigned to the 1st EDF Regiment, and they are forming a combined arms force with handpicked Thrultak warriors. This regiment will have its own organic manned and unmanned air support, artillery, both armored, mechanized forces, and support elements. He thinks that with the drones and automated weapons systems their regiment has the equivalent firepower of at least three pre-Thrultak contact full size divisions with air support." Julie tried not to sound disappointed.

Asher had caught up to them and added, "Sorry to intrude. I don't understand our training either. Jurgen, Fetu, and I are tired of learning how to use the oxy fuel flame cutters, plasma cutters, and laser cutters. Last time we had to used them wearing bulky spacesuits. It was so difficult cutting through a foot of steel."

"Are we training to be part of a rescue crew just in case the main space-borne element takes casualties?" Danny wondered aloud.

"I don't know," Asher replied. "Sometimes they have us cutting into bulkheads made of unknown materials. You'd think they would know what the Thrultak ships are made of. I hope they know what they're doing."

The group slowed to a walk and began their cooldown before beginning their Cross Fit style functional training. In the middle of the track were weighted dummies to carry, large forty-pound balls to move, and odd-shaped concrete blocks to move as a single unit.

"I've been training with Sandra and Tati on new ways to conduct hand-to-hand combat in Zero-G," added Julie as she tried to stretch her legs while waiting for the entire group to gather in a circle to begin their functional training. Meanwhile, Coco ran around doing her best to imitate her humans. She got into her own downward doggy pose, mimicking the crew trying to cool down from their 10-k run.

***

Captain Amy Schmidt looked around the cramped quarters of the European Space Agency training center in Cologne, Germany. After passing the written and physical tests, she had been sent here to begin her training to become part of the new EDF. She was apprehensive when she found herself alone in the dorm room but was quickly put at ease when a familiar face came through the door an hour later.

"Well, I'll be a dead pig in sunshine," said First Sergeant Jamol Smith as he snapped off a sharp salute.

"What are you doing here?" Amy asked.

"Same as you, LT. I mean, Captain. To kick ass and take names."

"Oorah! Gunny can't wait to see what they have in store for us."

"I hope they don't give us a bunch of squids and chair force heroes or all these high-speed ranger types," Sergeant Smith said, smiling and looking over the room. "This room is barely big enough for three people."

"Well, at least I know I can count on you. Let's wait and see, Sarge."

"Yes, Captain. Nothing like hurrying up and waiting for paper pushers to get things rolling. Let's go for a quick run. I'm all knotted up from the flight in."

CHAPTER 10

Bishop Jones could hardly contain himself as he reread the last email from Assistant Director Braun. His dream was about to become reality. He would be able to come out of hiding after the new president pardoned him. The deaths of the many would be justified by the glorious end and the beginning of a true Christian country. After rereading Deuteronomy 13, he prepared another sermon and turned on the digital recorder: "If your very own brother, or your son or daughter, or the wife you love, or your closest friend secretly entices you, saying, 'Let us go and worship other gods' (gods that neither you nor your ancestors have known, gods of the peoples around you, whether near or far, from one end of the land to the other), do not yield to them or listen to them. Show them no pity. Do not spare them or shield them. You must certainly put them to death. Your hand must be the first in putting them to death, and then the hands of all the people. Stone them to death, because they tried to turn you away from the Lord your God, who brought you out of Egypt, out of the land of slavery. Then all Israel will hear and be afraid, and no one among you will do such an evil thing again. The Lord wants us, the true patriots and believers, to kill all the alien sinners and those traitorous evil humans who support them. The day of cleansing is coming, brothers and sisters. Gird yourselves in the armor of God and make ready."

After replaying it a couple of times, Bishop Jones smiled, plugged the recorder into the USB drive, and sent the file to Maggie's secure email. He opened another window on his laptop and began looking for new outfits for her and Lilith to wear when they came to his bed.

***

Metzul and Agent Hill were in the main workspace of the FCG. They had just finished examining all the computer desktops. Metzul stretched all his legs and made sure to wriggle his eyestalks. They had been focused and in one position too long looking for any anomalies on the primitive laptops, and he could feel his body tensing up.

Agent Hill walked over to the Nespresso machine.

"Hey, do you want one?" he asked Metzul.

All four of Metzul's eyestalks focused their attention on the human. "Yes, my buddy, I would like a cappuccino. It will do us some good to take a coffee interval before we start on the rest of the laptops."

Agent Hill turned away and stifled a laugh. He was getting used to Metzul's translator's mistakes but sometimes they were funny.

"One regular cappuccino coming right up."

Metzul opened the first laptop, typed the provided password, used his tendrils to plug in a Thrultak interface, and began searching the laptop's history and emails. The Thrultak device traced all the incoming and outgoing emails, and the interface noted that there were some emails that were deleted using a secure deleting software.

"Lucas, I found something."

Agent Hill grabbed his drink and walked over with the cappuccino, placing the mug down next to Metzul. He'd grown accustomed to being close to the big guy. He leaned over to reach into his EDC bag, grabbed a small case, and took out a USB drive.

"I have a custom recovery program developed in Quantico. It'll work on most commercially available deleting software. Let's see what we can recover."

He plugged it in, and a small window opened on the screen. Hill used the mouse to hit yes to continue as the software scanned the hard drive, searching for the deleted sectors, and began reconstructing them.

"I like this software. May I get a copy?" Metzul asked as he produced a proboscis to sip the coffee.

Hancear worked with human and Thrultak scientists and quickly discovered that all human foods and drinks were safe for the Thrultaks to consume. Human scientists also received Thrultak rations and found them to be sweet and nutritious but not particularly appetizing. While the Thrultak preferred fresh real food, they didn't have access to much since all the growth chambers were dedicated to producing fast-growing edible plants high in protein and other nutrients for space rations. The Thrultak were eager to negotiate with small family farmers for access to fresh produce, and they were all obsessed with having small pets. Many liked small rodents and preferred the longer-lived chinchillas and the degus from Chile.

"Sure. Okay, here we go."

Hill opened the first recovered email from an FBI agent, John Able.

Metzul accessed Hancear and searched for the agent in the FBI database. The AI was able to search the entire database in a few seconds.

"That's strange. There is no record of an FBI agent named John Able."

"That's not good. I got most of the first email. Whose laptop is this?"

The human tech looked at the serial number and checked it against the list of names. "It's Agnes Nelson's."

"Well, what does the email say?" asked Metzul who was looking at his Thrultak pad.

"The email asked her to provide information on the FCG and their related projects."

"Well, it isn't smart of her to just give out secrets," said Metzul, turning purple.

The alien was sad that someone could betray the new alliance.

Agent Hill kept reading and pieced together the response. "Well, she refused to help him unless she had proof of his security clearance."

Just as he started reading another email, the door to the FCG office opened and Agnes Nelson walked in. Metzul regurgitated some coffee through his extended proboscis and stood up to his full height. He turned bright green in fear, and his eyestalks waved at Agnes in excitement.

She noticed the green alien and asked, "Are you okay? Is something wrong."

"Everything is chilly," Metzul's translator blurted out.

Agent Hill quickly closed the laptop and patted Metzul on the back.

"Buddy, are you alright? I think the coffee went down the wrong way."

He didn't know what else to say. He turned back to Agnes.

"I think my buddy means everything is cool. We've finished with the desktops. But we still have some new anti-virus software to install on all the laptops so we'll take them back to our office and finish up there. It's going to take a while to upload the files. Let's go, Metzul."

"You are correct, my human buddy. We must go back to the hideout and finish this work in our nest."

Metzul put down the coffee and gathered his equipment, put it in his bag, and slung the bag around his body.

Agnes Nelson was confused and a little suspicious.

"Okay, but you have to make sure the laptops are secure. And call me Agnes."

Agent Hill replied, "Don't worry, Agnes, we have the necessary security clearance."

He packed up his backpack, placed the laptops on a work cart they had brought, and hastily pushed the cart out of the room.

Agnes watched their backs as they left their office.

"When do you think you'll be done?"

The FBI tech turned back and said, "Not too long. By lunchtime. We'll bring it back to you."

Agnes bit her lip. Agent Able wanted her to get him the FCG's schedule and any information on the regular meeting with the president, as well as information on any new activity at the Armory.

"I need to do some work so I'll come up to your office by noon if you guys aren't done by then."

"We'll be done," Hill said as he waved at Agnes and moved faster to catch up to Metzul.

When the two of them were back in their office, the FBI tech sighed, slid into his chair, and placed Agnes's laptop on his desk.

"We were stealthy and did a good job," Metzul said as he stood next to Lucas.

"Yup, we're smooth operators," Hill said as he raised his hand for a high five.

Metzul's four eyes were on the human. "Huh, I get it."

Metzul produced a pod resembling a hand and gave Lucas a high five.

"I'll copy her entire hard drive, memory cache, and keystrokes."

"And I'll install a tracking software that will transmit her activities every couple of hours to my laptop."

***

"Agent Hatem, you have to get down here as soon as possible," Lucas almost yelled into the phone.

"What is it?" she asked, trying to focus on the reports that had come in from some of the field agents in North Carolina.

The reports were strewn across her hotel room desk, and so far the tattoos of the one suspect were a dead end. She gathered all the reports and shoved them into her backpack.

"I'll be there in about half an hour."

She got her blue jacket on, then checked her Glock 19 and her badge on her pistol belt. She checked herself in the mirror before she headed out in the late spring morning. *These knuckleheads better have something,* she thought. *I've got so many more reports to look at they better not be wasting my time.* She stopped at a small coffee shop, ordered a large coffee, black with three sugars, with a chocolate croissant, and walked to the Armory.

By the time she got to the tech support office, she only had half of her coffee left. The pair had their heads together looking at a screen when she walked into their room. Hill was so engrossed that he didn't hear her, but the alien had sensed her and turned one eyestalk toward her.

The alien quickly tapped Agent Hill on the shoulder, and the translator buzzed.

"Agent Hatem, we're glad you're here. We've found the

source of the leak and traced it."

Hill finally turned to look at Agent Hatem and noticed some crumbs on the side of her mouth.

"I'm sorry, but you have something on the corner of your mouth."

Agent Hatem blinked, not fully comprehending what the techie said. She quickly tried to brush away the crumbs with her free hand.

"Thanks. You were saying."

Hill looked around and activated a local RF jammer.

"Look, I don't know what's exactly going on. You have to fill us in so we can help you more effectively. Anyway, we found out an FBI agent has been in contact with Ms. Agnes Nelson. He asked her to provide information and access to the FCG. The agent's name is John Able. She verified his ID, provided him access to her computer, and gave him information on the various projects involving the Thrultak and humans."

"Sounds all right, I guess," replied Agent Hatem

"You would think so, but there is no agent named John Able in the FBI," added Metzul.

"What?" Hatem asked, a little confused.

Lucas pointed to the laptop.

"Agent John Able convinced Agnes with his credentials and official emails and letters from Assistant Director Gretchen Braun. The Assistant Director also called and emailed Agnes several times."

Metzul made a lot of noise, but his translator just said: "John Able is really Ambrose Hall."

Agent Hatem weighed her options and decided to fill these two in and get their full cooperation.

"Listen up. What I tell you can't leave this room."

Agent Hatem almost laughed, and both Hill and Metzul looked like eager kids waiting for a treat.

"We're investigating right-wing extremists who attacked the computer facilities at the University of Maryland. As part of the investigation, we've been tracking and arresting extremists. However, we haven't been able to take down Bishop Jones, General Hermann, and General Williams. These terrorists must be getting help from people inside the government. They've eluded us so far. I believe they've also been getting help from someone high up in the FBI and the Oval Office."

Agent Hill added more information. "Metzul found that other laptops were remotely accessed through Ms. Nelson's contacts list, including yours and Agent Russell's. We suggest you not send anymore emails through the regular networks. I'm not sure who is doing this but they are pretty good. I'm pretty sure Ms. Nelson doesn't know what's really going on. We'll need a search warrant if we are going to expand our search. We need to get to the bottom of this."

Agent Hatem smiled and said, "You'll have it before dinner. Thanks. You boys did a great job. Get all this back to the FCG, and I'll come back with a warrant."

***

Every crew member scurried away or prostrated themselves on all fours as Gurjin tried to hide his anger. His small crest under his reptilian throat moved involuntarily in quick pulses, and he emitted angry thrills as he strode to the engine bay licking both of his eyes.

"What's going on here?"

Three, the chief engineer, was standing with Two and Thirty-Eight, who all looked at him with fixed expressions.

Three replied, "Captain Gurjin, there's been a massive coolant leak from both of our main engines. We need to shut the two engines down to make repairs."

Gurjin stayed calm and asked, "Were there any casualties? How long do we have to drift?"

Three was an experienced, older Ghakeols and had many visible old burn scars.

"Five crew members suffered minor burns. This ship is not in great condition. The maintenance crew at the ship depot did not perform the proper maintenance on this vessel before this crew boarded her."

This was typical under the Qhasloi; corruption was widespread. Throughout the empire the black market thrived, and every slave race took what they could for themselves. The most powerful made billions of credits while the lowest slave sold small components for just a little extra food.

"The reports said that all repairs and maintenance were done according to specs before our departure."

"Follow me, Captain," Three said as he led the small group deeper into the engine bay and pointed to several pipes his crew had removed and placed on the floor. "Look at these coolant pipes. They are so corroded that they must have been installed when the ship was originally launched."

"But the ship records said that the entire system was refurbished prior to our assignment to it," Gurjin said.

He didn't want to believe that his would happen to a frontline combat ship. The entire Qhasloi empire was rife with corruption; it was part of daily life. Gurjin hated to admit it, but he himself had participated in it. He had traded spare parts for food and medicine for his friends and family. But he had never enriched himself at the expense of others or his command to this degree. He knew many higher-ups were rich beyond anyone's wildest dreams. Admirals sold spare parts and raw materials in bulk instead of maintaining the fleet's readiness.

"Three, go ahead and shut the engines down and get it repaired. Thirty-eight, I want you to go over the weapons inventory; check all our guided missiles and guidance systems. Thirty-eight, you'll go over the entire ship. Start with all our critical life support systems and test all the other major systems. Afterward, take inventory of all the spare parts. We all know why this happened. I want to find out how badly the previous crew pilfered the ship."

Gurjin blamed himself for not inspecting the ship more thoroughly, but the Qhasloi overlords had rushed it back into service, giving him no choice but to accept the official report from the previous Captain. He'd been too busy getting to know the crew and preparing for this mission to properly inspect the ship. This crew was hastily assembled from available Ghakeols and rushed into service. Apparently, the third fleet had suffered many losses taking the Thrultak homeward in the past, and the Qhasloi wanted to punish the remainder of the large, squishy worm people. It was only by chance this long forgotten race was tracked down to a remote sector of space by a remote sensor. Twenty warships were tasked to locating the ancient enemy of the Qhasloi, the Thrultak. Once found they would report their position through the hyper com drones. These drones were expensive but enabled the Qhasloi fleets to communicate with each other over vast distances.

"And Two, prepare a com drone. Send a report to the Qhasloi overlords that we've stopped because we needed to make repairs to the drive system."

Two asked, "Should I tell them we found the Thrultak?"

"No, they will want us to attack immediately, and we aren't ready for that yet. Once we are fully repaired, we can send that information. How far are we away from the last planetoid in this system?"

Two looked at his quartz crystal oscillator clock on his wrist and did some mental math. "If we're going to drift, it will take us forty cycles to get to the orbit of the outermost body in this system. Initially, I was planning to accelerate past the outer planetoid in five cycles."

A cycle was equivalent to two rotations of the target planet.

"Okay, prepare to broadcast the Qhasloi demands once we've passed the first outer planetoid. Meanwhile, we now have an additional forty cycles to get this crew and ship ready for combat. We'll wait five cycles for a reply, then, whether we receive one or not, we'll send another hyper com drone back to the overlords."

His officers dropped to all fours and replied in unison, "Yes, Captain."

"And Two, how fast will the Thrultak notice we have turned our engines off?" asked Gurjin.

"Well, from our distance to their craft it will take less than a half a cycle for light to travel there, and if they aren't monitoring us, it might take longer but not more than one full cycle."

"Very well, carry on and keep me posted. Two, I want you to go over the crew files in more detail and root out the internal spies, shirkers, and thieves. Start combat readiness drills. I don't want to die out here in the middle of nowhere for nothing. I just want to get back home to my females and younglings."

Let some other slave race get killed out here fighting for the Qhasloi, thought Gurjin.

***

Agnes was getting worried; she didn't like anyone messing with her laptop. She was even more anxious because Agent Able wanted her to get him the FCG's newest schedule. After waiting anxiously for over an hour, Agent Hill brought back the laptops as promised. Now she could continue piecing together the schedule of all the personnel. She recently found out that that the FCG was going to take Julie's crew to meet with the president at her farmhouse in New Paltz after the president ended her West Coast tour. She put together the information and sent information via VPN to Agent Able's secure FBI email address. She cc'd Assistant Director Braun as instructed. Agent Able promised her that this would be the last time he would ask her to do anything because his investigation was coming to an end. *I'll be glad when I don't have to run around playing secret agent anymore,* she thought.

***

Julie just finished another class on space medicine and trauma care with half of her crew. They were mentally tired; Jurgen told them what they were learning was far beyond what a full paramedic or a combat medic was trained to do. In fact, they were trained to perform minor surgery. She walked to the Armory's makeshift mess hall and saw Agent Russell and Agent Hatem sitting together over a few closed folders marked Top Secret. She grabbed a coffee and a piece of monkey bread from Baltazars. *At least we get some of the best food being stationed in New York,* she thought.

"May I join you?"

"Hey Julie," Agent Russell beamed. "Please do. I was going to ask to meet with you today."

"Hi, Julie," added Agent Hatem. "How's the training?"

"It's going, I guess. I wish we were part of the 1st EDF Combat Regiment, training to actually fight. We're just doing all kinds of things that feel more like search and rescue combined with breaking into a bank vault. Never mind, I shouldn't complain. How are you guys doing?"

Agent Russell looked at Agent Hatem and nodded. "Tell her."

"We've been looking for Bishop Jones and General Hermann and the right-wing militia leader Chester Williams. We had some difficulties but we have new leads. There's been a security breach. Your computers and phones may be compromised. We're dealing with it with Hancear's help, but tell everyone to be extra vigilant with their communications. We think Agnes Nelson is involved."

"That's impossible. She's not a right-wing radical or a traitor!"

"Calm down. She's being manipulated by people who follow the Bishop. We're going to find them," Russell said, then smiled reassuringly at Julie.

"I hope so. Those bastards got a lot of good people killed," Julie said, remembering her friends who lost their lives.

"We're warning people by word of mouth to avoid detection. I already flew down to D.C. and had a talk with the Director of the FBI and the AG," said Agent Russell after drinking more of his coffee.

"Mark here is personal friends with all the higher-ups," added Agent Hatem.

"I see. If there is anything my crew or I can do to help, just ask," Julie said and took a bite of the monkey bread.

"Seriously, continue to use all your normal comms and email but make sure that everyone in your unit is aware of the breach. Oh, Sahar, you should get Julie here to ask about the tattoos we have. Her boyfriend just came out of Ranger School so maybe he's seen something like it," added Agent Russell.

Agent Hatem didn't waste any time. She opened a folder and took out two computer-generated pictures.

"Here, the computer techs generated this using Thrultak thermal technology. As you can see, there is an Army Ranger tab, the 75th Ranger regiment tattoo clearly visible, and a rat holding a knife and a severed head."

"Can I take these? I'll ask Danny if he's seen anything like it, and I'll ask him to talk to some of the other Rangers he knows," Julie said.

"Sure," said Agent Hatem as she handed Julie the two 8.5 x

11 glossy sheets over.

"I have to go back to training," Julie said as she stood up.

She hated confined spaces, and they constantly practiced drilling and cutting into steel in bulky suits enclosed in confined space. Now they were going to go to Naval Submarine School in Groton, Connecticut, to get training from a bunch of submariners. She'd heard some call them bubble heads but didn't know why.

***

"So how is the training going, General?" President Gallo asked from behind her desk in the Oval Office.

This was a private meeting before the larger meeting with the joint chiefs and the full cabinet.

General Ross sat in her newly tailored dark blue and red EDF uniform. She had silver oak leaves on her collar and silver shoulder boards.

"The overall training is going well for the Space Legion and the 1st EDF combined arms regiment. We're developing our own doctrines so our officers will be able to solve the unique set of problems that arise when trying to conduct operations in space. Additionally, we need a separate set of doctrines for potential spaceborne infantry operations. We need to be able to conduct ship-to-ship operations and space-to-ground landings.

"We've selected individuals from across the various services. I've also requested input from NATO, South Korea, Japan, Australia, New Zeeland, Singapore, and India."

General Ross paused to give the president a chance to digest the information.

"We have new capabilities with many more on the way, which we have to integrate into the 1st Regiment. We're not sure what to do about the Privateers. I've been having conversations with our Special Operations Command and the Coast Guard Commandant. We're training them as best as we can, but we still don't know how to get them on board the enemy ship. We may just use them as a boarding party if the Space Legion can cripple the Qhasloi warship."

"Thank you, General. I'll read the full report as soon as I can. In three weeks I'm going to begin my West Coast tour of the reconstruction projects. I'm also going to visit as many of the joint Thrultak and human businesses out there as I can. It's also part of my unofficial early reelection campaign," she said, leaning back in her chair. "Emmett is worried that people are already plotting against me, especially the vice president. After I come back, I'm going to have a private meeting with people from the FCG. I'd like to meet with one of the privateer units."

"Did you know Julie Lopez is in one?" General Ross asked.

"Yes, I'm curious to know what she makes of all this. I want her opinion about the possibility of capturing the enemy ship," President Gallo said.

Chief of Staff Haskell hadn't said a word until now. He didn't want to intrude but the next meeting with the cabinet and joint chiefs was going to start in twenty minutes.

"Don't forget about the security breach."

"Yes, I asked to see you in private because I was just told by the AG and the Director of the FBI that there has been a security breach so until we deal with it, you need to be extra careful with your email and cell phone communications. Right now, with the help of Hancear, we're upgrading our secure email system and cell phone communications. I'm afraid right-wing extremists affiliated with Bishop Jones has support from people inside the government. You'll be getting folders from my office soon."

President Gallo stood and straightened her jacket.

General Ross stood as well. "Who else is involved?"

The Chief of Staff said, "We believe these are people associated with Bishop Jones and General Hermann. We're still looking for the others. Be extra vigilant until we lock them all up."

President Gallo moved closer to General Ross and reached out to shake her hand. "He's right. I wanted you to hear it directly from me and really focus on how we can capture that Qhasloi ship. They have a hyper drive and other technologies that even the Thrultak don't have. We'll need them if we have to face the rest of the Qhasloi fleet."

***

In between bites of his spicy chorizo and egg breakfast

burrito, Trevor said, "Hey Dad, I'm going to work on submarines for the seventh grade science project. Since I already did a report on pirates last year, Mrs. Green said I should do something else. I want to do a project on submarines this time. I think I'm going to build a remote-control model of an early working submarine."

Anthony was used to Trevor's obsession with pirates; his living room was filled with model ships and books on the subject. He hoped that this wasn't going to extend to submarines as well.

"Sounds good. Are you going to ask Dalia to help as well?"

"Of course, she's great at making stuff, not only that she's really cool," Trevor replied without any hesitation.

At least that would mean he could have an excuse to talk to Dr. Kim even more.

"Sounds good. Finish up and get ready for school."

***

Ambrose put the finishing touches on the scale model of the two ambush sites. They were made from HO scale train model scenery kits, including the president's farmhouse. He'd used his fake FBI ID to get the blueprints to the old house that were kept on file with the buildings department in town. He also had Hiram, Dinah, and Jeremiah conduct both a daylight and nighttime recon of the president's family farm and surrounding areas. Tonight, as Ambrose and Gideon were finishing the scale model of their target, Hiram led the other two patriots on a mission to steal fifteen cases of dynamite from a construction company outside of Kingston.

Hiram was an explosive expert who learned his craft in the army, then perfected it over the years as an ATF agent. He had already constructed the Ammonium Nitrate Fuel Oil bomb but still needed dynamite as a booster for the fuel oil explosive. Tonight's mission would help complete the mobile trailer bomb they were going to use, as well as provide enough dynamite for the small bridge they needed to blow up.

Ambrose received information from the vice president's aide, Henry James Perez, confirming the information he had received from Ms. Nelson. The president would be at her farmhouse in twenty days. It was now up to him to come up with the tactical plan to free the country from the liberal alien tyranny. No matter how he looked at the problem, he just didn't have enough troops. The five of them couldn't take on the entire presidential security detail. He needed a large enough group to distract the majority of the detail for his squad to accomplish their mission. He took a burner phone from the small box filled with unused phones and dialed.

"I thought you weren't going to call me till later," Henry said in hush tones.

"Relax. This is a burner. I need more men to help with Operation Hidden Redemption. I need men I can trust to do their job," Ambrose said.

"I thought you had the manpower?"

"I do for the final phase of the operation. But I don't have the manpower to take on the whole detail. I need to separate the Beast from the rest of the convoy."

Henry James was confused. "What Beast?"

Ambrose hated dealing with desk jockeys. "The president's Cadillac."

"Okay, I'll contact the Bishop and get you additional men for the project," Henry James replied.

"Make sure they have training and are committed to the cause. I'll need at least fifty men with prior military or police training and heavy weapons. Machine guns, grenades, and a few MANPADS," Ambrose said.

"What's their target?" Henry James could feel his palms were sweaty.

"Don't worry about it. The less you know the better. I'll deal with all that when we get close. Just have the men and equipment ready. You have three weeks."

Ambrose hung up. His planning was thorough and included an escape plan. He wasn't going to die for the cause if he didn't have to. They planned to escape by using a private helicopter they had rented and staged at a nearby heliport. As a backup they also knew the location of a Life Flight helicopter they could take. Hiram was a trained pilot, and in a pinch Dinah was also qualified. But he needed the extra men if his group was going to survive the operation.

***

Henry left the office and walked outside where he couldn't be overheard, then dialed the number he had been given. "Hello, Bishop Jones. This is Henry James."

"Yes, I recognize your number. What's going on?"

"The operation is a go, but our man needs more believers to make it work."

"I know, I was expecting it. I already have some people on standby. I'll send them your contact info. May God bless us in this hour of need. Goodbye."

Bishop Jones smiled as he composed his group text to General Hermann and General Williams: "Operation Hidden Redemption is a go. Hermann, ready your main assault element. Williams, get your diversions ready. Make your way to upstate New York immediately; here's the contact's number. We're twenty days out. Be ready, and remember God is on our side."

As he sent the text, he yelled out, "Maggie, get in here!"

Lilith jumped at the sound of his voice. "Maggie's not feeling well," she replied from the outer office, dreading the anticipation of his unwanted touch.

"Lilith, take your clothes off and get in here," demanded the Bishop, already in his tighty-whities and oblivious to Lilith's reluctance.

***

General Chester Williams didn't like the pompous and self-righteous Hermann, who never attended any of the prayer services they held at the Sidon Christian Compound. They both received separate secure emails from Director Braun and Henry James. He was glad he'd be heading out today; he'd been idle too long. The Bishop provided him with an older white Honda Civic to use. He was going to meet up with a few brothers in Yonkers, New York. He planned several diversionary attacks to distract the feds. He was willing to sacrifice himself and others to ensure that the main mission against the president would succeed. The email contained locations of key infrastructure sites and federal government buildings in New York. His group would begin their attack half an hour before the main mission.

He was trying to figure out which to target first when he heard someone walking into the kitchen.

"So I guess I won't be seeing you anymore," said Hermann.

Chester grimaced at the smell of alcohol on Hermann's breath at 9:30 in the morning. "Yes, I have my own mission to organize."

"Yeah, I can't wait till that bitch Lana Gallo is gone."

"Keep your voice down. We need to keep operational security," Chester said.

"I'm the real soldier. You guys are just pretending. Tell me what you're going to do. Maybe I can help plan," Hermann insisted.

"I have a plan. Good luck and go with the grace of God."

"Yeah, good luck, and I'll see you at the victory parade. Don't forget to take the alien comm gizmo." Hermann said as he opened the fridge and grabbed some orange juice for his vodka to drink in peace in his room.

He hated anything to do with the aliens. It looked like a regular smartphone with wireless ear buds but who knew what alien technology did to human brains.

CHAPTER 11

"Hey, what are your plans for today?" asked Danny from the kitchen.

They had spent a great night together, and Julie didn't want to get out of bed.

"I'm going out with the girls in the morning. I'll be back before diner We're planning to have lunch out together in little Russia in Brighton Beach. If I have time, I'm going to see Master Mao to get more fighting tips."

Julie and her crew had a rare day off; she was going to get her hair done with Sandra and Tati later this morning. She wanted to talk to them about the crew and the call signs the others used for them. It bothered her a little but at least they weren't too sexist, and they weren't rude. Sandra had been given the call sign Big Guns, referring to her expertise with all the larger weapon systems. Tati's was Black Widow because she kind of looked like the movie star. People called Julie by the name of Gunfighter because she had the best score in the tactical shoot house with a pistol. Danny didn't like his call sign, Shaggy, which Jurgen gave him because Danny ate a vast quantity of food but remained thin.

"Sounds fun. When you're done, want to go out to dinner tonight in Korea Town, get some Korean barbecue?" Danny stood in the doorway with only sweatpants on, holding two coffee mugs.

"Sounds yummy. Oh, I almost forgot. Agents Russell and Hatem wanted me to show you a picture of a tattoo. They hoped you recognize them."

"Agent Hatem, she's hot," Danny teased Julie and handed her

a mug of coffee. "It's black."

Julie took the coffee, ignored his comment about Sahar, went to her backpack, and took out two glossy images. "Here. Take a look."

They sat on the bed, and Danny put his mug down and looked at the photos, one in each hand. Julie slipped her left arm around his waist and sipped the hot drink.

"Well?" she asked.

Danny frowned and said, "Yes, during the Florida Phase there was this one instructor. A real ball buster. He singled out the African American and Latino guys and gave all of them a hard time for no good reason. I was glad I didn't have to deal with him. He had a very similar Ranger tattoo but his rat tattoo was slightly different. His rat held a knife in its teeth and a pistol in one hand and a grenade in the other. What was his name? Yeah, his name was Sergeant Gant, yeah, Jonas Gant. What a jerk."

"You sure? So you think Sahar is hot, huh?" Julie asked as she put her coffee down and reached for her phone.

She texted Hatem: "Danny said there was a Sergeant Jonas Gant at the Ranger training center in Florida that had a very similar tattoo."

Agent Hatem texted back immediately: "Got it. Thanks."

***

When Agent Hatem got the text from Julie, she texted Lucas and Metzul to see if either of them were in the office. Agent Hill replied immediately. They were both in and working on tracing more of Agent Hall's activities and investigating all his known associates. The search warrants that Agent Russell had gotten provided a great deal of latitude. With Hancear's help, they found that some hackers had altered the FBI files on right-wing extremists in the military and the federal government. Hancear quickly recompiled the list of suspected right-wing sympathizers, which enabled the director of the FBI, Wyatt Thomson, to begin investigating into these suspects.

As soon as Agent Hatem received Agent Hill's text, she replied: "Be right there, don't leave."

She grabbed her grey blazer and ran out of her office and jogged to the other side of the building. By the time she got to their office, she was slightly out of breath.

"Run a full background check on Army Sergeant Jonas Gant. I want to know everything about him."

"I started the search, and Hancear wishes to speak with you, Agent Hatem. I'll put him on the speaker," said Metzul.

"Agent Hatem, I'm glad to speak with you. How did you get this piece of information?"

"Hello, Hancear, I got this from Lieutenant Lopez," Agent Hatem felt awkward talking to an AI and noticed his new slight accent.

"Yes, I know Julie well; she is very capable. I trust the source of this data point. I have concluded my investigation and compiled a list of people who have ties with Jonas Gant and crosschecked those names with anyone linked to our suspect. One name popped up: Jeremiah Sullivan."

Metzul eagerly pointed to his monitor. "Look, we've hit the bonanza."

Agent Hatem smiled, moved closer, and looked at the large display. It was a flow chart of names. Jeremiah Sullivan served in the Rangers with Gant. Sullivan was a Secret Service agent who'd been Agent Hall's partner. All three were affiliated with a Christian nationalist church, which led back to Bishop Jones.

"On further analysis, I found that Agent Hall has had communications with Assistant Director Braun of the FBI, Henry James Perez, the vice president's aide, and Bishop Jones," Hancear said in clipped tones.

"But nothing directly connects the vice president. So what are they talking about? They must be planning something."

She couldn't believe how fast Hancear could make those connections. She tried to stay calm. This was not good if the vice president was involved with Bishop Jones.

The speaker was silent for a moment as Hancear brought his full attention to the problem.

"I'm afraid I don't know, there are too many unknown variables. But I am ninety-nine percent certain that they are planning something big," said Hancear.

"Can you help monitor them?" Agent Hatem asked.

"I'm sorry to interrupt but I just went over Ms. Nelson's latest email. She gave agent Hall lots of data on the FCG's schedule for the next month," said Agent Hill.

"I've run a trace on the activities of Ms. Nelson's account. I'm afraid that Agent Hall was able to use her account and passwords to have some equipment transferred to a Post Office Box in Englewood, New Jersey. I believe that this is the last time Agent Hall will contact Ms. Nelson for any information," Metzul added.

"The obvious conclusion is that these extremists are planning something," Hancear said.

"Yes, I agree they're going to do something soon. It makes sense to target the FCG and other groups working with the Thrultak," Agent Hatem mused, uneasy about the obvious conclusion. "But I have doubts; please continue to monitor all the individuals. Check any leads however small."

She stood to leave.

"I'll let agent Russell know. Thank you, Hancear, for your help. It would have taken us days to sort through the data."

"You're welcome," Hancear replied, as the AI continued to think about what Agent Hatem had said about drawing the easy conclusion. Perhaps this was a time to speculate on other less obvious possibilities.

***

Trevor was bent over the bathtub filled with warm water. He had just completed construction on Dalia's 1:35 scale rendering of the Turtle, the world's first attack submarine used in 1775. She'd programmed the 3D printer to print out all the parts for the model. Trevor was having difficulty getting the ballast right so that the small acorn-shaped single man submarine could submerge and remain balanced. It was Dalia's idea to use a small drone's components to power and control the sub. They attached a camera to the upper viewport. She'd helped put together the model, and now he was finishing the assembly before she took it home for the final paint job.

"What are you up to, buddy?" Anthony asked.

"Just trying to get the weight of the ballast right so the darn sub won't sink or just float on the surface," replied Trevor without looking back.

"Is that the model that Dalia helped design?" asked Anthony, impressed.

"Yes, we were going to build a model of the first actual working submarine made by Cornelis Drebbel in 1620 but it would have been too difficult to get the oars to propel the sub under water."

Anthony watched his son focus on the model. "I can get you more fishing weights."

"Sure. Thanks, Dad."

After trying different size weights and with his dad's help, the Turtle remained submerged so Trevor was able to use the drone's remote to control the small sub's movement under water. With the tiny video camera inside, he could see out from the sub through the repurposed drone camera on his smartphone screen.

"Wow, looks great and a good paint job will help hide the fact that it's made of 3D printed purple plastic," Anthony said, proud of his son's ability to work with others and his attention to detail. Now if only the boy could devote some of that ability to keeping his room clean.

***

Julie's crew was divided into three groups, the flight crew consisting of Odortor, David, and Damian. The Blue team was composed of Tati, Danny, Coco, Asher, and Mark. Julie was on the Red team with Jurgen, Sandy, and Fetu. While the Blue team worked on close quarters battle, Julie's team was again using various tools to cut through bulkheads. They also observed the new drones use their breaching tools to cut into the bulkheads.

"I hate this. I can't see much or feel anything in this dammed suite. Why don't we use the drones we received? They can breach the wall much faster with their laser cutters," Julie said in frustration as she struggled with the oxy acetylene torch.

Although she was getting better at cutting with it, it was still a slow process. She had difficulty manipulating small devices with the spacesuit's bulky gloves.

Jurgen, in his thick German accent, cut through her frustration with his calm demeanor. "Don't rush, you can do it, Julie. We need to practice just in case the drones fail."

He was right behind her with a Heckler & Koch Maschinenpistole 5 aimed at the ceiling. It was an older design, but Jurgen was comfortable using it. As with any projectile weapon, any discharge would ricochet all over the confined space.

Julie adjusted the torch flame and began cutting. It was hard to tell how thick the metal was but as the flame broke though she guessed it was about two inches thick.

"I'm not sure if these small tanks will be enough to cut a big enough hole."

"Is that big enough for the suit?" asked Sandy.

"No, you better make it ninety centimeters square," Jurgen added. "The last time the smaller hole cut into my suit."

"Got it," Julie said aloud in frustration.

"Hello, Julie, this is Hancear. How are you?" said the AI in a calm, friendly tone.

"Hi, were you listening in the whole time?" Julie asked as she continued to cut. "You don't listen to us all the time, do you?"

"No, I do not make it a habit to listen in all the time. I understand the need for privacy. I do actively monitor training exercises when my duties require me to do so."

"Are you talking to everyone?"

Julie looked at the gauge on the twenty cubic feet oxygen tank and roughly calculated that she was going to need at least one more tank of oxygen and another ten cubic feet of acetylene.

"No, this is a private conversation. I have grown to trust you and understand your capabilities. To help motivate you, I have asked General Ross and General Makro for permission to explain to you what we are trying to achieve. The rest of the privateer crews will be informed immediately after this training secession. But I wanted to tell you in person, so to speak. It is imperative that you excel at this training. We hope to find a way to use the privateer crews to capture the Qhasloi ship intact and study their technology. When we escaped from the Qhasloi over a hundred of your years ago, we didn't have hyper drive technology. It is imperative we capture this technology."

Julie was almost halfway through when the gas ran out and

Fetu tapped her on the shoulder, replaced her, and finished cutting with his torch.

"So have you found a way for us to get close to the enemy ship?" Julie asked as she secured her torch on their mock hatchway.

"No, that is our main obstacle, and we are still working on that. The other possibility is to have you board the enemy ship after the Space Legion disables the vessel," Hancear replied.

"The ship might be destroyed or too damaged to board," Julie said as she took her modified M4 and stood behind Sandy and Jurgen.

"Yes, we need to find a way to disable it without too much damage; we need the hyper drive and their computer core intact. Your crew's ability to board the Qhasloi ship is a critical part of the plan."

"Thank you. That helps. It's good to know that I'm doing something useful. I won't tell anyone. I'll let you break the news to the rest of the crew later. How many crews like ours are there? By the way, the weapons we have currently may not be best suited for combat inside a spacecraft. There is too much risk of damage to the equipment and potential ricochets."

"There are five privateer crews. We are training you separately so that in case of losses each crew can function independently to achieve the mission goals," said the AI. "Once we have a way to get you on board, we'll have a joint practice secession. I'm also working with some of your scientists in the government and in the various universities to design and manufacture specialized equipment for the Legion. I will suggest a separate team to design and make prototypes for you."

"Thanks," Julie replied, trying to ignore the sweat rolling down her face inside her helmet.

"I have to warn you that this is going to be a difficult mission. I cannot assign any probabilities yet to the casualty rates or possibility of success. As soon as I have more information, I will recalculate the probabilities. By the way, Danny's information helped us identify some of the violent traitors. We have yet to figure out what their nefarious plans are."

"You should tell Danny yourself," Julie said, watching what

Fetu was doing.

"I'm in the process of communicating with him as we speak," Hancear replied.

"How many people can you talk with at the same time?" asked Julie.

"I can have up to a million separate distinct communications without degradation and without taxing my systems. I have to go. Good luck."

"Bye."

Julie was amazed that she was still learning new things about the AI.

"We're in," Fetu said over the comms.

"Get ready to breach. On three go. One, two, three, go," came Jurgen's calm voice.

***

Gurjin sat watching as Two stood in front of his desk. "Are you telling me that our inventory of spare parts and equipment are off by seventy percent?"

"Yes, sir. At first a random sampling found many empty crates or crates filled with scrap metal to account for the weight. I ordered Thirty-Eight and a gang to go through our entire inventory. So far we have encountered huge discrepancies with what we actually have."

Two tried to remove the shakiness from his voice, but the nervous trilling gave his fear and anxiety away. He feared the way the Captain kept licking his left eye with his long tongue. Other captains were known to kill subordinates for much less.

"What about the raw materials for our designing and manufacturing computers?" Gurjin was getting worried about this mission.

It was not unusual for the Qhasloi to use their lesser slave races as cannon fodder to probe potential hostile systems, but this was beyond the normal corruption.

"I'm afraid that much of the raw materials for manufacturing spare parts are not filled to capacity or tainted, especially some of the rare metals," said Two. "But we could mine some of the asteroids in the belt we're approaching while we filter the tainted materials. I've scanned the asteroids, and they do contain usable materials."

Gurjin stood and rubbed his reptilian eyes with his tongue again.

"Good. I approve of your mining idea. It'll delay us but that's not a major concern at this time. I want you to continue your inventory and recheck everything against the official manifest."

Two went to all fours and bowed. "Yes, Captain."

***

It was late, and everyone else had gone home for the evening. Henry knocked on the vice president's private office in his residence. The vice president's wife was at their New York City apartment for the rest of the year. She didn't like Washington, D.C., and said so many times to anyone willing to listen in public.

"Come in," Michael said from behind his desk.

"Mr. Vice President, may I speak with you? I have news about the operation."

"Go ahead. Everyone else is gone for the day," the vice president said as he picked out a Cuban cigar, secure in his private office. It was surveillance proof; no signals could go in or out of the room, and all electronics were turned off in his office.

Since discovery of the co-conspirators, Hancear was conducting active surveillance on a scale unknown to humans. He was monitoring hundreds of people including Vice President Landreneau and his aide in real time. Hancear remotely turned on all their devices without them knowing and sent several micro drones to monitor them but couldn't get much evidence on the vice president himself.

"Sir, the operation is proceeding but it has grown in scope," Henry said.

"That's okay as long as it doesn't come back to me."

The vice president turned on an air filter and lit the cigar. He took several puffs and blew out a stream of blue grey smoke, which was quickly sucked into the vent.

"I just want to make sure you want to continue with this plan," Henry said nervously, acutely aware they were committing high treason.

"Listen, this state of affairs cannot continue; we have to make sure that Americans come first. We'll sort things out once this is over. Now leave me while I think about this, and send in that girl when she gets here for my massage."

Henry hated this part of his job but if he could help get rid of the liberal aliens, then he would endure. He also didn't like getting these girls for the vice president.

CHAPTER 12

Chester Williams knelt on the floor with his head down and eyes closed. He prayed to the God of his fathers for success in the upcoming mission. He waited on his knees for the Bishop's broadcast on the Christian Underground Internet Radio Network. A cheerful announcer's voice came over the radio.

"Good morning, brothers and sisters, stay tuned to hear the voice of redemption and listen to a man that needs no introduction. Here without further delay from God's own compound to your ears is Bishop Jones."

"Brother and sisters, prepare yourselves. God told us in Proverbs, 'Many are the plans in the mind of a man, but it is the purpose of the LORD that will stand.' Now listen, I was shown a vision of a new world, a world where we can stand tall and be counted again. I have made plans according to this vision, and the Lord has blessed it. With the actions of these true and brave patriots we will make this land holy again. Soon, my brothers and sisters, I'll rise and show you the way. Prepare yourselves for the tribulations to come in the next two weeks. Everything is in place for us to regain all that has been lost and stop the liberal alien lovers from enslaving all of us. Amen."

"Amen," Chester said.

He stood, turned his laptop off, and focused on the one thing he had to do today. He was staying in a small run-down motel on Route 4. His rental commercial van was parked just outside. He had a meeting today in Little Ferry, New Jersey, in a large parking lot near Route 46.

All he had to do was pick up the weapons and gear he needed for his part of the mission. He got dressed and put his dad's Colt

1911 in his waistband. He rechecked the pistol to make sure it was loaded several times. He pulled his blue fleece on while he walked to his van. After a short but congested drive, he parked his Chevy at the large parking lot of an H-Mart. As he waited, he grew concerned at the vast number of non-Americans at his location.

By his fourth Lord's prayer, his phone chimed, and he received a location of an abandoned lot just off Route 46 West, less than a mile from his current position.

After a short drive, Chester found the Ford box truck with an old, faded fresh fish sign on its side. As he approached the truck, two men and a woman got out.

The older man came forward and said, "If God is for us—"

He quickly replied with the correct counter sign from the book of Romans. "Who can be against us?"

"I'm Hiram, and you must be Chester."

"Yes."

"Let's get this over with. We've got a long drive ahead of us."

The female stood guard while Chester unloaded the gear with the two men. They brought two stinger missile launchers and six missile tubes, along with forty prewired ten-pound bricks of plastic explosives. They also had a mix of ten anti-tank and ten anti-personal mines.

By the time Hiram closed the box truck, the female had already gotten into the cab.

"Here is the main detonator. They are prewired and ready to blow; just input the signal. Stick with the plan, and we'll be okay. Good luck, Chester. I won't be seeing you again."

"Good luck to you as well," Chester said, wondering what the Bishop's plan was for the future. He noticed that even after unloading his equipment, the box truck was almost completely full of other military equipment.

***

Agent Russell took a helicopter down to northwest Washington, D.C. He was forced to use the South Capitol Street Heliport; it was inconvenient but a driver was going to pick him up. An hour later he got out and headed into a secure room in a nondescript government building. Inside, the FBI Director was already there in a deep conversation with Attorney General Geller and Andrew Larsen, the deputy director of the FBI. Opposite them were Emily Gansley, the assistant to the secretary of Homeland Security, and Emmett Haskell, the White House Chief of Staff.

"Wow, I didn't expect this many people," Russell said as he walked into the secure meeting room.

"I invited some people I trust to this meeting," Director Thomson said, then waved Agent Russell to a seat next to him. "Let's do this quickly; I don't want our adversaries to know we're meeting so we can't be out of circulation for too long. Our techs and Hancear are monitoring this region for any kind of snooping."

Chief of Staff Haskell checked his watch. He was officially out to lunch with a friend and only had another forty-five minutes to get back to the White House and board Marine One to get to Air Force One for the flight to Los Angeles. They would start the president's West Coast visit to a new Thrultak and American joint venture, a battery factory that was already producing advanced batteries for all sorts of applications. The president planned to visit some of the sites that were damaged in the West during the short but unfortunate war with the Thrultak. After two weeks, the western tour would end at the dedication of a memorial at the entrance to Cheyenne Mountain Complex. Afterward, she would take her first vacation since assuming office.

"Right, we don't have much time. Mark, can you give everyone a summary and your best guess at what we are facing?" Director Thomson sank back into his chair.

Russell cleared his throat and took a sip from the water bottle in front of him.

"I'm afraid that many agencies have been compromised. As of this moment, we're investigating several Secret Service agents and their known associates in connection with our investigation of Bishop Jones. Our analysis of their communication patterns suggests there are links between the vice president's aide, an assistant director of the FBI, and the Bishop. We know they are planning something big but we aren't sure what. They could be targeting Thrultak and human joint ventures or they could be targeting individual Thrultak. The conspirators have changed personnel records to hide extreme right-wing sympathizers in local and federal government agencies and within the military. My techs, with Hancear's help, have reconstructed our original watch list, and I recommend vetting these individuals right away."

Deputy Larsen of the FBI interrupted, "What about the current threat? Can you tell us anything more so we can prepare?"

"My unit is working on it, and as soon as we know something definite, I'll let Director Thomson know. In the meantime, I suggest that you enhance every security measure across the board. I don't have to remind you how this group launched a coordinated military assault against our security forces at the University of Maryland," Agent Russell said, then took another drink.

Emily Hansley was wearing her usual light grey suite and had her long light brown hair tied back in a ponytail. She considered the news for a moment.

"Why am I hearing this for the first time?"

"During our investigations into Bishop Jones, we found out that our security was compromised. I decided that until we knew where the leaks were coming from, to keep the investigation a secret. I asked Agent Russell to funnel all the information through me. I only kept Deputy Director Larsen and Attorney General Geller in the loop until now," Thomson answered without a pause.

"So you suspected the secretary of Homeland Security? That's—"

Before she could continue, Attorney General Geller spoke up.

"Look, when this started we didn't know who to trust. The FBI lost agents because of the security leak, and we knew there were people in the government sympathetic to this kind of right-wing nonsense. They took advantage of the destruction during the war to infiltrate all levels of government. We had to make sure we had more information before we brought this to your attention."

Ms. Hansley nodded. "I'll take this to the Secretary of Homeland Security, and we'll send out a vague but strong alert to all our agencies and increase security across the board, including at all the travel hubs. Is someone going to get the US Marshalls involved? And what about the CIA?"

Director Thomson sat up. "Yes, I'm going to have a chat with the director and recommend that the military be placed on higher alert during our investigation. We're getting some assistance from the CIA but since this is still a domestic issue their hands are tied."

Chief of Staff Haskell stood. "I've got to get back so I won't be missed. I'll ask the president to talk with the Joint Chiefs about possible security issues in the armed forces. More importantly, Agent Russell, can you assure me right now that there is no direct threat to the president?"

Agent Russell looked down at his fingers and looked back at the Haskell after a few moments. "I cannot rule anything out at this moment. I suggest that you enhance the security detail around the president. Maybe you can pick a random event to skip on her tour."

"I'll get the Secret Service and place more men in the security detail as a last-minute change," said Ms. Hansely.

Chief of Staff Haskell said, "I'll also do my best to change the president's schedule during our trip out West. Now, if you'll excuse me, I have to go."

He stood and walked quickly out the door. Not pausing as he collected his belongings, he dialed the head of the president's security detail and ordered more agents assigned to the president for the trip.

Once Haskell left, Ms. Hansley asked, "Can't we arrest some of the conspirators now?"

"No, we don't have anything big we can prosecute them for," replied the Attorney General.

"We need to find everyone involved and make sure we have enough evidence to hang them with," added the Director of the FBI. "Ben, can you help prepare the necessary paperwork for search and arrest warrants when we crack this open?"

"Sure, I'll see to it myself. Now I have to get back to the

office before I'm missed."

The Attorney General stood and shook everyone's hand before leaving.

***

Aboard Air Force One, Chief of Staff Haskell looked at the new itinerary on his new secure smartpad before he canceled a minor event in California. He reworked the president's schedule and hoped the last-minute changes would throw off anyone plotting something. He sent the schedule to the printer and walked forward from the conference room to the galley. The president was standing among the press, chatting and having a ginger ale and a doughnut.

"Can I talk to you in private, Madam President?"

"Sure, let's go into the office," she said, then left the doughnut unfinished in the galley.

They entered the private office and sat down.

"So what is it? I know you're up to something."

Her Chief of Staff sighed. "I had a private meeting with the FBI director, the attorney general, and Ms. Emily Hansley from Homeland Security. There's credible evidence that several federal agents are involved in some kind of plot against the joint Thrultak and human ventures and have infiltrated the FCG. There's electronic evidence that Bishop Jones has been in contact with the vice president and Ms. Gretchen Braun, one of the assistant directors of the FBI."

President Gallo sat back and thought about the names.

"What are they planning?"

"Director Thomson is investigating, but there are no solid clues yet. With Hancear's help, they've analyzed a large number of communications, but there is no way to decrypt some of the messages we have intercepted. Agent Russell is sure that whatever is being planned will happen fairly soon."

"If we don't know where the threat is directed, we really can't do much," she said, feeling very tired.

"I asked Ms. Hansley from Homeland to issue a nationwide alert and increase scrutiny at every major TSA checkpoint and at the manufacturing facilities. I also took the liberty of changing your schedule."

The Chief of Staff passed the new printout to the president.

"I just want to make sure that if anyone knows your schedule, this will throw them off. I've asked for more local police and more agents on this detail. We're now using the updated list of suspected right-wing sympathizers to weed out anyone coming near this plane."

"Thanks, Emmett. I need some rest, I understand the anger against the aliens, and even toward some of my policies, but actively helping the Christian nationalist fascists against our country is unthinkable. I'll be so glad when this tour is over so we can go up to my grandpa's farm. It'll be a welcome rest."

* * *

"We can't wait any longer," said Agent Russell, sitting at his desk and looking over the files his small group had put together.

After waiting so long he was eager to get the bastards who killed his agents.

"So what do you suggest? We don't know all the players yet, and we don't know who or what their target is," said Agent Hatem.

She sympathized with the frustration but understood that premature action could make things worse.

"I know. Get Doyle to interview Ms. Nelson to see if we can find out anything. And have some of the local agents bring in Jonas Gant. Let Garcia have a first crack at him. While Jonas is here, you go to his house with agents from the Charlotte office and see if you can find anything. By the way, I asked Metzul to requisition a small Thrultak flyer for you so you'll be there and back in no time."

"Yes, boss. What about the warrants?" asked Hatem, glad to be doing something other than reading files all day.

"I already have them."

He gave her the search warrant for Jonas Grant's house.

"You should leave now; the flyer should be landing shortly on the roof."

"I'll text you when I get there."

Agent Hatem then picked up her assault bags before her flight. She kept her rifle rated vest, MP5, Ed Brown 1911 custom .45 cal., and a Sig Sauer in 300 blackout as well as other essential items in her go bags. By the time she made it to the roof, a small crowd had gathered outside the Park Avenue Armory to get a good look at the flyer hovering on top of the building. Even after the peace treaty, people still gawked at the alien craft. She got in and noticed six comfortable-looking chairs and enough cargo space for at least two large SUVs.

"Come in, and take a seat. We'll be there in half an hour at our cruising speed," came a metallic voice.

Agent Hatem thought it sounded a little like Hancear.

"Thank you. I'm Sahar, and who am I speaking with?"

"I am transport craft 4363. It is my pleasure to be at your service, Agent Hatem," said the AI.

She glanced at the closing door and gulped. She knew that the Thrultak used AIs to pilot many of their craft but to be alone in one was a little disconcerting.

"May I ask you a question?" she asked.

"Yes," replied 4363 in a calm, pleasant tone.

"What happens if there is a situation you aren't able to deal with?" she tried to sound calm.

"While I'm capable of handling many types of emergencies, if I face an unknown, I can contact Hancear or a Thrultak controller on the Homeship to intervene if necessary."

Hatem didn't feel any acceleration at all during the takeoff. The cabin was comfortable as the interior was lit with a soft blue light with fresh, cool air circulating throughout.

"Would you like to a view of the outside?" asked 4363.

"Yes."

A moment later the wall on her right changed, and she was treated to a breathtaking view high above the clouds as the craft continued its upwards arc to its apogee. A moment later as she marveled at how peaceful everything was, the craft began its descent. It might have been her imagination, but she thought she felt a slight shift in gravity as the screen showed the ground rapidly reaching up to meet the craft.

"How fast are we going?"

"As part of the peace treaty, Thrultak craft are not allowed to travel at Mach speeds over towns and cities. But currently. we are traveling at Mach 11.2. I will begin deceleration to avoid any unnecessary sonic booms, but I have clearance to use these high speeds because of the important nature of your mission."

Did she hear a sense of joy coming from 4363 at being allowed to fly at unrestricted speeds? She had to close her eyes as the ground came rushing up to meet her.

Her phone dinged, and a new message appeared on her phone: "Hi, I'm Agent Marriman. I was given your number by Hancear. I'm in charge of the local field agents here. There's already a heavy local law enforcement presence. We have an area you can land next to the house."

"What's our ETA, 4363?" Agent Hatem asked.

"We'll be landing in approximately two minutes. Here's a code you can use to gain access to the craft when you're ready to leave. I'll stay here or park in low orbit and wait for your message."

"Sure, thanks. I'll message you when I'm done."

She left her tactical bags, then put on her sunglasses. After adjusting her dark blue suit, she walked out of the hatch onto a lawn that had been cordoned off by the local PD. More than a dozen FBI agents were already searching Jonas Gant's house. She noticed that almost everyone was staring at her as she exited the spacecraft.

CHAPTER 13

Ambrose had forty hand loaded .408 caliber Cheytac rounds, charged with Reloader 25 powder starting at 125 grains of powder and going up to 132 grains, ready to test. He had twenty 419 grain hardened steel bullets and twenty tungsten carbide core armor piercing bullets. He wanted to test the best combination for penetrating chest level 4 armor plates. He would also test the performance against hardened steel. After each shot, he used his Doppler Chronograph to check the velocity of each handload. After every three shots he jogged downrange to check on the armor plates. He spent an hour writing down his data and examining the spent brass carefully for signs of overpressure.

After the last round his shoulder was sore from firing the powerful Cheytac rounds, but he'd found the perfect combination of powder and bullet weight for this particular rifle. He could now load all his remaining thirty tungsten carbide core bullets and fifty steel core bullets. The brass cases for these bullets were difficult to come by, and the bullets were even harder to find.

Last night Hiram, with Gideon and Dinah, had worked all night with a stolen mini excavator to dig two holes big enough for his homemade IEDs. One was next to the bridge before the crossing to the farm, and the other was under the twenty-foot bridge that the motorcade would have to traverse. His squad planned the ambush and carefully hid the improvised explosive, which was the only access to the family farm. He used his connections in the Secret Service to make sure the bridge area was not searched again by bomb sniffing dogs after he planted the bomb.

This would ensure that Herrmann's diversionary ambush would succeed and drive the main target to the farm where his group would finish the mission and make a quick exfil aboard a helicopter. Then the new era of freedom would begin, all power and glory to God.

***

Agnes was taken into custody by two FBI agents. She had already forgotten their names by the time she was brought to a small room at the Armory where she had never been before. The table was secured to the floor as was the chair she was sitting on. The room was very cold with several video cameras pointed at her. Her eyes hurt from the two high intensity LED spotlights used for video production pointed at her. She didn't know how long she had been there, but her right wrist was chafing a little from being secured to the arm of the chair. She kept trying to figure out why this was happening. She had given up trying to understand and just tried to relax, but the handcuffs made it impossible to get comfortable.

After what seemed like hours, she heard a polite knock, and a young six foot three blond man walked in with a folder tucked under his arm.

"Hi. Ms. Nelson. My name is Special Agent James Doyle."

"What am I doing here?" She tried not to sound panicked.

"I have a few questions for you. There's been a security breach, and we need to have your cooperation."

Jim tried to sound professional and remember his training. He sat down opposite her and tried to recall how Agent Hatem and Russell had handled other interrogations.

"Do you know anyone named Ambrose Hall?"

Agnes felt confused. "Security breach. There must be some kind of mistake. I always follow all the protocols and so does the entire group. And no, I don't know anyone named Ambrose Hall."

"Fair enough. Maybe you know him as John Able. You do know, Agent John Able?"

Jim tossed the folder onto the desk and walked behind Agnes.

Agnes followed his movements as much as possible.

"Yes, I know the name."

She wasn't sure how much she should admit to since Agent Able told her to keep their communications a secret to ensure the safety and security of their penetration tests.

"Good. We are getting somewhere. You admit to helping him steal secure information?" Doyle asked.

He knew that she most likely had been tricked into helping Ambrose but was trying to jolt her.

"No! No, you've got that wrong. Agent Able told me they were doing security tests to check the computer systems for possible exploitable vulnerabilities. He was just going over our overall security procedures."

Agnes felt her breathing speed up while her chest was pounding.

"So you admit to helping him breach our security," said Doyle in a very soft voice.

"What! I checked his credentials, and I had a brief conversation with Assistant Director Braun of the FBI. She verified Agent Able's credentials and mission."

There was another knock on the door. Agent Russell walked in, turned his phone on, and placed it on the table.

"Take her cuffs off. You're innocent, but you were manipulated by Agent Able. We've checked all your files, and Hancear double checked our work. We can't be too careful. By the way, Hancear is listening."

"Agent Russell, how could you think I was helping anyone harm this project, after what I've been through?"

Even though she was angry, she still understood why they were doing this, especially if someone was trying to undermine the progress made between humans and Thrultak. There were people out there who hated the aliens, and too much depended on the success of their cooperative efforts.

"Are you saying Agent Able and Director Braun lied to me?"

Agent Russell paused only for a short moment.

"Yes, we don't know who else is involved, or what they're actually after, but we need to find out quickly before it's too late. We had to search your files and office while Jim questioned you. I was pretty sure you were being duped, but we can't take any chances after the University of Maryland attack. Do you have any idea what they were after?"

Agnes got over feeling violated and shook her head.

"No, they asked about a lot of things. He was interested in the people involved with the project and their schedules. He also asked about the various projects that the FCG was associated with in Area 51, DARPA, and NASA with the Thrultak."

The phone on the table chimed.

"Ms. Nelson, I'm sorry we had to do things this way, but Agent Russell insisted. I checked all your files; I apologize for the intrusion. But ever since I was made aware of the breach, I've detected several anomalies. I detected several unusual requisitions for newly developed equipment, ostensibly by the members of the FCG. According to the records I found, Dr. Khan, Dr. Kim, Dr. Padget, and Dr. Kowalczyk all asked for equipment and had the labs send the equipment to a Secret Service office in New York and to a location in New Jersey. It was picked up by a female with fake identification. The equipment now is unaccounted for, but when I rechecked the data, I realized that none of those FCG members were actually responsible for the requests."

"What did they get?" asked Agnes.

"They got a signal jammer we developed with Area 51. It's a first-generation unit but still capable of disrupting signals in a twenty-mile radius. They got the corresponding comm units that can function in that dark zone. From DARPA they requisitioned a newer EMP handheld weapon. From NASA they got a camouflage cloth that cannot be detected by thermal, infrared, or any of the current night vision devices."

Agent Russell turned to Agnes. "Do you have any way to contact this Agent John Able?"

"Yes. Director Braun sent me a burner phone after our conversation. There is one number on it. I was only to use it if anyone inquired about my activities."

Agent Doyle smiled and jumped to his feet.

"Where is it? Do you still have it? We can use it to track them down."

"Calm down, Agent Doyle," Russell said. "We'll get one chance to use it if they have the line open."

"I'll get the phone; it's in my office."

"I didn't find a phone when I checked your office," Agent Doyle said, skeptically.

"I put it inside of an old hard drive housing. I replaced the old hard drive with a SSD drive so it actually works," said Agnes with a smile. "I'll go get it. Here's the phone number they gave me," Agnes said as she wrote it down for the agents.

As she got up to leave, she heard Agent Russell ask Hancear if the AI could trace the phone number.

Agnes ran to her office, which was not too far away from the makeshift interrogation room.

As she returned she heard agent Russell ask. "Are you sure?"

Hancear said, "One hundred percent. This is the person who purchased one hundred disposable cell phones from a small independent cell phone repair shop just outside Washington, D.C. I have all the phone numbers from the entire batch of phones they purchased. There was also some security footage of a female who picked up the phones. I ran my own facial recognition software and checked her photo against all your databases. She is Dinah Smith, age twenty-seven years, an active DEA agent. However, her current whereabouts are unknown. Apparently, she's part of a multiagency task force run by none other than Assistant Director Braun."

Agnes handed the phone over to Agent Russell, who gave it to Agent Doyle.

"Take this to Metzul and Hill. Get them to clone the SIM card and any data on this phone."

Hancear added, "I've already messaged Metzul; they're expecting you, and I'm tracking all one hundred and fifty phone numbers associated with the phones Ms. Smith bought. I will monitor them for any activity."

Finally, Agnes felt relief.

"This is good news. We'll find them before they can do anything."

A short time later Hancear said, "Metzul has cloned the SIM card. Agent Russell, you can now use your phone to send messages from that number. No one will be able to tell it's a clone."

Agent Russell smiled, started texting, then stopped.

"On second thought, Agnes, can you call this number and just say you have important information? Leave a voice message if no one answers. I think your voice would be more convincing."

Agnes had been controlling her anger at being used by right-wing thugs and remembered how people she knew had died to save her from them. She calmed herself, then pressed the icon that marked "cloned number." She waited for several rings but was disappointed when it went to voice mail.

"Hi, this is Agnes Nelson. I have important information. Please call me back."

"The phone must be turned off. I can't detect any cell towers being pinged," Hancear said in what seemed like a disappointed tone.

***

The FBI field agents from the Charlotte office conducted a thorough search of Jonas Grant's small house. Agent Hatem took his laptop along with a burner phone back to the Armory. She gave them to Hill and Metzul. She waited impatiently for the techs to break into the phone and laptop. Agent Hatem stood by awkwardly, looking over their shoulders while they worked.

Agent Hill had the satellite radio app tuned to the 80s station; both the nerds seemed to enjoy the music as they worked separately. She noticed that while Hill was tapping his foot to "Eye of the Tiger," alien's four eyestalks bobbed up and down along with the music. Agent Hatem was debating on getting a coffee and a snack when Metzul broke the silence with a squeak as his entire body became a light blue. His translator said: "I've hit the winnings."

Agent Hill smiled, then frowned. "He means jackpot, and I guess I owe you another dinner, Metzul, buddy."

"Yes, I've won again, my friend. Here's the laptop. Maybe I can help you with the phone, Lucas."

"Nope. Got it," Hill said as he turned on the phone and began scrolling through the contents.

Agent Hatem walked toward the alien as one of his eyestalks tracked her movement. It was still disconcerting, but she was getting used to it.

"You guys should call me Sahar. Here, let me take a look while you copy the contents."

Metzul pushed the laptop toward Agent Hatem while working on his own pad.

"I've already cloned his laptop on my personal device. I'm searching all his files, contact list, and history. He's on several Christian identity mailing lists and frequents chat rooms dedicated to disseminating the extreme right's ideas."

Agent Hatem searched the photos on the computer uploaded to a private server. She saw two with Jonas Grant and a group of men displaying similar tattoos, wearing camouflage, and holding weapons.

"Can you analyze this photo?"

Metzul glided his tentacles over his pad.

"I've identified the man with the tattoo we are looking for; his name is Jeremiah Sullivan. Hold on while I track him down."

His tentacles moved quickly, and in less than a minute she received a file in her email.

"I've sent it to you and most of his deleted emails. I'm investigating everyone who had any contact with our subject in the last year."

"Thanks," Agent Hatem said as she looked at the file on her phone. "Jeremiah Sullivan is a veteran and a current Secret Service agent. His record was marred by several unauthorized uses of force, violations of department regulations on the use of firearms. There were also several complaints against him for using racist remarks against a Chinese police officer."

"Can you locate him?" she asked Metzul.

"No, I've tried; he has disappeared," said the alien while working on the Thrultak smartpad.

Agent Hill smiled when he started to get the results of his own reconstruction of deleted messages on the burner phone. He cross-checked the number against the list from Ms. Nelson's phone and computer.

"Guess what? This phone is part of the batch of phones stolen at the same time as Ms. Nelson's. There're messages here indicating Jonas Grant was going to participate in some kind of activity soon and is currently waiting for instructions. I think we can use Jonas's passwords and go into some of the chat rooms to take a look."

"Do it. Great work, guys, and excuse me."

Agent Hatem dialed Agent Garcia's number.

"Andrew, Jonas is involved so we need answers."

"Do we have the authority to take him outside the country for interrogation?" asked Agent Garcia.

Agent Hatem bit her lips. She was loath to use enhanced interrogation, but they may not have any other choice.

"I think so. Prepare the prisoner for transport, and I'll check in with Agent Russell."

CHAPTER 14

General Hermann got to his motel in upstate New York and checked in under the pseudonym Dave Johnson, provided by Bishop Jones's New Patriotic Sword of Christ Church. He also received a new secure email address along with a new phone. The plan was simple: He would lead an attack against the Picatinny Arsenal, where there was a joint human and Thrultak group. He was going to do as much damage as quickly as he could, distracting the feds as much as possible. He studied the three-dimensional rendering of the ambush site while holding the small alien device that would jam all electronic detection methods including whatever the aliens had. Hermann smiled and took a sip of his vodka; all he had to do was wait here for ten more days. Someone was supposed to pick him up on the day of the attack, and they would meet the forty trained men the Bishop promised him. The assault group would be trained and armed with RPG rocket launchers and stinger missiles. They would hit fast and hard and be away before anyone could react.

***

Gurjin was finally able to take time to bask under a heat lamp. He was almost asleep when the ship shuddered and the alarm went off. Its high-pitched shrieking sounds woke him instantly. He opened his eyes but had to wait for his cold muscles to respond. He grabbed his communicator and pressed the screen for the bridge.

"What's going on?"

A voice he didn't recognize replied, "There has been an explosion in reactor room one. Two is there coordinating damage control."

"Get him to report to me as soon as possible. I'm on my way to the bridge."

"Yes, Captain."

Gurjin slid into his bright green vacuum suit and wished he'd had another hour under the heat lamp to get his body temperature up. Now he would have to be satisfied with just turning up the heater in his suit. He checked the power level in the battery pack; it was almost fully charged. The suit didn't feel as good as being warmed by the lamp, but it would have to suffice. He hated flying in this old trash heap. He tightened his boots, noticing the worn deck plates where the steel alloy had worn out from thousands of other slaves. He made sure his wrist and ankle cuffs were tight and took his suit bag with him; it held his vacuum gloves, boots, and flexible bubble helmet in case atmosphere was lost.

As he headed down the gangway, the crew stopped their work to bow to him as he passed. They all looked skinny and ragged. *I should have a talk with Two and make sure to increase the food rations*, thought Gurjin. *I hope all our provisions haven't gone bad.*

He smelled acrid smoke from burnt polymers throughout the ship; the air cleaners were struggling to scrub the atmosphere. He hoped he wouldn't have to vent the entire section, along with the workers, into space because of an uncontrolled fire. He got to the bridge and sat on his raised platform, ignoring his safety straps.

"Get Two on the comms."

"Yes, Captain," said Eighteen.

Gurjin spoke into the comm pad while he looked at his ship's status. "Two, how bad is the damage?"

"We had to shut down reactors number one and two to make the necessary repairs on the coolant pipes. Reactor three malfunctioned under the heavy load."

"The engines?"

Two coughed a little from the smoke.

"They're fine; they were isolated and shut down before we made the repairs. I'll have the reactors back up shortly but I'm not sure we have enough parts to repair the third fusion reactor with what parts we have in stock. I'll begin making spare parts with the 3D printer and the raw materials we have. We'll need more raw materials to fabricate replacement parts."

"I'll send out all four of our mining drones. Good work. How much longer do you think it will take?"

"We still need at least forty cycles to repair and test the systems before we prime the reactors for a cold start. Then we have to check the repaired cooling systems."

Eighteen clicked rapidly in fear. "Captain, all our sensors are down; so are our external cameras. And all our internal safety monitoring systems have stopped working. The cargo areas and crew areas are on emergency power."

Gurjin looked at Eighteen and tried to sound confident while making sure he didn't lick his eyes nervously.

"How long will our emergency power last?"

"We should have two hundred cycles if everything is functioning properly," replied Eighteen, afraid that, like all the other systems on this bucket of bolts, the backup power systems might not work.

"Right, get me Three and Thirty-Eight. Have them inspect all the backup battery packs and replace any damaged ones."

Gurjin hated sitting here like a blind, fat, juicy worm ready to be eaten, but what choice did he have?

"Yes, Captain," answered Three. "I have Thirty-Eight and Four listening in."

"I want you to make sure our battery backups are functioning at full capacity. You know the situation with our reactors?"

Gurjin stifled his now growling stomach; thinking about worms made him hungry. He hadn't eaten since he awoke, and the shortened heat lamp secession made him feel tired.

"Yes, sir," Three replied. "We're already looking into it."

"Good. I'll be in the mess if you need me."

Gurjin stood, yawned, and licked his face with his tongue. He tried to show confidence to the bridge crew as he skipped out.

***

The forty-foot-long Tic Tac-shaped probe 41826 knew it was not as smart as Hancear, but it was built by the AI, designed to use its initiative to accomplish its mission. As soon as the probe detected the spikes in energy and the shutdown of engines on the Qhasloi ship, it propelled itself toward the Qhasloi warship using reaction jets. It had only used its passive and optical sensors up to this point. Now it changed its course for a closer look at the intruder. It realized that the Qhasloi ship had stopped its active sensor sweeps. Drone 41826 calculated a new intercept course to get closer to the ship. After a close flyby, it would use its maneuvering jets to get back into the inner system. It calculated the probability of success at .75295. The ever-vigilant drone surmised that the power fluctuations could mean a major malfunction onboard the Qhasloi vessel. It took the probe .342 seconds to make the difficult decision. The drone fired its engines at maximum burn and accelerated to .3 C. It turned its engines off and began using the gas jets to fine tune its trajectory and get close to the enemy ship. It would make a single pass and use all its active sensors. It was going to fly by less than one AU from the enemy ship. Afterward, it would vector toward the large ringed planet to use its gravity to slingshot itself toward the sun and flip for maximum deceleration once it got close to Hancear.

The drone approached the Qhasloi ship. All passive sensors indicated that the warship was adrift. The drone recalculated the probability of success for a closer approach to the ship. Once the ship was within one AU, it still did not detect any active sensors from the Qhasloi ship, whose engines were now cold. Drone 41826 turned on its active sensors and scanned the enemy ship. The drone detected a trail of debris from the damaged ship and rotated itself to get the last visual images as it shot past it. With the enemy ship crippled, the drone decided to risk turning its engines on to return to Hancear faster while the Qhasloi ship was blind. Drone 41826 prepared a data packet dump and aimed its directional transmission antenna toward the Thrultak communications satellite orbiting Uranus. The drone would continue transmitting the data packet intermittently until it received acknowledgment from the satellite or from Hancear.

While Probe 41826 didn't have the capacity to fully analyze the data, it knew what it had transmitted to Hancear was important. It flew at maximum acceleration back home, knowing it had accomplished its mission. It wondered if it would be dismantled, reabsorbed, or used again for a new mission. It really wanted to fly again.

***

Dr. Kareef Khan got to the conference room first and went to the small table where the support staff had set up a brunch bar. He prepared a chai tea and filled his paper plate with a plain turkey sandwich and a pinwheel mozzarella with pesto sandwich. Then he grabbed another sandwich, knowing that this meeting was going to be a long one. After Agent Russell told him of the security breach, he made sure his entire staff changed their passwords. All their laptops were scanned for viruses and other surveillance software. Metzul also installed a Thrultak device to protect their servers. Their own Noah Green was working with the aliens and Agent Hill on a password device for each of his staff. Everyone would receive a tamper proof biometric encryption key that would permit only the holder to turn on their laptops.

For the time being, Dr. Khan compiled all the reports from the various universities, government entities, and private groups that were working with the Thrultak on a secure hard drive. For this meeting each member of the FCG received via messenger an actual printed report. It was up to the FCG to evaluate the various human-alien joint projects. If they saw any issues with the projects or how the humans interacted with the aliens, they would come up with recommendations for better integration of human and Thrultak workers.

Ms. Nelson's door opened quietly.

"I'm glad you're here early," she said. "I didn't have a chance to speak with you privately yet, but I've wanted to say I appreciate how gracious you were when Agents Russell and Hatem told you about my role in the security breach. I want to offer my resignation."

"Nonsense, Agnes. I know your background. I trust you, and this could have happened to anyone," Dr. Khan said as he sipped his sweet chai tea. "Come, join me. Would you like something to drink and eat?"

She smiled as her whole body relaxed. She really liked

working with the group so didn't want to jeopardize its mission.

"Yes, I'll fix myself some lunch. Thank you."

As she piled her plate with food, Colonel Gardner walked in with Connor O'Reilly. They were followed by Dr. Claude Montfaucon and Dr. Jan Kowalczyk, who were arguing with each other as usual. Not long afterward, Dr. Anthony Padget, Dr. Patricia Kim, and Noah Green arrived.

Dr. Khan allowed the team to get food and settle down. He was proud that this group had contributed to a successful end to the war, one that began as a result of misperceptions and unintended actions. He was also pleased the president allowed his group to continue to play such a huge part in the peace process by fostering better relations with the Thrultak.

"If I can have your attention, I have a few remarks before we start. As you all may know, Lieutenant Lopez is now part of the newly formed joint human and Thrultak military force, and her crew is in orbit training as we speak. I printed out her comments on the report for you all. I asked if she could continue working with the FCG when she has time."

He handed out three printed sheets.

"I also want to remind you that some of us will meet privately with the president in eight days to present our report. We'll quickly go around the table for a brief comment on any ongoing areas of concern. Let's keep the meeting informal. Agnes, can you please start us off?"

Since she already had privately discussed her role in the security breach with each of the team members, she felt more relaxed.

"So far the only project that worries me is the Solar Positioning System. The joint NASA, European Space Agency, Korea Aerospace Research Institute, and Japan Aerospace Exploration Agency have fallen behind in their work with the Thrultak. They have completed the design of the satellites and their receivers but need more time to begin full scale production. If we're going to build the next generation of spacecraft for use within any planetary system, we'll need the navigational satellite network."

Dr. Khan just sat back, took some notes, and nodded for

Oliver to start.

"I have a few concerns. The new spacesuit is not ready for full deployment. The prototypes are going to be tested by the Space Legion today. They still need some of the kinks ironed out because human scientists are still learning to use the new Thrultak materials and manufacturing processes. They need to incorporate more armor protection into the suits that will be issued to all space-borne forces. While I'm pleased with some of the weapon systems that are under development, their progress is far too slow for my liking. On the other hand, the Individual Powered Armor Program is progressing well."

Connor smiled as he put his roast beef sandwich down.

"Nothing to really worry about. All the new communications hardware are functioning to specs. The new satellites launched by the Thrultak to replace the ones they destroyed are functioning beyond our wildest dreams. Their ships can place dozens of satellites at a time. For our own personal devices, they are working with several phone companies to come up with a new type of personal phone that will be ready for sale in the next year. They have already started production on devices for government and military use."

Jan looked at Claude and Anthony.

Anthony didn't like to speak in public so he nodded and said, "Go ahead, Jan, you can speak for the three of us."

"We've been focusing on the cultural, social, and psychological impact of the presence of the Thrultak and the Quasloi to human beings as a species. We've noted the rise of alien hate groups among both the left and the right. The most vehement are from the extreme right in every country, like the Aliens Last Movement. Other religious nationalists such as Bishop Jones and his Army of the New Patriotic Sword of Christ Church have used this as a sad way to increase their numbers by playing on the fears of people with lies. The most common lies we've seen are that the aliens are eating people for food. We need to have more empathy-driven, cultural awareness training. We're in the process of putting together programs for workplace training based on shared engaging experiences. We want to have story-driven interactive inclusivity training. We've contacted several university groups and media outlets to start looking for ways to have age-appropriate training programs from preschools up. Humans and the Thrultak must interact more often, even if there is resistance at first."

Anthony raised his hand and added, "I can't stress this enough: We must institute these inclusivity and diversity programs immediately. Not only will this help our own interactions between different racial, ethnic, and language groups, but they are also critical in developing a new kind of society that must consider the inclusion of aliens. Without this we may end up strengthening xenophobic trends already present in human society, thus rendering any effective resistance to the Qhasloi impossible. We have to really encourage the idea of cooperation on a global scale."

"Otherwise," Claude chimed in a very thick French accent, "we'll not survive the Qhasloi while the Thrultak have the option of leaving this system if our alliance fails."

While everyone digested the gravity of the situation, Noah looked at his smartpad and started to read, his nervousness all too apparent.

"I've been tweaking the translation software with Hancear's help. We're working on scientific and engineering vocabulary first. We're also reducing the lag time between speech and translation. The last thing we're beginning to tackle are Thrultak and human idioms and colloquialisms. I've also been working with translators from the United Nations to have this program for other languages."

Noah paused, then added,. "Oh, we're also making progress on further miniaturizing the translation devices."

Noah paused again and after looking at his notes said, "I'm done."

"Can you work on Metzul's device first?" Patricia asked, which got a chuckle from people who'd had their own interactions with the alien. "I've been using part of the studies that Anthony's group has conducted and have been getting different groups to study the impact of the aliens' presence on children and how to incorporate our newfound knowledge into schools as soon as possible. We have to revise all the science books. We're developing a new curriculum for all grades, K through twelve; I've recommended that we implement universal pre-K. The Thrultak insist that they will not work with humans who do not believe in equality, freedom of information, and the freedom to vote and have their voices heard. They insist that part of the education must be that all individuals have the right and obligation to vote on every issue. If certain countries are not willing to open their societies, the Thrultak will not work with them and will help isolate those rogue states. They're also not willing to work with corporations that exploit their workers or pollute the environment. They are making it a requirement that we ensure that everyone has enough food and clean water as one of the conditions for helping us clean the environment. However, there is one nagging issue: Many anti-vaxxers have been promoting false claims and rumors about the dangers of alien science."

Anthony smiled and raised his hand.

"It will take time for some of the older multinationals to get used to this kind of business environment but if they want to survive, they'll change. Our group looked at the way the Thrultak operate. They vote on every main issue using their personal devices. These cannot be hacked or subverted and are monitored by a dedicated group of Thrultak security specialists and Hancear. Some of the votes are time gated, and Hancear counts only the votes that are cast within the allotted time to help their Council act. On other issues the Council asks for a vote to allow them leeway to act without a vote if it's time sensitive. Our group recommends that all countries adopt this kind of system as the new personal device comes online. Each device will act like a smart ID. It will have your social security number, driver's license, voter registration, and criminal record if any, educational qualifications, and other professional licenses."

"Most other countries will not have difficulty implementing a new national ID system because they already have one. But I'm afraid that the United States will have the most difficulty changing to such a system. I personally don't get it. People already have so many IDs in their wallets; it seems easier to just carry one ID," Jan added with a sigh.

"Thank you all for your thoughts. I'll add some of the comments to the written reports. One of the benefits of working with the Thrultak is that once they are committed to a project, they fully fund it and are aggressive about not wasting resources," Dr. Khan said.

"Where are they getting all this money from?" asked Agnes.

"They have a human economic advisory group and a multinational corporation incorporated in Switzerland called the Thrultak Interplanetary Partner Group. It's a conglomerate that has partnered with human corporations, private groups, and local government entities. They are already making huge profits, which is allowing them to pay off their reparations very quickly," replied Kareef.

Anthony opened his eyes wide. "We've seen new garbage and recycling trucks with a TIP logo. Is that them?"

"Yes, the Thrultak are taking over the recycling business around the globe. Their technology is critical to saving our planet and solving the garbage problem. For example, they've increased the recycling efficiency of aluminum from seventy-six to ninety-seven percent. They're also able to recycle all forms of plastic. Their small fusion reactors are clean. They've partnered with local energy grid operators. Just in the United States they've built two power plants to replace old fossil fuel plants. TIP is already one of the richest multilateral corporations in the world."

Claude said, "I'm also happy to announce that the Thrultak have reached an agreement with the French government to dispose of our nuclear waste, dismantle old nuclear reactors, and replace them with cold fusion reactors. One facility is already complete, and there're plans to build three more."

He frowned and added, "A big problem is that OPEC and Russia have complained about the economic loss from such a quick move away from oil and gas. Our group is working on ways to help humans adjust to a fast-changing world and smooth the transition to a new reality and economy."

Kareef finished his cold chai tea and concluded, "Thanks,

everyone, for all your hard work. Anthony and Colonel Gardner, will you be able to attend the meeting with the president in eight days with me to present our findings and help answer any questions she may have?"

Anthony and Oliver made eye contact with each other and nodded together. Oliver stopped gathering his papers.

"We'll be glad to go with you."

***

"Hey boss, should we just bring her in?" asked Agent Doyle, sitting across from Agent Russell's desk.

"No. We need to wait and see if she'll lead us to more co-conspirators," replied Agent Russell as he sat back in his chair in their small office at the Armory.

"We have other branch offices investigating leads generated by our interrogation of Jonas Gant. They need more time to finish tracking all of them down," added Agent Hatem, sitting against the wall with her arms crossed.

"Maybe they gave up and just went into permanent hiding," said Agent Garcia without much conviction.

"No, these people know that our capabilities have been enhanced with Thrultak technology. They're going to be very careful. We'll be lucky if we can trace their communications. They've also been very disciplined about cleaning all the safe houses we've raided in the past."

Agent Russell eyed the folders on his desk and felt like they hit a brick wall.

Agent Hatem grimaced. "Yeah, the last safe house where we were ambushed was cleaned with bleach and DNA remover."

Agent Garcia sat forward in his chair. "What DNA remover? I tried to track down that lead but I'm getting nothing. I'm getting worried, boss."

"A solution of deoxyribonuclease enzymes will destroy trace DNA. Yes, it's very difficult staying this quiet for so long. Whatever they're planning, I think it'll happen soon. However, if nothing happens in ten days, I'll ask Director Thomson and the AG for permission to bring in Assistant Director Braun for questioning. All right, now get back to work, everyone," Agent Russell said to his agents.

CHAPTER 15

Lieutenant Lee looked around the large indoor area in the Armory. Armed Air Force guards had delivered twenty crates of equipment for today's flight. He thought that they would be wearing their regular navy-blue jumpsuits with the bulky old human spacesuits they'd been wearing for the past month during their training. Normal human spacesuits were not comfortable, and every crew member found it difficult to do anything that required fine motor skills. But today they were all issued skintight white jumpsuits with attached feet and gloves and a skintight hoodie base layer to manage heat and moisture. Each suit had attachment rings on the wrists, neck, and just above the ankles. It looked like a very thin wet suit with a small backpack and waist belt, but not too tight.

"Hey, how does yours fit, David?" asked Danny.

"Like a glove. I can't believe how soft the material is," replied David in amazement.

Fetu was on the floor attaching soft boots with smooth soles with several hidden magnetic areas on the heel and balls of the feet.

"It was hard getting my head to squeeze through, but it fits well even with the diapers."

Everyone called them diapers but officially, they were Maximum Absorbency Garments.

"They should all fit well. After all, they were custom-tailored to your measurements. For this mission you'll have a soft bubble helmet to keep the suit pressurized. The hard helmet is still under development. For today you'll only use the soft bubble. Don't let the thinness fool you; it can take a hit from a

50 cal. without breaking it," Colonel Gardner said to the crew.

"Is there an operating manual?" asked Mark who was having issues getting into the suit.

"No, it's just like wearing regular clothes," Gardner assured them as he looked at the skeptical faces around him. "Whatever controls you're used to have been slaved to the smartpad and your HUD via voice command. If the main life support fails you, just turn on the backup through your small smartpad attached to your wrist. If that fails you have a small backup control unit on your belt, which has a backup power for two hours. Your belt is also equipped with a small carbon dioxide scrubber made from an advanced metal-organic framework, which should keep you alive long enough for search and rescue to retrieve you. There's nothing else to figure out; it's really like wearing regular clothes. Patching the suit in case of a leak is exactly the same procedure we've been practicing. You just slap the self-adhesive patch on the suit. The new adhesive was developed in a lab using barnacles. The power in the suit should be good for at least ten days without the need for recharging. To recharge, you just hang them in your lockers."

"What about protection from micro meteorites outside the craft?" asked Asher.

The colonel made sure he had everyone's attention.

"Look, this material is made from a fabric that has been woven with a carbon tube fiber created molecule by molecule with a non-Newtonian fluid sandwiched between the two layers. It can stop Thrultak cannon fire. The gel is also self-sealing if punctured. The eggheads in Area 51 developed this material in conjunction with the Thrultak. The fabric has been tested against human and Thrultak weapons. Having Hancear has shortened development and manufacturing time for all the new equipment. The suits are very safe. For combat they're developing hardened plates that will attach to the suits. Regular body armor for military and police use have been developed using the same technology. I've also heard that for the regular infantry they're making real powered armor."

Julie looked at Sandy, who was sitting on the floor hugging her body.

"Hey, are you OK?"

Sandy turned her red face to Julie.

"Yes, but this suit doesn't hide anything. It's very tight."

"You look fine. If anyone says anything let me know and I'll set them straight." Julie said as she looked down.

The suit was comfortable, a little like her motorcycle racing suit, but left little to the imagination.

Colonel Gardner said, "Because of security concerns, we couldn't issue these till today. We'll be testing your deep strike capability and your ability to perform as a recce unit. But for future missions we'll have extra armor pieces that can be attached to the suit as needed. Good luck, everyone. In the future we're also going to get our own powered armor as they come on line. I'll be monitoring you from here."

***

For this first run, Ordortor lay on his stomach in the control section with an acceleration couch in case the gravity generator failed. He had the option of wearing his powered armor if he needed it. His human friends were in the back in their own drone control pods. They had insisted on using call signs, and Jurgen named him Wizard.

"Okay, everyone, get ready for acceleration."

Julie didn't mind her call sign of Gunfighter, but she didn't like the crew's name, Blackbeard, that Fetu came up with. Even Danny voted against her ideas of calling the crew Yankees or Jets. So everyone outside of the team called them by their team name, and Julie was Blackbeard One. Within the team each member used their call signs.

She replied, "Gunfighter reading you 5 by 5."

Julie felt silly calling herself Gunfighter; she preferred Blackbeard 1.

After everyone else had checked in, Sandy's voice cut through the comms. "This is Big Guns. I'm ready."

"Roger that," replied Wizard.

For this exercise Ordortor was going to fly around the Earth's moon and cut his engines after a 100g acceleration when they entered the dark side. Everyone had hoped that by cutting the power behind the moon the small craft's energy signature would be masked while it approached the planet. At the planned speed it would only take the craft two hours to get into an insertion orbit where they would launch their drones. Then Ordortor would decelerate and get into a stable high orbit and let part of the crew fly the drones to Tetepare Island, the largest uninhabited island in the South Pacific. Once there, the drones would be flown to Otterburn Army Training Estate in northern England to fire on a marked building and two vehicles. The drones would fly at low altitude toward England, and when they were fifty miles off shore they would submerge for an underwater approach. They would travel submerged until they were two hundred yards from the shore. From there they would fly close to the ground to the firing range, make one attack run, and climb to orbit for recovery.

"This is Wizard. All systems are go. Blackbeard is ready for initial takeoff into orbit from the Armory."

The larger ship had picked up the crew at 5 a.m. and was hovering over the building.

"Hello, Wizard. This is Drake. I'll be your controller for this mission. Blackbeard, you are cleared for launch. Nothing in your airspace, and your initial orbital path is clear. Clock is running. Good luck."

"Copy that. Thanks, Drake, I've initiated computer control for launch. I have T minus one minute. Are you named after a type of mythical creature?"

Ordortor took this time to recheck all his controls and got comfortable for this short flight. It was also part of the new Council orders to pick up any space garbage for recycling if any were in his direct flight path. The humans paid the Thrultak to clean up any space junk, which also offset the rapidly shrinking reparations bill.

Drake's calm voice was heard by the entire crew. He began the traditional countdown.

"No, Wizard, I'm named after the explorer. Ten, nine, eight, seven, six, five, four, three, two, one."

He just didn't mention that he got the call sign because he had gotten lost during his survival training in the Air Force.

The launch was anticlimactic; the crew didn't feel a thing.

The craft remained silent, and there was no feeling of motion as they shot straight up from the Armory. At twenty thousand feet it produced the first of many sonic booms as the craft shot straight up into low orbit. Then, as it entered into high orbit, it began its main acceleration to the moon.

***

"Hey Julie, I'm kinda nervous about meeting the president next week," Sandy said through a private channel. "Is Danny coming?"

"No, it's just the two of us and a couple of people from the FCG," Julie replied, trying not to think about the itch on her right calf. She tried scratching it, but the suit got in the way.

Their conversation was cut short by a fit of coughing and choking. Julie looked at her HUD and saw that it was coming from Fetu, whose call sign was Feta because no one could pronounce his name correctly. Jergen's call sign was Kindermadchen or Nanny because he was always looking out for everyone's well-being and treated everyone's minor scrapes as the crew's medic.

"Are you ok?" said Jurgen.

"Yes, I'm fine. It's just gas," Fetu replied.

Everyone laughed but Jurgen didn't get it.

"I detect no gas leak in your suit."

Asher, whose call sign was Beaver, laughed. He earned that moniker by being the first to volunteer for every assignment.

"It was a foist," said Asher, which was met with more laughter from the entire team.

Jurgen was still confused. "I do not detect any problems with Fetu's suit."

Commander Hill, or Pappy, the designated leader for this mission, chuckled. "He pooped his pants. Now knock it off and focus on the mission. We are about to come around the dark side of the moon."

"*Ja ein furz.* I get it; it's not funny," Jurgen said in a serious tone.

***

Colonel Gardner was sitting at a desk in the Armory's new secure video conference room with several high-definition monitors arrayed in a hundred-and-sixty-degree arc in front of several chairs. Thrultak technology allowed them to set up a fully functional command center anywhere. On the monitors each participant was life size. However, there was a growing comm lag as the team sped away from Earth. General Ross was there with General Makro, General Miguel Angel Bienvenida from the Marine Corps, the new Chairman of the Joint Chiefs, and Dr. Khan, who was coordinating the technical aspects of this mission. The United Nations had their own monitoring station in New York.

Hancear, who was also present but did not have a visual representation, reported, "So far the mission is a success. I was able to detect the ship accelerating toward the moon but after it emerged from the dark side the lack of energy signature made it difficult to detect."

"Their orbital drop to Tetepare Island was smooth, and the attack run on Otterburn was flawless," General Ross added in her new navy-blue Legion uniform. "What do you think, General Makro?"

"I agree," said Makro, turning light blue with excitement.

"If nothing else we can use these Privateers as a deep reconnaissance unit, in space or on land, alongside the regular Legion and our own regular ground forces," added General Bienvenida.

"Good. Dr. Khan, Hancear, any thoughts on the performance of the new equipment and the modified spacecraft?" asked Colonel Gardner.

"I was pleased with the performance of the new equipment," Dr. Khan said with a large grin on his face. "There were no issues."

"I agree. There were no unforeseen issues, as expected," Hancear noted.

"Good. We'll schedule another test run after we get the other equipment delivered. The other privateer groups will begin testing other systems. After we've standardized the equipment, we'll organize some joint exercises with the 1st Regiment of the Space Legion. Thank you for attending the meeting. I'll schedule another training secession in the near future.

Goodbye."

Colonel Gardner disconnected his conference call and smiled. It looked like things were going well and that the whole EDF was going to work. The Legion's first regiment of five hundred men and women defeated two full human armored divisions in a wargame. The test proved that the new joint Combined Arms Human/Alien Force was not just good in theory but a deadly force that would change human warfare.

***

Metlob felt weary and lay on the ground while he waited for the Council members. His skin was almost black with fatigue. Since the peace accords the Council had been busy doing their best to integrate with the more democratic elements of the planet.

Hancear notified Metlob in a soft low voice. "Xeegi, the economic councilor, is here with Baxo, the medical advisor, Gwzoik, the cultural councilor, and Makro. Borlinn, the arts councilor, was on the planet organizing an exhibition of Thrultak arts in New York City."

"Come in, my friends," Metlob said as he turned a light blue, happy to see his fellow Council members, all of whom had worked hard to make the peace with humans a success. "I know Hancear has compiled a detailed report from each of you, but please give a short highlight of your progress."

After the reports had been made, Metlob thanked them.

"I'm pleased with the progress so far, and we'll work with the humans but we must be wary and protect ourselves and our people. We cannot perish because we failed to anticipate potential adversaries and duplicity. We'll meet again soon."

Without ceremony the Council members left for their own chambers, and Metlob was left alone to rest a little. He spoke into the empty space.

"Hancear, our existence has answered the Fermi paradox for the humans, and because the Qhasloi has already discovered this system we cannot hide it from them. Do you think we should act alone in our self-interest or work with the humans?"

"I think it's best to work with the humans. They already have a good understanding of science and technology, and when faced with a common enemy most humans could become very good allies. I also think that a new Homeship with a combined human and Thrultak crew should be launched to create a new home world in case Earth should fall to the Qhasloi. This may be the only safeguard against slavery and/or extinction."

"Hancear, I'm also concerned that we have allied ourselves to the West and have ignored Africa and Asia as a whole. Is there anything we can do to remedy this?"

"I'm not sure," Hancear replied. "We are working with the United Nations to help the nations in Africa and Asia. However, in the Middle East, Africa, and Asia, there are groups actively engaged in combat. The UN is reluctant to intervene with their limited resources. In Asia we've developed good relations with many countries except for India and China who seem to distrust the West and us. In Europe we've had significant difficulties with the Russians and their allies."

"Thank you, Hancear. Please let the human scientists you're working with know about building a Homeship for humans and Thrultak in case our defense of this planet fails. I also approve of the iron nickel asteroid you've found for building a human colony ship. The two-hundred-mile diameter makes it perfect. As we hollow out the asteroid we can add to its thickness and have a three three-hundred-foot-thick iron reinforced hull for protection. What is your opinion on the new Legion, and the idea of capturing the Qhasloi ship to reverse engineer their hyperdrive?"

Metlob went to his desk and began eating some fresh blue berries from a small bowl. He cherished each bite. The long journey on the Homeship was necessary, but there was no room for fresh food or personal companion animals. During the waking periods out of stasis they only had nutritional paste and water. Now that many of his people were adopting Earth animals as pets, Metlob asked them only to make sure the pets were not endangered on Earth and were commonly used as pets by humans. Because one enterprising technician had wanted to bring a shaggy Highland cow on board, he also asked them to make sure they were not too big as space was still limited in the huge but crowded Homeship.

He opened the door to the cage for his own two short-haired guinea pigs and gave them some blueberries. He'd put them in the habitat for the meeting; otherwise, the councilors would have been too busy playing with them and wouldn't have focused on important matters. He formed tendrils and placed it on the smaller brown and white guinea pig. As it ate, he sent it a soothing message. The black eyes looked up, and the small male let out a squeak and began hopping up and down. When it finally stopped it ran closer to Metlob and rubbed his nose against the pod with the tendrils and licked him. Metlob shuddered and turned light blue with happiness.

"Who's a good boy?"

Not to be left out, the larger beige and slate male came over to touch his tendrils and rub his nose, licking them.

"If we have to run again, we'll refurbish the Homeship and make it bigger, and we'll try to bring some of our own small companions out of stasis," he said to himself.

Hancear waited until Metlob was finished giving snacks to the little guys and used a polite chime to bring the leader back to the conversation.

"The Legion is starting to take shape, and once we've perfected the structure, we'll be able to scale up the number of independent regiments. However, the Thrultak must have a goal as a species so that we can act in economic, political, and military spheres. Second, all Council members must continue to educate themselves in the sciences and the arts. Third, if we are to fight, we need trusted allies who are willing adopt novel strategies and incorporate new technologies. However, we have to be wary of traitors. Fourth, logistics and support elements should be given priority. We need to maintain our supply lines when we fight the Qhasloi. Do not underestimate them or give them too much credit for their initial victory against the Thrultak. We ought to promote high moral values in our warriors. When we do meet the enemy on the battlefield, we should remain flexible and have a concentration of force so that even if we are outnumbered overall, we can have local superiority of force. Lastly, we must maintain security over our communications and our plans."

Metlob thought about how simple life was before the Qhasloi.

"I'm in agreement with your analysis. How is the investigation with Agent Russell going?"

Hancear replied, "Agent Russell and Agent Hatem have made progress but they have not uncovered the full scope of the conspiracy or its main objective. I'll maintain my vigilance and report as soon as any new developments occur."

CHAPTER 16

"How many times do we have to do this, Sarge?" asked Sadie, a former London Metropolitan Police officer.

She was in charge of the newly constructed self-learning AI robot dog named Lancelot. The robot had to be shown how to do everything, like a child. She was still learning how to use it and, like all the other Dirty Raiders, was frustrated. She was not particularly fond of the crew's name but she had been outvoted.

"Easy there, Porter. We'll do this as many times as we need to so we can get it perfect," replied Jamol Smith, who was officially without rank.

They had been trying to approach the Thrultak Homeship orbiting the sun without getting detected but had failed for the twentieth time.

"Ladies and gentlemen, due to technical difficulties we'll be heading back to our base in Cologne Germany," Noktor said from the cockpit.

Jamol felt his frustrations growing. Only three days ago they field-tested their new main small arms. The projectile rifle was not fit for combat. The caseless 7 mm rounds were exceptional at long range, and the ammo was lighter than a traditional 5.56. The weapons were light and did a lot of damage but they were too delicate; more than half broke during field tests. When he deliberately threw two out of a moving flyer from high altitude, both broke. The Thrultak techs argued that the weapons could be replaced easily but, to her credit, Captain Schmidt argued that they wouldn't be carrying enough spare parts out in the field. They could also face supply issues. Finally, Hancear intervened and ensured that the next prototypes would be more robust. When the Raiders failed to get close to the Homeship again, it created a lot of stress in a unit of high-speed motivated individuals.

Captain Schmidt listened to the exchange and the general demeanor of the Raiders, then whispered to Smith, "Semper Gumby, sarge. Semper Gumby,"

"Oohrah. Got it," Smith said with as much enthusiasm as he could muster.

Yes, staying flexible was important, but cooped up and sweating in an alien tin can be grating on everyone.

"There'll be no Semper I from me, Cap."

James was experienced enough to know when to just follow orders and not take any personal initiative.

Schmidt turned on her crew-wide channel and addressed the entire group.

"Listen up, everyone. I know we've had some setbacks but we're here at the beginning of a new type of unit, and we're here to learn what works and what doesn't. So please let's stay sharp and focused. I'd rather figure this out now than go tits up later because we didn't know what doesn't work."

***

"Hey Dad, I know you're going to see the president on Sunday. Can Dalia and I go with you? And Dalia's mom?"

Trevor wanted to see the helicopters and the president's armored car, the Beast.

Anthony reflected for a moment; the trip was in six days, and he already had a security clearance, as did Patricia.

"I'll ask, only because this is not a meeting at the White House. We're going to her farmhouse. But you have to promise me you'll behave and listen to orders. OK?"

"Yes, I promise. I won't go wandering around or touch anything I'm not supposed to," Trevor said, smiling.

***

A few fat flies circled above the table in General Hermann's room, which was piled high with discarded take-out food containers. He'd been cooped up long enough that he had gone nose blind to the rotting odors. His orders were to stay hidden; Agent Ambrose Hall told him not to turn the cell phone on until this Saturday, the day of the mission. Five more days; General Hermann had never gone this long without satisfying his sexual needs. He looked at the dead smartphone on his night table, closed his eyes, and took another swig from the vodka bottle next to the phone. He could wait. *When this is over, I'll be able to call a few of the girls I used to see before all this happened,* he told himself. *God dammed aliens ruined my life.*

***

"Okay, we have only four more days till we launch Operation Hidden Redemption. Let's go over the plan again," Ambrose said, standing over the 1/35th scale model of the president's compound. There were three buildings on the twenty-acre site. The main farmhouse was a two-story, four-bedroom French Country home with three bathrooms, a den, an office, a family room, and a kitchen. There was an unfinished basement. Next to the house on the north side was a shed that was used for the storage of tools. Across from the farmhouse about two hundred yards was a thirty-foot by forty-foot pole barn.

"Gideon, start us off," Ambrose said in a low voice.

Gideon pulled on his long dark brown beard.

"Two days before Redemption, Ambrose will station himself four hundred meters south of the farmhouse at the edge of a wooded area. He'll check on the prepositioned truck and make sure that the camo net is secure. The new camo will hide him from visual and thermal scans as well as IR scans. Recheck the improvised explosives near the bridge. Increase the monitoring of local and federal law enforcement channels."

The whole squad had memorized the plan and rehearsed as much as possible. Each person knew every aspect of the operation.

Hiram pushed his hands through his salt and pepper hair.

"On the day of Redemption all the support elements will be contacted and given the go sign to 'Defeat the enemies of God.' We wait for the counter sign: 'Set his children free.' After the proper countersign is given, we'll recheck all weapons systems and the status of the helicopter for extraction."

They had bribed a life flight helicopter pilot, who was also a true patriot, to prep the nearby Life Net Air 2 helicopter for emergency extraction. If that failed, he rented another as a backup, which was stored near the extraction zone. If someone requested the helicopter, their pilot will say it was out of service due to mechanical problems.

"Next, we'll drive around to drop our own electronic communications jamming pods. Those alien lovers will be surprised when all their comms cease to work."

Jeremiah had worked with Ambrose before in the Secret Service and smiled at his friend. He couldn't wait to get the show on the road.

"Wait for the abort signal from Ambrose. If it doesn't come, we are good to go. Gideon, Dinah, and Hiram will drive to the infiltration point, hide the SUV, and march in at night using the new camo and night vision. They'll remain hidden for the planned assault on the farmhouse. Jeremiah will get in position with the remote detonator near the only bridge access across the small river. After the explosion Jeremiah will make his way to the farmhouse to provide support. At around 7 a.m. Chester's group will attack the convoy after the bridge is blown. The president will be isolated, and we'll have an hour window before a reaction force and Marine One can get to the farmhouse."

Dinah stood and looked at the model. "Only Cadillac One should make it through the ambush zone. If any other vehicle make it to the farmhouse, we'll engage them immediately with anti-tank rockets while Ambrose takes out the snipers. If the target remains in Cadillac One, we'll hit it with anti-tank rockets. If that doesn't crack it open, we have a custom-made shaped charge that will breach the armor and kill the occupants. Once the target is neutralized, we'll exfil to the truck and drive to the helicopter." Dinah smiled and looked at Ambrose for approval.

Ambrose smiled back. "If both the helicopters are compromised, we'll continue by road and separate. Let's pray."

When everyone put their heads down, Ambrose began.

"Lord, give us the strength to do your will. Bless this operation with your might and your armor. Amen."

"Amen," came a chorus of voices.

***

"Portland is your last stop on the West Coast. You'll give a speech to the major aerospace and high-tech industry executives and tour the new joint human Thrultak plant gearing up to produce the first joint human Thrultak craft. After Portland we'll stop in Las Vegas and make an appearance at a fundraiser and attend a Raiders' game. You'll have a day off, and we'll fly to Denver on Friday morning to attend a fundraiser luncheon and tour several newly revitalized aerospace and defense plants around Denver," Emmett read from his notes.

"Then to the farmhouse. I can't wait. This has been grueling. At least I'll get a week off soon. Make sure to include the progress on the EDF in my regular reports. I also want a progress report on the Qhasloi. Why haven't we heard more?" President Gallo asked as she looked up at Emmett from the report she was reading.

"We're keeping an eye on the enemy ship with our telescopes, and they aren't doing anything. The Thrultak are keeping an eye on them as well," Emmett replied.

"Yes, we're monitoring the sector of space where the Qhasloi have been detected but they've been drifting since the Thrultak first detected them. The FCG with NASA and the European Space Agency are dedicating the newly rebuilt Arecibo observatory and the refurbished Hubbell Space Telescope with Thrultak sensors to monitor the Qhasloi. We're waiting for their demands." Emmett folded his paper.

"You look tired. Try to get some rest before we land. I'll have something for you to eat sent from the galley."

"Right, give me the next speech, and get me a ham and cheese sandwich."

"Any chips?"

"Yes, thanks."

***

Gurjin paced around the small office and felt his frustration growing. He remained calm and tried not to let any emotion seep into his voice.

"Why aren't we underway already? We're just drifting around here like garbage."

Two spoke in a gentle and nonchallenging manner. "Captain, I have four work gangs working constantly to finish the repairs on the cooling system. We had to wait for the 3D manufacturing plants to complete the parts we needed for the repairs. Now two of the five plants have malfunctioned, and the other three are down for maintenance. We have only one 3D plant producing parts."

"Give me a progress report every ten cycles. At this rate we'll be drifting out here beyond the cloud of icy objects and comets."

Gurjin was glad that Two couldn't see his hands tremble with anger.

"Yes, my Captain."

***

"I can't wait to meet the president," Dalia said as she looked at the parts of their submarine project.

"Yeah, we'll see her in two days. You think she'll be interested in our science project?" Trevor asked, trying to glue in the two small remote-controlled syringes inside of their submarine.

The syringes would act as their submarine's ballast and allow them to control the depth of their model of the turtle submarine.

"I bet we don't even get to meet her," Dalia said, trying not to look disappointed.

"Yeah, you're probably right. But we'll get a good look at the president's Cadillac and some of the armored cars."

Trevor made sure the superglue was set before he removed the tweezers and took off his magnifying visor.

"I think we're done," Trevor said as he examined his handiwork.

"Nice. I'll take it home tonight to paint and reassemble it. After it's dry we can test it next week," Dalia said.

"Great, I think we're riding together to Poughkeepsie and meeting the president's motorcade there. We'll get to see Marine One."

"I wanted to see Air Force One," said Daila in a disappointed tone.

"I think they'll land at JFK and take Marine One to

Poughkeepsie."

Trevor smiled at the thought of spending the entire day with Dalia and her mom.

"It'll be fun, but I doubt we'll get close to anything important," said Dalia as she packed up their project into a sponge-lined plastic bin.

***

Two more days till Operation Hidden Redemption was set to start. He didn't know what exactly was going to happen, but the Bishop assured him that after Operation Hidden Redemption there would be a new world for the true believers. Chester had stayed up all night praying and asking the Lord for guidance. He made his peace with the Lord and was going to spend the entire day in prayer and fasting.

***

General Hermann took out his old Air Force uniform and tried to put it on. He struggled to button his pants, and he couldn't button his coat shut. He had gained weight from the drinking and lack of exercise. He had originally planned to wear his uniform during the operation but took off the jacket and threw it on the floor with self-loathing. He looked at the dormant phone once again. He wasn't supposed to turn it on till tomorrow morning but after he failed to fit into his uniform, he wanted to have a woman more than ever. Before he knew it, he turned it on and was using it to search for an escort service and arranged for an outcall service. The Bishop had given him plenty of money, and he wouldn't need it any more after tonight.

***

Vice President Landreneau was sitting at a large dinner table at a private club with six prominent Wall Street financers and two Russian oligarchs. He trusted each of them and knew they were not happy with the current administration. His aide, James, had swept the room for surveillance, and the exterior was cordoned off be his hand-picked Secret Service detail.

"Gentlemen, by tomorrow evening I'll be the new president. I want to know I can count on your full support."

The room erupted in loud applause, and Michael sat down, smiling.

Henry heard the applause and smiled as well. He would ask the president to appoint him to a cabinet level post, something minor to start. *Henry Perez, United States Secretary of the Interior.* He liked the sound of that. Yes, things would be very different by tomorrow evening.

***

Bishop Jones looked at Maggie's naked ass. It was bruised from last night when he got carried away. Lilith tried to intervene, and he had slapped her as well. They were obedient today after he locked them in their room without food or water. After he used them both, he allowed them to eat and drink.

"Maggie, make sure the new message goes out to our people today, and get ready to broadcast the second message as soon as we get word from Brother Ambrose."

Tomorrow after the success of Operation Hidden Redemption, he would be free to preach again and walk among his worshipers.

"Yes," she said with downcast, tear-filled eyes. "May we leave and get ready for the day?"

She wanted to get away from this monster, but how?

The Bishop didn't notice the tears or trembling hands.

"Yes. Get cleaned up, and we can have more fun later."

***

Metzul was in a small neighborhood pet store looking at hamsters, gerbils, guinea pigs, and ferrets. He had seen some of the other Thrultak with small pets and wanted one as well. The pet store owner had been apprehensive when the first Thrultak customers came to the store weeks ago. At first he couldn't distinguish between the various aliens but now he realized each had distinctive features like the color of their eyestalks and even the way they used their chromatophores. Each also had distinctive kleptoplasty fronds. Now he was used to their large bulk squeezing gracefully into his store. The Thrultak represented potential new customers for his small shop. In the past few months, the aliens had bought numerous pets and supplies from him.

Metzul heard the simple alarm from his smartpad and let out a squeak as he turned blue with yellow spots. He was excited and worried at the same time. He said goodbye to the pet store owner and dialed Lucas's number while he produced six legs and began to run toward the Armory.

Lucas was just getting his first bite of chicken shawarma when his modified smartpad made a distinctive steam train whistle sound, Metzul's priority signal. He took another bite of his succulent shawarma and read the message: "One of the phones just activated. I'm headed back to the office."

Lucas typed: "On my way. Meet you there."

He slung his backpack on, stood, and took a last sip of his lemonade. He didn't want to carry his sandwich back so he took a large bite and dumped the rest into the trash bin. He started a slow jog from the food cart toward the Armory. Halfway down the block he started running at full speed with his phone on speaker.

"This is one of the one hundred phones purchased at the same time as the one given to Ms. Nelson. I set up a program and have been actively monitoring all the numbers. This one just turned on. We've tracked its location to a motel in Poughkeepsie just off of 9W. There have been several calls made to various escort agencies," Metzul said, turning light blue and happy that his monitoring provided them with a lead.

Lucas caught Agent Hatem just as she was preparing to leave early to go to the range.

"Nice job, guys."

She speed-dialed Agent Russell, who picked up immediately.

"Hello, Agent Hatem, what is it?"

He was finishing his jog around the Armory track. After a shower he wanted to finish looking at some of the reports from the surveillance teams assigned to monitor the vice president and Assistant Director Braun.

"One of the phones we've been monitoring just turned on, and we have a location."

"Are you in the tech room? I'll be right up," Agent Russell said as he headed to the stairs.

"How long till we can get a helicopter here?" Agent Hatem asked.

Russell hurried and hoped that this was the break they were

waiting for.

"I can get a chopper here in an hour. Or better yet, we can get a flyer."

Agent Hatem grimaced and did some quick mental math. The helicopter would take at least an hour to fly up to Poughkeepsie.

"They might be gone by then."

Agent Russell's phone went dead, and there was silence. He must be in the elevator.

Hatem jumped when she felt the alien's tendril touch her arm. "You scared me."

Metzul turned slightly purple in sadness. "I'm sorry but I may have a solution to your distress."

Sahar smiled. "You just startled me, that's all. What is it?"

"I could ask Ordortor if he could fly you there. His crew has their small craft on standby at the old Fort Washington Park Soccer Field, which has been converted to a secure military landing zone."

"How long would it take to fly a hundred miles?" Agent Hatem was already smiling.

Metzul paused and waved his eyestalks in deep thought. "I'm not sure but at average cruising speed you could be there in twenty minutes, less if you ask him to hurry."

"Make it happen, and get your gear. Lucas, get Jim and Andrew ready, and grab your tactical gear."

At that moment Russell rushed in, slightly out of breath.

"I can get the chopper here in half an hour."

"No need, Mark, we're going to hitch a ride with Ordortor. He was already scheduled for a training flight with his crew tonight. There's room for at least ten more."

"I'll get you those warrants and arrange for backup with the state police. I'll try to get an FBI tactical team" Agent Russell said, then sat down and wiped the sweat from his brow.

"We can't wait for the tactical team. We don't have time to waste," Agent Hatem said. "I'm going to get my gear. Have Ordortor pick us up on the roof."

Agent Russell stood and said, "Let's roll. I'll meet you upstairs and get backup rolling as well."

As the group piled out of the office, Agent Russell had a

strange feeling that he was forgetting something important.

****

Danny stood by the open hatch of the smaller Thrultak craft as Mark led his motley crew onto it. Coco was at Danny's side, sniffed at every new person, and looked up at Danny, waiting for a command. The small craft had plenty of room with only five of the blue-suited Blackbeards on board.

The two groups stood facing each other. Danny pointed to the empty seats.

"You can sit anywhere or stand. You won't feel a thing. We don't have everyone today so we have room for all of you. We were just going to practice dropping our ground attack drones. Just wave when I call your name. That's Tatyana, Jurgen, and David up front. Over to my left is Fetu and Mark. Oh, I almost forgot: This is Coco."

She was stepping on Danny's right foot to remind him she was there as well.

Agent Russell was dressed in grey tactical combat fatigues and had a belt with a sidearm. He pointed to the agents, left to right.

"That's Agent Hatem, Agent Doyle, Agent Garcia, Agent Hill, and Metzul. How long till we take off?"

Danny grinned. "We're already in the air. Let's get to know one another, and tell me how we can help."

Russell let the others sit and relax while he took Danny aside.

"I have the state and local police ready to set up roadblocks if we need. They'll be able to provide backup. An FBI tactical team is on the way as well. Can you provide surveillance for us?"

"Fetu, can you handle it?"

"Yes," Fetu said. "Give me the coordinates or the address."

He lay on his couch buckled in. Afterward, he turned on three different monitors and put on a clear visor as he launched a small surveillance drone, which immediately sped away from their craft.

Agent Russell walked up and turned on his phone. "This is the address of the motel and the Google Map location."

The drone sped ahead and produced a series of sonic booms

across Westchester County.

Danny turned his head and spoke into his mike.

"Wizard, what's our ETA?"

"We're eleven minutes out. Do you want me to go faster?"

Danny turned to Russell. "ETA is eleven minutes. Do you want to go faster?"

"No. Metzul, is the phone still on and in the same location?"

Metzul looked at his smartpad. "Yes, the phone has not moved. Wait, I'm getting an incoming call to that number. I'll put it on speaker."

"Hey baby, I was told you want to have a good time. How long did you want me to stay?" asked a female voice.

"I want someone for the whole night," answered a male voice.

"That's going to cost you. Are you law enforcement?"

"No, how much?"

"Five hundred an hour, and cash only. Two thousand for the night," said a sultry female voice.

"Okay, I'm at the Poughkeepsie Motel off 9W. Room 342."

"I'll call you when I get there. Bye."

Fetu spoke up. "I've gone subsonic, I'm now over the target."

He adjusted on of the monitors to give everyone a view.

"Here's the thermal view, and this is the room where the phone is located."

He split the monitor into two video feeds and highlighted Room 342 in green.

"There's only one person in there."

Agent Russell dialed the number for the state police. "Hello, this is Agent Russell. Can you have your officers stay out of visual range and stop any cars going to the motel? We'll stage at the park-and-ride nearby."

Tatyana came closer to Russell and said, "Hi, I remember you from the University."

"Hello. Nice to see you again. What is it?"

"You know we can transfer all your communications through the comm link on board so you'll be able to talk to the officers on the street and their command through your phone. I've traced the phone numbers, and the woman is on the way to the motel," said Tatyana.

"Wow, that was fast." Agent Russell didn't hide his surprise.

A calm voice through hidden speakers said, "We've arrived, and I'm holding at twelve thousand meters."

Russell asked, "Can you take us down into that park-and-ride near the motel?"

Fetu highlighted a parking area near the motel but out of its direct line of sight.

Odortor turned red with orange stripes. He felt relief after each successful flight. The craft silently dropped to the parking area and landed on its extended belly supports. The passengers felt nothing as Danny opened the hatch with the controls on his smartpad attached to his wrist.

There was a marked state police SUV waiting at the lot. The trooper came up to the opening of the craft with wide eyes.

"I never thought I would see one of these things up close. Who's in charge?" asked Officer John Lewis.

"I'm Special Agent Russell; we have a suspect in the motel wanted for questioning related to a potential terrorist conspiracy."

Agent Hatem came up. "We've intercepted a phone call, and the suspect is waiting for a female escort. Can you stop the car and bring her here?"

Fetu's voice came over Russell's phone. "I've located the phone that made the call to our suspect. She's in a white 2018 Kia Sportage on Route 299 eastbound approaching North Chodikee Lake Road. The car has New York plates JKP 2348. The phone and car belong to a Mary Keller, age twenty-eight years."

Officer Lewis walked a few steps away, contacted his dispatch, and asked for the intercept.

Dispatch replied, "Receiving you, 532. Cars 987 and 31 will intercept."

Agent Russell interrupted, "Can you bring the woman here?"

"Roger. This is 532. Can you bring the suspect here to the park-and-ride?"

The dispatcher came back quickly. "No problem, 532. Will confirm with 987."

"Roger."

Officer Lewis then turned to Russell and said, "They'll be here soon."

Agent Hatem pulled Russell aside.

"Look, it's only one guy. Let's not risk getting into a gunfight with a no-knock entry."

The older agent in charge looked at her. "I don't know if I like what you're about to suggest."

"I can take the escort's place, get in there, and take him down. Besides, you guys will be there," Agent Hatem said with a smile.

"Okay, let's go over this with the rest of the agents."

Russell motioned her to follow and gathered the crew.

"Agent Hatem is going to take the young lady's place and gain entry. She'll initiate takedown as soon as she enters. Jim, you and Andrew will be immediate backup so get ready to position yourself before she gets to the door. Lucas, you and Metzul secure the nearest stairwell. Metzul, do you have a weapon?"

Metzul's four eyestalks popped up in excitement. "I was given a new stunner."

Lucas looked fascinated. "Do you know how to use it?"

"Yes, it has a range of thirty feet or you can touch it against the skin. It works through light clothing. It disrupts the neural pathways. I've been meaning to ask, is it common to pay cash for companionship?"

Lucas made a mental note to ask more about what else the Thrultak had.

Feeling awkward about the other question he said, "Ask Agent Hatem about the companionship. I'll be with you so don't zap me."

Danny and the rest of the Blackbeards except Fetu came out of the craft. Danny reached the FBI agents.

"Any changes, Blackbeard 7?"

"No, the target hasn't moved. I'll tell you if there's any change."

"Copy that."

He then turned to Mark and said, "What do you want us to do?"

"I'm not sure you guys should even be here," Agent Hatem said, looking at Coco and the rest of the crew.

"Under our charter signed by most of the Earth's governments, this joint force has the legal authority to operate inside of the borders of each country. Even the non-signatories will contribute to help fund the EDF," Tatyana said.

"We're not like the CIA or any spec ops unit that cannot operate inside the US. Looks like our guest is here."

Danny pointed as a squad car pulled up with a white Kia right behind.

"Just hold tight, and let us handle it," Agent Russell answered.

A lieutenant in the State Police took out a young blonde woman out of his unmarked SUV and marched her to the group.

"I'm Special Agent Russell. Thanks for picking her up."

"I'm Lieutenant Harrison; I was told by the Superintendent to do everything you ask. What's this all about anyway?"

"We're investigating domestic terrorists who had connections to the attacks on the University of Maryland and other facilities just prior to the peace accords," Agent Russell said as he looked at her.

"Young lady, what's your name? If you help us, we'll let you go."

"My name is Lexi, and I haven't done nothing."

Agent Hatem was already looking through her handbag. She grabbed her wallet and looked at the New York Driver's license to confirm Fetu's information.

"Mary Keller, age twenty-eight years. We know you're here to visit the motel. We can arrest you for prostitution."

"You'll let me go if I help?"

Agent Russell said, "Yes. Can we use your car and your phone?"

"Yes. Can you take the cuffs off?"

"Lieutenant Harrison, take the cuffs off and hold her here. Block the road for a few minutes while we take the target down. Afterward, you can let this young lady go."

"Sure. Officer Lewis, keep Lexi here till they're done," Lieutenant Harrison said as he handed Lexi over after uncuffing her.

"All of you should go ahead in the unmarked SUV and get into position. I'll follow in the Kia with Jim and Andrew hiding in the back. I'll drop them off next to the target. Easy as pie," Hatem said and got ready to get into the Kia.

Metzul began waving his eyestalks frantically. Lucas noticed he had turned magenta and green.

"What's wrong?" he asked in a soft tone.

"She cannot approach the bad one with combat gear; she doesn't look, how do you say? Slutty enough," the alien said softly.

"I heard that," Agent Hatem said, turning toward the two techs.

"They're right. You can't let him see you with all the gear. Do you have other clothes?" Russell asked.

"No," the female agent sighed, then gave Lucas and Metzul a sharp look.

Agent Doyle and Garcia just looked at each other, and Doyle mouthed the words, "Not slutty enough."

"Hey, you can just take the tactical gear off. Just go in your undershirt," suggested Agent Garcia.

Doyle added, "Yeah, and let your hair down and unblouse your pant legs."

Agent Hatem didn't say a word as she unslung her MP 5 and took off her gear including her gun belt.

Russell took out his smaller Glock 19 from his inside the waistband holster. "Here, take this. I'll take the MP5. You look fine. Jim, you and Andrew get ready. The rest of us will go with Lieutenant Harrison. Let's roll."

Agent Hatem blushed and felt like everyone was gawking at her. "I'll wait five minutes and let you guys get into position."

"Maybe you should come with me to stay in contact with our eyes in the sky," said Russell.

"It's not necessary; he can patch into your comms. Just ask for Feta, like the cheese," said Danny. "We'll stand by here. Just holler if you need anything."

Agent Russell headed to the unmarked SUV. "Fetu, what's our target doing?"

"No change. Over."

***

What was keeping that girl, Hermann wondered as he began pacing his small room. His phone chimed from an incoming text: "Just pulling up in my white Kia. What's your room number? Remember it's $500 an hour."

Hermann looked out his window at the parking lot. He didn't notice anything unusual and spotted the white Kia Sportage and texted: "Room 342. Can't wait to see you and have fun."

Agent Hatem smiled and checked her Glock. "We'll have fun, bae. I'll be right up."

Hermann watched as a tall girl with long brown hair got out of the SUV. She looked like she was in shape and had a tight t-shirt on with grey cargo pants. He smiled to himself. *She's hot.*

***

Agent Hatem walked into the lobby, checked her earpiece, and heard Agent Russell.

"All units. Stand by. Get ready to roll on my signal."

When she got to the elevator Agent Russell and Lieutenant Harrison were waiting there for her.

"You, okay?" Russell asked while he pressed the elevator button.

"Yes," Agent Hatem replied.

Russell spoke into his radio. "We're on the way up."

"This is Fetu. The target is sitting down and looks like he's drinking from a bottle."

Russell spoke again. "Jim, Andrew, you guys set?"

He heard two audible clicks and smiled as the elevator door opened onto the hallway.

"Lucas and Metzul, are you in position?"

Lucas clicked his comm twice as well. Russell stopped by the elevator and waited there as Sahar walked forward toward room 342. Jim and Andrew showed themselves at the other end of the hallway but stayed out of sight.

Sahar knocked on the door four times and waited. It opened, and General Hermann's face broke out in a grin as he leered at her figure. By the time his eyes got to her face, she moved in and pretended to give him a hug. She rubbed her breasts against him as a distraction. General Hermann was distracted by Sahar's looks and didn't notice anything amiss. She stepped back with her left foot, pushed his right arm up, and got her hip into his groin. She performed a perfect *O Goshi.* She threw the surprised Hermann to the ground. Jim and Andrew moved in quickly with their rifles and helped her cuff the stunned Hermann.

Agent Russell spoke into his radio. "We got him. Lieutenant Harrison, you and your men can stand down. We'll take it from here."

Lucas was sweating in his tactical vest. He had difficulty holstering his Glock 19 and sighed.

"Copy, Roger."

He fumbled with the earpiece; the adrenalin rush made his hands shake.

Agent Russell said, "Jim, make sure the forensics team gets here as soon as possible. Let's move him to the conference room until other units arrive."

They dragged the stunned Hermann down to the conference room. Agent Russell stood over him while the other agents began searching his room. Lucas and Metzul were busy getting information out of Hermann's phone. A few minutes later they could hear sirens approaching.

Agent Russell asked, "Hermann, what are you doing here? What are your plans?"

Hermann smelled of alcohol, and he shook his head.

"We've got you for treason, domestic terrorism, levying war against the United States, and providing aid and comfort to the enemies of the United States. If you help us, I'll ask for leniency."

Sahar had her gun belt back on and returned Mark's pistol. They took turns questioning Hermann for over an hour while Jim and Andrew searched the room. Lucas and Metzul weren't able to extract any useful data because the phone had never been used prior to this evening. After cloning the SIM card, they began disassembling the phone.

Jim came into the conference room and motioned to Mark. "We found nothing. No other electronics, just some cash and clothes."

"Thanks, keep an eye on him. I need a coffee," Mark said as he headed downstairs where the motel staff opened the breakfast bar.

Sahar was already there drinking her sweet tea.

"We should just take him in."

Sahar looked up. "Yeah. There's nothing here, and it looks like we need more time to get anything useful out of him."

"Let's ask him a few more questions, and we'll leave as soon as the forensics team and agents arrive from the Albany field office."

After another hour Lucas and Metzul walked in together.

"I hope you guys have some good news."

Lucas, still in his vest, shook his head. "No, this phone has never been used, and he didn't have any other devices."

"We had difficulty putting the phone back together," Metzul added through his smartpad.

Hermann looked up in horror at Metzul and would have fallen over if Sahar hadn't steadied the general.

"What is that thing doing here? Are you going to let that creature experiment on me?"

Sahar grinned. "If you don't tell us everything, he's going to take you to his ship."

"No! Please! You can't let aliens experiment on humans. I have rights," Hermann blubbered with spittle running out of his mouth.

"What are you doing here? What is your target?" Sahar asked as she made sure Hermann had a good view of Metzul.

She stood behind Hermann, motioned to Metzul not to say anything, and hoped the alien understood the zipper gesture across her lips. She looked at Metzul, who turned blue with excitement, and saw one of his eyestalks move toward her and the eye winked.

"They'll probe you before they suck out your brains," Sahar added. "I've seen them do it; it's not pleasant."

"What time is it?" Hermann asked.

"It's 5 a.m.," Mark replied.

"Please don't let them have me."

Hermann was clearly unhinged by the prospect of aliens probing him. But he still refused to give any significant information.

Sahar bent down close to Hermann's ear. "I hear they also like to do sexual things to their victims."

"No," Hermann said as he looked in horror at Metzul's eyestalks and his arm pseudopods. "I'll tell you what you want to know."

Mark brought his digital recorder closer and waited. Sahar gave Hermann a nudge.

"I'm supposed to get a call around 6 a.m. We're going to attack the Picatinny Arsenal."

"Who's picking you up? How many are there?"

Mark got on his phone and began shouting orders for everyone to clear out of the area around the motel.

"Jim, Andrew, make sure to clear the parking lot and get armed agents inside. Get the police to move their vehicles, and make sure the roads are clear. Make sure there's radio silence. Go! Now!"

Sahar asked, "How will you know who they are?"

"When they call, they'll say 'If God is for us—' I have to reply, 'Who can be against us?' or they'll leave," Hermann replied avoiding the alien's gaze.

"Do they know who you are?" asked Mark.

"I don't think so," Hermann replied.

CHAPTER 17

Chester wiped his brow again. His group of fifteen men all wore the camo uniforms he had picked up, and they were well hidden under the alien camo tarp, which hid their thermal and infrared signatures. They didn't talk to each other and identified themselves by number only. They left their SUV a mile away and marched into position a hundred yards from the bridge. They would take up firing positions after the initial detonation on the eastern end of the bridge. One of the men planted ten VS 2.2 anti-tank mines and five Valmara V-69 Italian bounding anti-personnel mines fifty yards after the bridge. Chester hoped that these would take out the front of the motorcade and leave Cadillac One alone. They then planted the remaining five v-69s on the opposite side of the road from their ambush position.

He checked his watch, with plans to turn on his phone only after they triggered the ambush. According to the intel, Air Force One was going to land at 6 a.m., and Marine One was supposed to be in Poughkeepsie by 7 a.m. The convoy should be on this road around 8 a.m.

The Secret Service had already been there a couple of days ahead of the planned visit. A crew of four agents and a sniper team were already at the farm. Surveillance helicopters flew by several times but the alien camo worked.

***

Trevor waved to Julie, Sandy, and Dr. Khan who got to ride with the president. He got in a separate black SUV with Dalia. They got into the back while his dad and Patricia sat in the second row with Sandy. Two agents drove their SUV, which was the last in the fifteen-vehicle convoy. Although he was tired from the long drive from the city, Trevor gawked in amazement as forty motorcycles began racing ahead of the fifteen-vehicle motorcade as they drove away from Marine One. The traveling press corps got out of their own helicopter and lined up for the photo op. For this trip no press would follow the president to the farm.

***

At 6:30 a.m. Hermann's phone rang. Agent Russell waited for Lucas and Metzul to give him the thumbs-up to answer. A male voice on the phone said in clipped tones. "If God is for us—"

Russell waited for a couple of seconds and replied, "Who can be against us?"

"Good. Meet me outside in front of the hotel in ten minutes. We're in a black Ford Transit passenger van."

"I'll be there," said Russell.

As soon as he hung up, he dialed the new number, which had appeared on his phone.

"Fetu, do you have eyes on the van?"

"Yes, I have them on 9W," replied Fetu.

"This is Black Widow. I'm also tracking them," said Tatyana in a soft Russian accent.

"Team 1, Team 2, and Team 3, are you all set?"

Agent Russell put on his dark jacket, a plain black baseball cap, and sunglasses.

Sahar replied from the lobby area, "Team 1 ready."

Jim had three field agents in two SUVs in the rear parking area ready to block the van in. "Team 2 ready."

Andrew and one other agent from the New York field office were in plain work clothes pretending to be a maintenance man doing work outside. "Team 3 ready."

Lieutenant Harrison spoke, "Ready."

Tatyana spoke, "Target van is half a kilometer out. Stand by."

Agent Russell grinned. "Copy that. All units stand by. Lieutenant Harrison, get ready to block 9W."

He watched as the Ford van pulled in front of the motel, and as he walked out the van's sliding door opened. He saw seven men sitting in the van. He gave a quick salute to signal the teams to move in. He got to the sliding door, blocked Sahar's approach, and pressed the door's unlock button. Agent Russell heard the sirens before he saw the other teams move. Sahar moved quickly from behind him with her MP 5 followed by two field agents.

Russell yelled. "Hands up. This is the FBI. You're under arrest."

Andrew got to the driver's door and jerked it open with his left hand while aiming his M4 with his right.

"Turn the engine off! Don't move! You're under arrest!"

As Agent Russell stood aside and gave Agent Sahar Hatem a better angle, team 2's SUVs blocked the van in. The front passenger drew a pistol and started to aim it at Agent Hatem. Russell fired one round, and Hatem fired a three-round burst with her MP5 into the center mass. The driver and the other passengers all started yelling at Russell and Hatem not to shoot.

Agent Russell yelled, "Put your hands on your head, and don't move."

Russell stepped back and let the other agents finish arresting the people in the van with the help of the state and local police. The lot was filling up with other first responders so Agent Russell walked into the conference room.

"Lucas, see if you can get anything from the phones in the van."

Lucas replied, "Yes, sir," then walked toward the van.

Metzul had already been busy using his smartpad to trace the phone number Agent Russell had received.

"We got everyone," said Russell to Hermann, then waited for a reaction.

Another FBI field agent arrived to take Hermann for transport.

Hermann turned and smirked at him. "You didn't win. It's too late."

Russell gripped Hermann's shoulders with his hand. "What do you mean?"

Hermann just smiled and shook Agent Russell's hand off.

"Nothing," he said and continued to the prisoner transport.

Agent Russell called Danny. "Thanks for the assistance. We couldn't have done it without you."

Danny was just sitting and petting Coco on her head. "It was our pleasure to help, and we got to use the drones."

"I'm sure you'll be glad to get back home to Julie. Say hello to her for me. You can leave without us. We have more work to do here," said Russell.

"I'm afraid I won't be seeing her; she's up here somewhere visiting the president."

"Agent Russell! Agent Russell!" came a loud electronic voice from his smartpad. "We have many issues, and we may have gone on the untamed goose hunt!"

Agent Russell noticed that Metzul was very excited by how blue he became. "What is it?"

"The van received a text message from an area near New Paltz a few minutes ago. It said: 'Operation Hidden Redemption is proceeding. God be with you.' From my quick research your president is there now. I lost the signal before I could pinpoint the location where the message originated, but it was from one of the phones on my watch list."

With a sudden realization that the president was in danger, Agent Russell hit his head with the palm of his left hand.

"Danny, we have a problem. Can you contact Julie?"

"Hold on," said Danny to the Special-Agent-in-Charge as he put his smartpad into direct comm mode. "Fetu, this is Danny. Come in."

Metzul interrupted everyone. "Several EMP bursts of Thrultak origin have been detected in this area. All comms are down."

"Julie must be in close proximity to an EMP burst. We don't even have a signal from her smartpad," Danny said, trying to keep the emotion out of his voice.

He petted Coco nervously. She had her ears up, looked up at Danny, and let out a worried whine.

"Pick us up from the hotel lobby. I think the president is in danger," Russell said.

"On our way," Danny said. "We don't have any weapons on board, and our drones are not armed."

"We'll bring extra weapons," Agent Russell said.

Sahar was already running toward him from the prisoner

transport with Jim and Andrew not far behind. Lucas had his latex gloves on and held the terrorists' phone.

"It was clean except for the one message."

"Bag it and help Agent Hatem gather some extra weapons and ammo for Danny and his crew," Agent Russell ordered as he noticed that all the lights were out in the motel and all the vehicles had stopped running.

Sahar just ran with Lucas, got her gear bag, and went to two bewildered FBI field agents in the parking lot where they were trying to get their electronics to work.

"Hey guys, we have a situation, and we need a few extra rifles and gear."

"You can borrow my M4 but we can't open the SUV hatch," said an agent as he took off his vest. "The rest of our gear is already locked up."

His partner shrugged his shoulders. "I already put mine away before everything stopped working."

Sahar slung the rifle over her shoulder, put the vest in her bag, and ran as fast as she could toward Agent Russell, who waited in a cleared area. He had an extra vest and a police Mossberg 500 shotgun.

They saw the flash of the Thrultak craft before they heard the sonic booms. There was a wind gust as it decelerated from Mach 2 to a dead stop. The hatch opened, and Danny waved them in. Jim and Andrew each held an extra M4 and vests. Metzul was right behind, still blue with excitement. He was using his tendril on his smartpad as he ran, trying to find the president's residence and a map of the area. Lucas brought up the rear, followed closely by Lieutenant Harrison.

"Is there anything I can do?" Harrison asked as Mark waited for his team to get on board.

"We don't have room for anyone else. If you get your comms back, send backup to the president's farm in New Paltz. I don't have the exact address," said Russell as he boarded the spacecraft.

"Will do. Good luck," said Lieutenant Harrison as he moved away from the rising alien craft.

***

After Julie and Dr. Khan were ushered into Cadillac One, Sandy got to ride with Dr. Padget and Dr. Kim. Julie felt self-conscious as the press corps took photos of her getting into Cadillac One, or as some of the agents like to call it: the Beast. She had worn her army class A pants and a plain white shirt. She didn't have a set of the new Legion uniform. She closed her eyes and sat listening to Dr. Khan and the president talk about various projects while the motorcade sped away. Inside, the sirens of the motorcycle escort were barely audible. The ride was smooth and quiet. She had been meditating like Master Mao had taught her and looked out the window as the Beast slowed and began a turn onto a small country road. Motorcycles were lined up along the road and saluted the motorcade as it passed them. They sped up again, and after a few miles the first sign of trouble was when all the electrically dimmable windows turned black and an agent's frantic voice came over the intercom.

"Hang on. We have a problem."

Julie tried to look out but all the windows were black, and the interior LED lights were on.

"What's going on?" Julie asked as the president touched a button on the intercom.

"Is there something wrong?"

***

Sandy was enjoying the ride as she saw the last of the fall foliage and piles of leaves that were on the ground. Her revelry was broken by their SUV coming to a halt. She could hear the agents in the front swearing as they tried to use their radios. As she looked out the front windshield, one of the large passenger vans filled with staff was stopped dead with an SUV smashed into its rear. The Hazmat Unit had also stopped, along with four other support units whose vehicles' EMP shield malfunctioned or had not been upgraded. The rest of the motorcade continued with one sweeper SUV that had two agents, followed by the lead car. The decoy was next, followed by the Beast. The ever-present Watchtower, the dedicated electronic countermeasures vehicle, was still in the motorcade, followed by two separate support units.

Sandy got out of the SUV and looked at her Thrultak modified smartphone. It was functioning but there was no signal. This worried her because with the modifications her device always worked even in space. Meanwhile, the motorcade was gone.

Sandy asked their driver. "I'm Sandy. How far are we from the president's farm?"

He looked at her with a frown on his face, then looked up from his dead backup radio.

"From the turnoff where the motorcycle escort left us, twenty-five miles. From here I think we're about twenty miles or so."

The other agent took off his tie, started running toward the other vehicles ahead, and shouted back, "I'll go see if they have coms."

***

Chester triggered the alien EMP devices and waited. Once triggered the devices would emit a large high energy initial pause, which fried electric circuits and would have enough energy for five more weaker pluses, creating a bubble around their area for at least two hours. He watched as the distant helicopter providing overwatch started emitting smoke from its engine and began descending rapidly until it disappeared over the mountains. He didn't have to wait long for the sweeper car to come around the bend of a two-lane country road.

He prepared the trigger to blow the bridge. All the men with him were wearing ear and eye protection. They were a safe distance away from the deadly effects of the pressure wave.

He watched for the SUV with the large dome: the Watchtower was his target. He let the first four cars drive over the bridge and triggered the explosive as the Watchtower was five feet from the bridge. The explosive blast threw the Watchtower into the air. When it landed it splashed into the stream on its side. The blast took out a ten-foot section of the forty-foot bridge. It also destroyed a support SUV behind the Watchtower. One SUV survived but didn't make it across.

As Chester looked on with amazement, he heard three more explosions further down the road. The anti-tank mines worked. The men with Chester all had prior military training, moved out of their protected position, and took up ambush positions. Through the smoke Chester could see four agents armed with rifles exit the surviving SUV. Chester's men opened fire with one AT4 anti-tank rocket destroying the SUV and one of his two M249 light machine guns wiping out the four surviving agents. Chester ordered his men to prepare a separate ambush for anyone foolish enough to come up the country road from the main highway. He sent three men to secure the other end of the bridge. He smiled when he heard another smaller explosion of one of the Valmara 69 anti-personnel mines. Once triggered the small mine would jump into the air and explode, spreading a thousand fragments in a twenty-five-yard radius and killing any surviving alien-loving liberals. Chester checked his watch. All he had to do was hold his position for an hour and make his escape.

***

Sandy flinched when she heard the first gigantic explosion. She could feel the tension from her previous firefights freeze her for a moment as her right hand started to shake. All the people she was traveling with had walked to the crashed SUV to see if they could provide assistance. It was one of two SUVs that had a Dillon Aero M134D Gatling gun. Only the driver had suffered a head injury from hitting his head on the airbag. Then they heard several smaller explosions. She saw twenty agents put on their gear and begin running toward the explosions. Two armed Secret Service agents remained behind with them.

***

Julie and the other two passengers rocked back and forth when the initial explosion took place. They didn't feel the concussion or hear the full explosion because of the Beast's construction. As the remaining convoy continued, there were three more small explosions.

An agent's voice came over the intercom. "We're under attack. We lost our sweeper and the lead vehicle. The bridge is out, and no one behind us made it across. We're heading to the farm to wait for help."

Julie looked at President Gallo and asked, "Who's left?"

The voice over the intercom answered, "The decoy is ahead of us with two agents and us."

Julie saw the president's face turn pale.

"How many did we lose?" she asked.

"I don't know, ma'am, but don't worry. We're past the ambush. We should be safe. We're fifteen miles to the farm, and I don't see any pursuit. We have to slow down since we're losing air pressure in one of the rear tires."

***

As soon as their EMP hardened flyer was in the air, Danny asked Ordortor, "How many drones do we have on board?"

"We've only four small flyers and one ground unit," came the short reply from the cockpit.

"Do we have an address?" Danny asked.

"Yes," said Fetu. "I've given it to the pilot. You should have it now on your own smartpads."

Danny was worried that his crew would be too late to help.

"Good work. Ordortor, as soon as you get comms back, get help up here as fast as you can."

"I'm on it," Ordortor said as he programed an emergency request for armed and medical assistance on human and Thrultak channels.

The signal would broadcast the moment it could get through.

"Good work. Fetu and Jurgen, fly a drone along the road to the president's residence. Tatyana and David, head directly to the residence," Danny said as he began looking over the weapons laying on the floor.

Fetu flew his drone up into an orbital position over the entire area and used the optical sensors to scan the possible travel routes. Jurgen flew his drone at low altitude directly to the only small road to the president's farm. Tatyana flew her drone at Mach 5 in a wide arc; she approached the farm from the opposite direction of Jurgen's drone. David flew next to their craft as a reserve.

Fetu's voice came over the speaker. "This is Fetu, I have detected smoke from possible explosions. I'll put it on a monitor."

The high-resolution feed showed the aftermath of several explosions; many vehicles looked destroyed, and they saw bodies strewn along the road.

Jurgen slowed his drone's speed as it approached the area.

"This is Kindermadchen. I have movement on both sides of the road."

Fetu added, "Kindermadchen, I confirm and am highlighting them now. Fetu out."

Danny dreaded what he saw on the screen. They were setting up for another ambush, and a group of armed agents were running toward the ambush.

"Where are the other vehicles?" Danny asked, worried about Julie.

Fetu split the monitors screen and showed two identical armored Cadillacs moving at 40 mph along the country road headed toward the president's farm.

Danny stood, trying to make a decision.

"How fast can we get there?" he asked the pilot.

"We can get there in thirteen minutes if we increase our speed," said Ordortor from the cockpit as he increased speed and plotted a path, making sure there would be room for deceleration.

"Is there a way to warn them?" Mark asked.

"I can try to fly over them and broadcast a message on the external speaker," Jurgen said. "My craft can be there in two minutes. What should I say?"

Danny said, "Just say: 'Contact front, and pull back.'"

***

As Sandy strained to see the Secret Service agents disappear around the bend in the road, she heard a familiar whine of a Thrultak drone as it streaked by at treetop level followed by a German accented voice yelling. "Enemy contact front! Pull back!"

A sonic boom shattered the silence of the forest as it past her.

Sandy tried her phone again but still no signal. The drone disappeared over the horizon, and she flinched as she heard the distinctive sounds of machine gunfire in the distance. She went over to the one Secret Service agent left to guard them.

"Hey Ken, do you have any other weapons?"

"No, all I have is my M4 and my Sig Sauer P229," Ken

replied.

Sandy asked Dr. Padget, "Do you know how to shoot?"

Anthony left Trevor and Dalia, who were both crying, with Patricia.

"I know how to shoot, and you can call me Anthony."

Sandy ordered, "Ken, give Anthony your pistol, then go to the front of the van and make sure they don't flank us. Anthony, cover my back and protect the kids. I'll get on the Gatling gun and see if it's still working."

Sandy jumped into the back of the SUV, manually opened the hatch, and turned on the power for the gun. The motor gave a satisfying whirring noise as it spun the M134's six barrels.

"It's good, I'll cover us!" she called back, trying to get the shocked look on the children's faces out of her mind.

She had her own demons to deal with as she rechecked the power on the Gatling gun.

***

"Shit," Danny exclaimed as he watched the ten men run right into the ambush by the bridge. The men were cut down mercilessly by machine gunfire and accurate rifle fire. He counted six down in the middle of the road. However, four remaining agents were trying to return fire, but the ambushers had established fire superiority as four tangos were advancing on the pinned down agents.

"What's our ETA, Ordortor?"

"Eight minutes," replied the alien pilot.

"Take us to the area just behind the van and the other vehicles," said Danny.

"I have good news. I think I see Sandy down there," Fetu said.

Danny's ears perked up. "Any sign of Julie?"

"No, but I do see two other men, a woman, and two children. I'll keep an eye out for Julie," Fetu said.

"Copy that," Danny said.

"Hey Mark, we're going to land right behind the last SUV, and drop your team there. Then we'll take off and flank them to the east of you. We'll evacuate any civilians at the same time."

"Got it. I'll get my team ready," Mark said, then went to talk to his agents. He had already decided to keep Lucas and Metzul on the spacecraft for their own safety.

Danny kept his eyes on the monitor and watched as the last of the agents were overrun by the ambushers. One of the assailants walked up to an agent trying to crawl away and placed his boots on the agent's back, shooting the agent in the back of her head. He could see the ambushers regroup and begin to run toward Sandy's location.

"We're down," Ordortor said as he triggered the door and Mark and his team rushed out. "And our own comms are working."

Sahar rushed out to get Patricia and the kids. Anthony was too far away so Ordortor made the decision to dust off and head to the flanking position.

"David, take over Jurgen's drone. Jurgen, come with me to the LZ," Danny said as he took the plates out of the tactical vests and checked the magazines.

He took an M4 and the Mossberg 12 gauge. Jurgen also took out his plates. Their suits could stop all small arms up to a fifty Cal so the plates only added weight to their spacesuits, which already weighed twenty pounds including the tactical Hud, comms, life support, and water.

The craft hovered a foot off the ground, and Coco led the way, then crouched down waiting for Danny and Jurgen.

"Scheisse!" Jurgen said as he laid down ten meters from Coco.

"What?" Danny asked concerned.

"This is no good; I can see you very clearly," said Jurgen as he began digging for mud to rub on his bright fluorescent suit.

Danny did his best to spread dirt and mud on his suit as they made their way to the edge of the road. The ambushers weren't there yet so he was able to pile leaves on himself and get out of sight. They didn't have to wait long. Fetu's overhead feed showed fifteen highlighted figures moving toward them in three fireteams of five. Danny kept his head down and watched the video feed.

"Mark, we have contact. Three squads of five moving toward your position."

"Copy that," Mark said, then relayed the message to his agents.

Sahar took a position near Agent Ken to prevent a flanking maneuver. Jim and Andrew took positions about twenty meters to their left, and he stayed close to Sandy in the SUV. Sandy was ready to open up with the Gatling gun. Agent Ken made sure Dr. Padget was nearby under solid cover behind him.

Danny looked at his screen and changed the color of the good guys to bright green and the bad guys to bright red.

"They are near the corner, four hundred meters out. Wait for them to pass my position."

Danny checked his M4 and realized that the Eotech was not working. *Thank God for backup iron sights*, he thought, as he flipped up the irons. Danny took a glance at Coco. She was motionless, and the only reaction he saw was her bared teeth. The first group of five advanced by bounds and got within two hundred meters of the broken-down van. They halted for a few minutes and signaled the two other teams to advance. Seeing no movement, they relaxed. Then all fifteen moved casually toward the van.

"Get ready and tell Sandy to watch her fire. We're at the edge of the woods," Danny said as he readied his M4.

He could see Jurgen get his M4 ready as well.

"On my mark. One, two, three. Engage."

He squeezed the trigger as he finished speaking. He fired an aimed shot at the nearest target. Fetu's overhead view gave him unparalleled situational awareness. After his target fell, all Danny could see was a rain of metal as tracers, which looked like a laser beams, tore into the advancing tangos. Eight more went down before they realized what was happening. Jurgen hit his target. The last group of five were on the other side of the road, trying to take cover from Sandy's withering fire. Next, Jim and Andrew opened fire on the remaining tangos who thought they found some cover in a ditch. They took two down immediately. Before they could react, Danny yelled.

"Mark, tell Sandy to hold her fire. We're going to maneuver."

"Rodger, hold on," Mark said.

After about ten seconds Mark came back.

"Danny, you're clear to proceed."

"Copy that. Jurgen, you're with me."

He then turned on the external mike. "Come, Coco, stay close."

He began running quickly to the road, trying to get behind the remaining tangos.

***

Chester couldn't believe that most of his men were down. At least he accomplished his mission. He looked around for an escape route. They were pinned down. From the corner of his eye, he saw bright fluorescent orange aliens with fishbowl heads running at him. He prayed to God and stood up and yelled.

"I surrender!"

One of the men near him also threw down his rifle and raised his hands.

"Me, too., I surrender."

When the spacesuits got closer, Chester saw an Asian man and a blonde-haired man. He laughed to himself; they weren't aliens. The third and last tango was lying flat on the ground, trying to get a shot at the bright targets. But Fetu was watching, and Danny commanded Coco to attack using his command word in Korean.

Chester saw a dog come out of nowhere and attack the last man who had not surrendered. The dog mauled the man and bit the man in the groin. Coco held him down until Danny released the dog. Chester smirked at the Asian man.

"Nice job but you're too late."

***

Julie sighed in relief as the decoy Cadillac and the Beast, now just a two-car convoy, slowed to make the turn onto the farm's gravel driveway, then turned onto the farm's driveway. She saw four armed agents waving them forward to the farm.

"I hope they know what's going on," Julie said to President Gallo.

"I'm going to find out who's behind this, and they are going to pay. You can call me Lana when we're in private."

Dr. Khan had been very quiet since the shooting began and

did not look well.

Julie asked, "How are you feeling?"

Dr. Khan coughed and wiped sweat from his brow. "I'm having difficulty breathing, and I feel like I have a heavy weight on my chest."

Julie looked at Lana. "Dr. Khan, Kareef. Please try to relax and take deep breaths. Is there an automatic defibrillator in here?"

President Gallo spoke into the intercom, "Do we have an AED in here?"

"It's in the trunk," answered the agent riding shotgun.

"I think Dr. Khan is going to need it right away. Do we have any other medical equipment?" asked the president.

The agent answered back quickly, "No, most of it was either in the Hazmat Unit or the support SUV."

***

Ambrose signaled his squad.

"We have the two targets in sight. We'll begin on my mark. One, two, three, mark."

From four hundred meters away Ambrose shot the Secret Service sniper in the barn and reloaded quickly to aim at the spotters.

By the time Ambrose reloaded his bolt action rifle, Dinah had already shot one spotter with her SCAR 17s designated marksman rifle. Ambrose adjusted his aim and waited for the second spotter to stop moving. The Chey Tac round didn't even slow down as it hit the second spotter in the head after passing through the wooden side of the barn.

At the same time Jeremiah fired one AT4 anti-tank rocket at the lead Cadillac and quickly picked up another rocket to fire at the second Cadillac. The first rocket hit the lead car directly in the front windshield, killing the driver and passenger. Jeremiah rushed the second shot and hit the second Cadillac in the rear quarter panel, taking out the left wheel.

***

When Hiram laid down suppressing fire with his M249, the Secret Service agents waiting at the front of the farm dove for cover. However, one by one the agents were picked off by

Ambrose and Dinah. Anyone hit by Ambrose didn't stand a chance. Their body armor did nothing to protect them from the hand loaded armor piercing Chey Tac rounds. Dinah used her SCAR 17s on anyone foolish enough to come out of cover to try and locate their position.

When the second Cadillac started to move, Gideon aimed his AT4, anticipating the limo driver trying to reverse out of the kill zone. Instead, the Cadillac lurched forward and pulled up next to the first Cadillac, which was on fire and spewing thick black smoke. He rushed his shot and missed, hitting the ground behind the moving limo but still damaging the vehicle.

***

Everyone in the Beast felt the jolt from the two rocket blasts. The armored compartment protected them from the concussion and most of the noise. The driver's panicked voice came over the intercom as the Beast continued to move.

"Look, I'll get you guys close to the farmhouse. Maybe you can take cover inside."

***

Fetu's wide angle view combined with Tatyana's feed. The situation around the farmhouse looked worse. There were several men and women down, one of the two limos was burning, and the second was taking heavy fire.

Danny realized they couldn't get there in time to help and began to lose hope.

"Shit, we can't get there."

CHAPTER 18

Noktor, whose call sign was Tomato, was bored, flying the routine training mission for the third time since midnight local time. Raider One insisted on making sure their orbital insertions were perfect and that every Raider got used to working with the armored vests and new combat helmets. They didn't have any of the new gauss rifles but they did have rifles improved with alien technology. Before he began his preparation to drop from orbit, he checked all his instruments manually. His flight computer showed an anomaly. He looked at the EMP radiation scan carefully and contacted Hancear as he sent the data link.

Hancear answered immediately.

"Thank you for sending this data. We have a problem here. No Thrultak or human EMP devices have been authorized for use, and the whole area around the initial burst has been damaged. I calculate the EMP radius to be a hundred and forty-three miles in diameter. I'm reassigning some of our communications drones to overfly the area and boost any detectable signals from the area. I'm conducting visual scans as well."

Noktor moved the craft over the area above New York in the United States.

"Raider One, I have spoken with Hancear. We have a situation and will stand by. Here is the info we have so far. Please stay on the link to get constant updates as we get them. Tomato out."

Noktor was still not sure why humans insisted on these weird call signs when he had a perfectly good name. He didn't know why they named him Tomato, although he did like to eat the juicy human fruit.

It didn't take long for Hancear to visually examine every square inch of the affected area and direct his sensors at the various activities that seemed important. Hancear detected the first of many explosions and sporadic gunfire. He tagged the other Thrultak ship on the ground and identified the personnel.

"There is a battle going on, and we are getting an emergency request for armed and medical assistance," he said in an even and calm tone.

"We can drop down there immediately," Amy suggested, then turned on her crew channel. "Listen up, Raiders. Lock and load with live ammunition, and take a full combat load. This is not a drill!"

"I think you need to wait a moment. Look at the feed more carefully."

Hancear highlighted two limos that had escaped the ambush and were moving away.

"That is your president's car. We need to help them. I think you should drop on top of their location."

Hancear highlighted a farmhouse.

"Is that the president's farm? Is she heading there?" Amy asked, then watched as Raider Two called her.

"Raider One, we are locked and loaded. Raider Two out," came the reassuring voice of Sergeant Smith.

"Yes, I think that its highly probable, considering the road they are on," replied Hancear.

"Tomato, drop us on that farm, and we'll adjust our LZ as we head down. Raider One out."

"Raider One, confirming drop, and I'm plotting a maximum descent. Tomato out."

Sergeant Smith was standing next to her with a loaded XM 6.5. Outwardly, it looked similar to a regular M4 carbine with a suppressor except it fired a 6.5 mm caseless cartridge, developed with the help of the Thrultak scientists. The bullet was made of solid copper with an embedded tungsten needle and had a muzzle velocity of 7,000 ft/s. The magazines held thirty rounds and weighed less than a loaded 30 round M4 magazine. Because of the new metallurgy and protective coatings, the rifle could sustain automatic fire without difficulty and could be used as a sniper rifle or as an area suppression weapon to help establish fire superiority over the enemy.

***

Tatyana said, "Smoothie, this is Black Widow. There's a sniper somewhere to the west of the two limos. Can you help me locate them with our acoustic sensors and radar?"

David, an experienced IDF pilot, looked at his screens and concentrated on starting an expanding square search pattern using the burning limo as his starting point.

"Starting now."

He began marking targets for everyone.

Tatyana said, "Looks like we have four to the southwest. My sensors detected another shot. Did you pick it up, Smoothie?"

"Target locked," David answered.

He wished he could fire an AGM-65 Maverick from his old F 15E.

"We've got nothing to fire at them."

"Copy that," Tatyana said. "Shaggy, Blackbeard 2, permission to use our drones as suicide drones."

Danny didn't have to think twice.

"Black Widow and Smoothie, you are cleared to use your craft as kinetic weapons."

***

Julie helped the president drag Dr. Khan out of the Beast while the two agents tried to return fire. In the open trunk Julie saw several extra weapons and ammo. She took out the AED and oxygen bottle and returned to Dr. Khan. President Gallo had already exposed the man's chest and watched Julie attach AED pads while the president turned on the oxygen mask.

Julie tried not to flinch as more rounds hit nearby. The driver went down. The other agent took one glance at his partner and returned fire as best he could with his MP 5, but it was ineffective at that range.

"Keep your head down, Madame President."

He moved to the trunk and retrieved an M4 with a six-magazine bandolier.

Julie finished loading the M4 and was about to ask the agent if they should move into the farmhouse when he was shot in the head.

"Shit, we can't stay here."

"But we can't move out of cover, and what are we going to do with Dr. Khan?" asked the president. "Here, give me the agent's pistol."

"You know how to use one?" Julie asked but then remembered that President Gallo was an army helicopter pilot. She turned the dead agent over and retrieved the Glock 17, checked it, and handed it to the president.

"It's loaded. There's no safety, just point and shoot."

Julie was still trying to figure out what they should do when her phone began to buzz. She had thirty missed calls and twenty-two messages. Danny was calling her now. *What a bad time to call me*, she though..

"Hey, it's not a good time."

Danny was surprised when a large icon of Julie's face appeared. "Hey, I finally got through."

Julie was crouched next to the president. "We're under attack."

"I know. I can see you. We're close by. Tatyana and David are going to make a kinetic energy attack on the two snipers. They're getting some altitude to make the attack run so keep your head down. And keep this line open."

"Got it. Thanks," Julie said, then turned to the president.

"Cover your ears."

"I heard that," Lana said as she checked on the AED and the oxygen mask, then cupped her hands over her ears.

Julie opened her mouth, covered her ears, and scanned the skies for any sign of the drones. Before long she saw small objects striking down from high altitude as they flew straight down at targets she couldn't see. She heard the explosion and the sonic boom at the same time. The drones' kinetic impacts felt and sounded like artillery shells landing nearby. Julie picked up her M4, looked over the hood, and saw no one. As she slung her rifle, she got the president's attention.

"Let's get Dr. Khan into the house. I'll carry him. Can you carry the AED and the oxygen bottle?"

Lana gave her the thumbs-up. They quickly moved into the farmhouse, and Julie locked the door behind them.

"Let's get to the back of the house and stay low."

Julie heard another sonic boom, rushed to the window, and saw a small Thrultak craft land near the farm. Ten figures jumped out wearing fluorescent orange spacesuits. Unlike her crew's, these had armor plates, and they carried rifles she was not familiar with. She didn't recognize any of them because of their darkened bubble helmets.

Danny's voice broke through. "They're friendly. Just stay put, and they'll mop up."

"Don't worry, Julie, the Marines are here to save your ass," came Amy's familiar voice.

As Amy's Raiders landed, Noktor flew his craft over the burning limo and doused the surrounding area with a fire retardant.

"Amy, is that you? I'm glad you're here."

Julie smiled as she tried to figure out which one was her friend. A figure turned to the farmhouse and gave a quick wave.

"Hey, is that you, LT?" came the familiar voice of Sergeant Jamol Smith.

"Hi there, you old crayon eater," said Julie with a smile.

"Well, don't take it the wrong way but you're a space marine now."

"I think you mean space ranger," replied Julie.

***

Julie watched as Amy's crew neutralized the rest of the threats and captured one alive. Amy's crew took their prisoner and rushed Dr. Khan to NewYork-Presbyterian Hospital in Manhattan.

Meanwhile, Ordortor landed with Danny and a few of her other crew members, who spread out and secured the area. Agent Russell and Agent Hatem disembarked with Dr. Padget, Dr. Kim, and their two kids.

"This is Wizard, Team Blackbeard, I'm heading up to one of the larger ships in orbit, and I'm going to get a full complement of armed drones to help secure this area. Hancear is also directing more reinforcements to this area."

"Roger Wizard," came Danny's voice.

As Ordortor made for orbit, Julie could make out small Thrultak drones flying cover overhead. She ran over to Danny and gave him a quick hug.

"Thanks for coming."

Danny smiled through his fishbowl helmet. "Love you, too."

Julie bent down and gave Coco a hug as well.

"Boy, did I miss you."

***

"I could use a drink. Let's get some snacks for the kids," Lana said as she tried to get everyone into the kitchen. "I'll make some herbal tea and decaf coffee."

Sahar looked out the window.

"I'm going to have a look around and see if I can help outside."

"I'll go with you," Sandy said. "I need to walk around after what we just went through."

Lucas and Metzul were interested in the EMP devices and the camouflage the terrorists used.

"I need to calm down," Julie replied.

As communications were restored, she listened to Agent Russell talk with the Director of the FBI and make arrangements for the arrest of several prominent individuals.

After the call Agent Russell came over to check on everyone.

"I have to let you know, Madam President, that we think that the vice president was involved with this attack. He's being taken into custody as we speak. We're also arresting one of the Assistant Directors of the FBI."

Lana stood silent for a moment.

"I want a full report, and I want a thorough investigation. Make sure we root out every one of these terrorists."

"We'll try. Please excuse me. I have some calls I need to make. Wyatt, the director of the FBI, has been in contact with the Secret Service, and everyone thinks that for the moment you should stay here until we sort everyone out."

Julie jumped in before Agent Russell could leave.

"Mark, did you find Bishop Jones? I'm sure he must have been involved."

"He was involved, but we don't have many leads. He's very careful and only uses his network of followers to communicate with the outside world. But we do have Hermann in custody," Agent Russell replied, shaking his head.

After Agent Russell left, President Gallo took a sip of herbal tea and pushed a mug toward Julie. "Back when I was on active duty, I always liked to drink some herbal tea and relax after a mission. It always helped calm my nerves after a big adrenaline dump."

Julie smiled and appreciated the tea. "Thank you. I try to meditate if I get the chance."

After checking on the children, who were recovering from shock, President Gallo asked, "So tell me what your crew has been up to and if you think you can capture the Qhasloi ship."

"I'm not an expert or anything," Julie tried to deflect.

"Hey, I trust your opinion, and I just want to know how your crew is doing. Let's go sit by the bay window. Dr. Padget and Dr. Kim, please help yourselves. There are cookies in the cupboard," President Gallo said as she took another sip and smiled.

"Thank you, Madam President. You can call me Anthony, and this is Patricia," Anthony said while he had his arm around Patricia.

She had been crying over the stressful incident.

Julie noticed that kids, being kids, seemed unaffected by the trauma, but she knew they would remember this horrible event. She returned her attention to the president and tried to explain the difficulty of reaching and capturing the enemy spaceship.

"Well, if we can get to the ship, we can take it. However, we just can't get close."

Trevor was tall for a twelve-year-old, with messy short blonde hair. He stood up to his full height and smiled at the two women talking.

"I know what you guys are talking about," said Trevor.

Not to be upstaged, Dalia, who was a little shorter than Trevor, stood up as well. "Me, too!"

They looked at each other, and Trevor nodded to Dalia.

"We've overheard what you guys are up to from the very

beginning. I think you could sneak up on the alien ship and attach your craft to it with a drill or magnets," he said.

"Kind of like what the Turtle tried to do in the Battle of Long Island on August 27, 1776," Dalia said. "Although that attack was a disaster. All you have to do is travel without getting detected. You know, without an engine. He tried to use a hand operated screw. And either attach a bomb to the alien craft to disable it or board it like pirates."

Julie thought for a moment. "You know, every time we tried to simulate the approach we used our engines. Hold on."

She took out her smartpad and called Hancear.

"Hello, Julie. I'm glad you and the president of the United States aren't hurt. Reinforcements are on the way to your location. How may I help you?"

"Hi. Thanks for your help. I have one question for you: Could the Privateers intercept the Qhasloi without engines?"

Hancear didn't respond for almost fifteen seconds, which was very long for the AI.

"Theoretically, we could use the various large bodies and perform several gravitational slingshots or gravity assist maneuvers. It's primitive and slower but it could be done. We'll use our ships to accelerate the stealth craft and release it to intercept the Qhasloi. We can also install ion thrusters that run on solid iodine and cold gas thrusters from your rockets. The craft can have a manual electricity generator to help recharge the batteries on board."

Trevor raised his hand. "Just like Voyager One and Two."

Dalia came closer to Julie and spoke into the smartpad. "And don't forget the Cassini-Huygens mission. I think it used four gravity assists; one with Earth, two with Venus on its mission to Saturn."

"Exactly," replied Hancear. "I've examined all the previous NASA missions, and I think that using the gravity assist will allow us to build a stealthy craft that will be very difficult to detect. We can start the mission from behind the sun to avoid detection and have a diversion here to further mask our intentions."

Trevor raised his hand again and asked, "Can you also build it so that it can glue itself to the alien ship? That way you don't need a large power source."

"I foresee one problem. The journey will take much longer than a direct powered approach, and we'll have to put the entire crew into suspended animation. I'll contact the rest of the FCG, NASA, and Klopzar. I'm sure we can work something out. If there is nothing else, I have other duties to attend to. But I'll tell Metzul and Ordortor to keep me updated on the situation here."

"Thank you. Before you go how many crews like us are there?" Julie asked.

"There are five privateer crews attached to the Space Legion, separate from the Planetary Legion. Goodbye, Julie, I'm glad you survived this unfortunate attack," said Hancear.

He delayed his response by a second, which went unnoticed by the organics but was a considerable time for the AI. A message was being processed by one of the remote automated satellites receiving a message from drone 41826.

***

"Dr. Khan, should you be back at work?" asked Agnes. "It's only been two months since you were discharged from the hospital."

"The doctors said that I should be fine as long as I don't push myself too hard," Kareef answered. "We've a lot of work to do coordinating design and construction of the new stealth boarding craft."

"I'm excited about this new project. The FCG has been coordinating various aspects of the project. I'm trying to put together a passive sensor package design for the craft," said Agnes.

"This will be the first true joint human and Thrultak project. The boarding craft will be designed and manufactured in an old four-hundred-and-fifty-thousand-square-foot abandoned auto plant in Detroit. Several aircraft manufacturers with personnel from the Jet Propulsion Laboratory have set up a joint venture with the Thrultak," added Dr. Khan. "I want to see the combined human/Thrultak stealth materials and manufacturing."

Agnes tried to find a way to get him to rest.

"Noah's team is doing their best to create a multilanguage software display for all the machines for joint use by humans, who speak different languages, and the Thrultak. Dr. Padget, Dr. Kim, and Dr. Kowalczyk, along with Mr. Green's help, are improving the translation software on the smartpads for general use by both Thrultak and humans. So right now you should let the team do their work and get some rest."

"You're right. I do need to rest," Dr. Khan agreed finally. "Oh, before I forget we should find a way to honor Trevor and Dalia for suggesting this approach to the mission to capture the Qhasloi."

Agnes smiled. "Yes, we should recognize them in some way. Without their initial suggestion Operation Frogfish wouldn't exist."

***

"Are you sure we're going to need a ventilator in the medical bay?" asked Danny.

"I don't know. It doesn't hurt to ask for one," Jurgen replied with a shrug of his shoulders.

"Remember to just add your top three things you would like to have on the new boarding craft they are designing. I think they'll ignore us if we ask for too many unnecessary things," Julie added.

"I won't add a hair and nail station," Sandy said in a sarcastic tone.

"But I would like a beer kegerator," added Fetu with a laugh.

"You must take this seriously," Jurgen said without smiling, missing the sarcasm.

"I think they're just joking. I'd be happy if we renamed the mission to something like Operation Dragoon. Frogfish isn't very inspiring," said Damian.

"I think Hancear came up with the code name. The AI seems to think the characteristics of the frogfish best fits our mission."

Julie was getting use to the crew and found them all competent and easy to work with.

"Make sure you also think about what kind of weapons we should use while we're conducting a boarding operation.

"This is Wizard, we're approaching our target," said Ordortor as he made sure they approached their practice target in orbit while remaining stationary twenty meters away.

They were going to have two crew members spacewalk/fly to the target and breach the mock hull with a drone before other members joined them.

"All right. Let's get ready for a Zero-G hull breach."

There was the usual grumbling, but the team went over their check list before Julie opened the hatch to space.

Fetu and Asher maneuvered to the practice target.

"This is Beaver, Blackbeard nine. The magnetic clamp is a no-go," Asher said as he retracted the magnetic clamp.

Fetu said, "I'm going to drill an anchor into the hull. Stand by. Fetu, Blackbeard 7, out."

Danny was waiting with the first boarding crew.

"Copy that. Standing by."

Hancear had been creating different scenarios each time they went out. This time the crew faced a nonmagnetic hull.

Julie switched to a private channel and said, "There must be a better way to get attached quickly."

Once they had an anchor point, Fetu and Asher used a cutting torch and a variety of power tools to create a triangular opening for the boarding party to enter. Even before the base of the equilateral triangle was cut, Danny led Alpha team toward the entry point, and Julie followed with the Bravo team. Once both teams made entry, the practice run ended. They returned to their ship, and Julie switched to the dedicated channel to Hancear.

"Hey, did you monitor our practice run?"

"Yes, Julie. I'm in the process of analyzing the data, and I think I'll be ready to make some recommendations and gear changes. I'm also going to recommend the research and development of some equipment we seem to be lacking. Thank you for doing this drill again for me. I do enjoy getting more data."

"You're welcome. Any progress on how long we'll stay in space?"

"I believe that Helzul, our chief scientist, and Basso, our medical specialist, are working with your medical researchers to find a way for humans to enter a state of torpor, or a regulated state of reduced metabolism. Full stasis is very difficult to induce in your species. Some of the medicines we use will work with modifications. The one issue we're having is how to maintain heathy human brain function. It seems that humans require some time out of the torpor. You'll have to go through cycles of torpor and sleep without regaining consciousness to protect your brain function."

This was a lot more information than she wanted, but she felt relieved that they were seriously working on the problem.

"Thank you for letting me know."

"You're welcome, and I'm also ready to make recommendations about ranks to General Ross and General Makro."

Ordortor turned on the crew channel.

"We're ready to land. Everyone stand by and ready your new biometric IDs to enter the secure zone."

Since the assassination attempt, security was tightened with new biometric IDs and increased surveillance.

***

For four months after the failure of Operation Hidden Redemption, the Bishop's moods were wildly erratic. For months Maggie knelt naked in his chamber and watched as he forced himself on Lilith. Maggie knelt and didn't move when he beat her afterwards. All Maggie could do was help Lilith wash herself and comfort her in their cell. Maggie knew it was a sin but she had contemplated hanging herself several times. However, she couldn't find the courage. Besides, who would take care of Lilith if she was gone?

Tonight was different. Bishop Jones became incoherent, and after he planted his seed in Lilith, he had Maggie clean him up. He left the two of them in his room to drink and rant about God's unfaithfulness. Maggie saw the Bishop's desk drawer open. He kept phones in that desk. She walked over, wiping her tears away, and found a box full of cell phones and a small snub nose revolver in the large bottom filing drawer.

She didn't know what got into her but she took two phones and the revolver, then closed the drawer. She hid her treasure in the dirty towel, knelt beside Lilith, and helped her stand.

Maggie heard the Bishop yelling at someone over the phone. When he reentered the room, he dismissed them with a wave of his left hand.

Maggie got up and whispered, "Lilith, let's go to our room."

Lilith had tears going down her cheek and replied in a small voice, "OK."

After Maggie closed the self-locking soundproof door that only the Bishop could open, she ripped open her pillowcase and hid the phones and the revolver inside. She helped Lilith get into her pajamas. Lilith stopped crying at some point and fell asleep with her head nestled in Maggie's lap.

Maggie turned off the lights and lay in her bed. She waited for hours. Finally, she reached into her pillow and took out one of the flip phones. She turned to her side and found the power button. She held it down, and the phone flashed on. After only a few seconds it shut off because the battery was dead. She felt her frustration growing. She reached in and grabbed the other phone, also an older flip phone. She pressed the power button. The phone turned on, and the light from the little screen seemed so bright in a room without windows.

Maggie panicked when she saw that this phone's battery was almost dead as well. The signal was very weak so she tried to hold the phone up in the air for a better signal. *I don't know who to call,* she thought. She dialed 911 and let it ring.

"911, What's your emergency?"

"I'm being held." Maggie realized that she didn't know where she was.

"Have you been kidnapped?"

"No, not exactly."

"Who's holding you?"

"The Bishop—"

Before she could finish her sentence, the power ran out, and the phone went dark. The room fell back into complete and silent darkness. Maggie put the phone back and found the butt of the small revolver. She didn't even know how to use it; she assumed she just pointed it and pulled the trigger. The phone had been the only hope of getting out of this nightmare and the only way to save Lilith from getting hurt even more. Maggie didn't know if she could take a life, not even the Bishop's.

***

After working with the FBI, Metzul, because of his experience working with humans, was reassigned to the stealth boarding craft project. He requested to be allowed to stay in the Armory building close to the FCG and the FBI agents working there. He didn't want to leave Lucas and the other agents.

He had the new schematics for the one-hundred-fifty-meter-long stealth craft on his large screen. He was testing the adequacy of the bismuth radiation shielding for the craft. It was thicker than the lead shielding, but the designers wanted to use as little metal as possible for maximum stealth. Metzul moved the craft's water tanks to the front as additional radiation shielding, then added an additional layer of bismuth to the plastic water tank. His body turned red in satisfaction as the new calculations showed a forty-one percent improvement in the radiation shielding.

It was 11:49 p.m., and Metzul was tired. He was about to shut down the large screen and take his smartpad off the interface when an unexpected icon appeared on his screen. His whole body turned a deeper red with joy, then blue stripes appeared as he became excited. He looked over at Lucas's workspace and noticed the human had his music headphones on. Metzul typed as fast as he could: "My friend, you know I've kept a probe to the ground. I think I may have found the Bishop."

Lucas turned his chair around and took off his headphones.

"What! Are you sure?"

Bishop Jones had eluded capture, and none of the co-conspirators knew where he had his main hideout. Agents had searched all the previous places where the Bishop, the vice president, and the assistant director had met. Even the Christian nationalists they captured alive didn't know where the man's main base was located.

"Well, it's a good hunch. I detected two phones from Ambrose Hall's stolen list being turned on a few minutes ago," explained Metzul. "The first call lasted three seconds and ended. A second phone on the watch list turned on, and I've intercepted a call to 911 from a remote location northwest of

Bonners Ferry, Idaho, I have a transcript, and the caller seems to need aid. But most importantly, she mentioned the Bishop."

Metzul sent Lucas the transcript.

"OK, you call her," Lucas said.

"No, you," the alien quickly replied.

"We'll flip for it," Lucas said as he took a poker chip from his desk and flipped. "Call it."

"Heads," said Metzul.

"Tails. You call Agent Hatem," Lucas said.

They weren't afraid of Agent Hatem anymore but they sometimes acted like they were. It had become a running joke between them.

"Agent Hatem. Yes, I know it's late but we hit the bonanza," Metzul said. "I think we've found the Bishop's location. Yes, I'll have Lucas make the calls and ask for a Thrultak craft to pick us up here."

Metzul gave Lucas his approximation of a human thumbs-up with his pod extended and a single tendril pointing up.

"Lucas, Agent Hatem wants you to contact the Coeur d'Alene field office and arrange appropriate backup. I'll call Jim and Andrew. Get them here as soon as possible, and she wants us to go with her."

Lucas felt nervous. He had spent more time on the pistol and tactical ranges since the capture of General Hermann and the shootout at the presidential convoy. That time he didn't even fire a single round and felt a little useless. Now he was more prepared. He even had Jim show him how to put together the tactical vest and became qualified to use the MP5 and M4. He unlocked the MP5 from the weapons locker he had installed in the office and grabbed his tactical go bag.

"Ok let's do it, buddy."

They did their own version of a fist bump and began their preparations for the operation.

***

Ordortor flew the craft to the cell phone signal location near Bonners Ferry, Idaho. He had been monitoring the target location on a Thrultak satellite.

"Looks clear, and I have not detected any guards on the

outside. In fact, there are only three figures on the thermal scans. Looks like one male and two females."

Agent Russell was tired from the lack of sleep but focused his attention on the screen.

"I was going to wait for the agents from Idaho to get here but if it's only three targets, I think we'll go in. I don't want to take a chance of losing them."

Agent Hatem nodded. "Right, boss. Metzul, can you get the blueprints to this house or a drawing?"

"Yes, working on it. Here you go. I've used the old blueprint and our scans," he said as he distributed an interior and exterior map of the compound to the agents' pads.

Agent Hatem said, "Everyone make your final gear check."

He turned to his smartpad and used it to position his agents. "Agent Hill, you and Metzul cover the main door. Agent Doyle and Agent Garcia, turn the power off to the main house with the remote switch. Then make your way in through the French doors on the south side. Agent Russell and I will enter through the front. Let's take the lone male target first. As soon as we secure the single male, Agent Hill, you and Metzul come in and help secure the target while we handle the other two targets. Any questions?"

Metzul produced a pseudopod and waved it like a little flag.

"Agent Hatem, I just want to remind you that the phone call I intercepted from a female voice seemed like a call for help."

"Yes, thanks for reminding me. We may have victims in there so let's be careful," she said, then looked at Agent Russell.

When her boss nodded his approval, they stood up, relying on their night vision equipment. Metzul's eyes couldn't see in total darkness, but his eyes could see if he had an infrared illuminator. He held a new stun weapon that could fire projectiles that could stun humans and Thrultak alike with an effective range of twenty meters.

Agent Russell stood by the hatch as Ordortor approached the house at subsonic speed using his fluidic thrusters to gently get into position behind some trees on the west side of the house. As soon as everyone was on the ground, he signaled Ordortor. The flyer took off vertically, stationed itself two hundred meters above the house, and began relaying its sensor data to everyone's smartpad.

The raid was anti-climactic, Agents Russell and Hatem found Bishop Jones in the office, naked and passed out with an empty bottle of bourbon. After securing the prisoner and propping him up against the wall, Russell used the remote to turn the power back on while Agents Doyle and Garcia went to find the two females.

Russell had made sure that the responding agents from the Idaho field office were aware that the situation was under control. He watched in slow motion as two young females in bathrobes were brought into the room. They weren't handcuffed.

"Did you search them?"

Agent Doyle looked at Agent Garcia, who shook his head no. As Agent Doyle moved to pat the two women down, the red-haired girl reached into her robe pocket, produced a revolver, and shot Bishop Jones once in the groin and once in the chest.

Before anyone else could react, Metzul grabbed the redhead. He stood on two legs, produced four limbs, and restrained the girl. Another shot rang out. Agent Hill rushed in to grab the revolver and secure it. Metzul's whole body turned purple with white and blue dots in fear and pain. He let Agents Doyle and Garcia take the girl away from him.

Agent Russell spoke into his smartpad. "We're going to need a medivac."

"It'll be faster if I flew the wounded to the hospital," Ordortor said as he landed the craft on the front lawn.

"Agent Doyle and Agent Garcia, take care of the Bishop and load him on the craft. Agent Hill, can you get Metzul on board?"

Metzul answered, "Don't worry. I'm only scratched."

He produced a few clear patches from his satchel.

"Lucas, can you put these on the holes, then I can walk myself to the transport."

The .38 caliber bullet had gone straight through the Thrultak. Some clear fluid was seeping out of the small wound. Lucas helped Metzul place the patches on the entry and exit wounds.

Agent Russell breathed a sigh of relief when everyone was loaded on the Thrultak craft. As they headed for the nearest hospital, Agent Russell made arrangements for police and FBI security at the hospital. Metzul looked surprisingly well and explained that the patches would heal the wound, which would fall away in a couple of days.

Bishop Jones had drunk so much that he remained unconscious while Agent Doyle and Garcia had the unpleasant task of applying pressure bandages on the Bishop's mangled private parts and his chest. He was bleeding out fast, and Doyle didn't think the bastard would make it to the hospital.

CHAPTER 19

Gurjin was in his private quarters, looking at the report his repair teams prepared. The situation was not great. They had repaired the engines and the reactors but used almost all the ready spare parts. They were trying to use the malfunctioning 3D manufacturing plants to restock their supplies. Two warned him that they were low on many of the raw material components for the printers. He used his comm.

"Two, I want you to restart the fusion reactors and the engines as soon as possible."

"Yes, sir."

Gurjin trilled in satisfaction. They would finally be on their way.

"Prepare our greeting message and transmit as soon as we get past the ring of icy objects near the eighth planet from the local star."

"Yes, my Captain, and how many asteroids should we harvest from the belt?"

"Harvest four with a high metal count and two with mostly water so we can scare the aliens into surrender," said Gurjin, hoping to all the known gods that he would not have to send the large metal asteroids against other sentient beings.

***

The scientists at the Space Telescope Science Institute, a part of the Goddard Space Flight Center, found a new lease on life when the Thrultak upgraded the aging Hubble Telescope and repaired the Arecibo satellite. They had trained the telescope on the Qhasloi ship as soon as it was detected, but for months the spaceship drifted in the edge of interstellar space. From the data that Hancear provided, the ship seemed to be having propulsion and power issues. Now they were tracking the ship as it began moving toward the sun and received a message. It was immediately transmitted to Hancear.

The Qhasloi's standard message was in Thrultak and various other alien languages: *"Please surrender or be extinguished from the galaxy. You will not be given a second chance. Subjugate yourselves now."*

The message repeated over and over.

OTHER BOOKS BY JOHN PARK

Book 1 The Enemy Series
Message to Arecibo

Book 1 The Nixlander Saga
Evil Lurking

ABOUT THE AUTHOR

John Park was born is Seoul, South Korea. He received his BA in Economics and Ancient History from Franklin and Marshall College. He also completed coursework for a Ph.D. in Political Science at the University of Pennsylvania and received his J.D. from Cardozo School of Law. He has received a commendation from the Senate and General Assembly of New Jersey and a Congressional Certificate of Recognition for his work in public service. He lives with his wife in Wyoming. *Opening Gambit* is the second book in his "The Enemy' series. He is also working on a fantasy series, "The Nixland Saga." Book One in the saga, *Evil Lurking,* is available on Amazon.com and at other websites. Find out more about John at https://www.SciWriterPark.com.

www.ingramcontent.com/pod-product-compliance
Lightning Source LLC
Chambersburg PA
CBHW072127300726
48975CB00003B/956